THE FRAGMENTS

ALSO BY TONI JORDAN

Addition
Fall Girl
Nine Days
Our Tiny, Useless Hearts

Toni Jordan's previous book, *Our Tiny, Useless Hearts*, was shortlisted for the 2017 Voss Literary Prize and longlisted for the 2018 International Dublin Literary Award. *Nine Days* won the Indie Award for fiction in 2013 and was shortlisted for the Colin Roderick Award and the ABIA General Fiction Book of the Year. Her debut novel, *Addition*, was shortlisted for the Barbara Jefferis Award and longlisted for the Miles Franklin in 2009, and has been published in sixteen countries. Toni lives in Melbourne.

facebook.com/authortonijordan
@tonileejordana

TONI JORDAN

TEXT PUBLISHING MELBOURNE AUSTRALIA

textpublishing.com.au
textpublishing.co.uk

The Text Publishing Company
Swann House, 22 William Street, Melbourne, Victoria 3000, Australia

The Text Publishing Company (UK) Ltd
130 Wood Street, London EC2V 6DL, United Kingdom

First published in 2018 by The Text Publishing Company

Book design by Imogen Stubbs
Typeset in Granjon 13/18 by J & M Typesetting

Printed in Australia by Griffin Press, an Accredited ISO AS/NZS 14001:2004 Environmental Management System Printer

ISBN: 9781925773132 (paperback)
ISBN: 9781925774047 (ebook)

A catalogue record for this book is available from the National Library of Australia

To Robbie, of course.

Part 1

1

Brisbane, Queensland, 1986

When Caddie Walker thinks back to this morning, she will try to remember everything. She will lie in bed and sift the moments for a clue. The first thing she recalls will be the heat, even before the scarf.

Deep summer. At home the corrugated iron horizon was already glinting and shimmering. Later, hanging on a bus strap, she swayed among the clammy shoppers and musky teenagers. Felt the barest hesitation. She could be on her way to the pool. She could be in the bath. In the kitchen in her knickers with one arm wedged in the freezer.

Now that she is here, though, waiting out the front of the art gallery, those thoughts have gone. She's halfway along the queue that weaves across the forecourt parallel to the river, among pink-faced women and a few damp-shirted men, children pulling their mothers' arms and the crumpled elderly fanning their throats with the free souvenir guide from the paper. The Botanic Gardens are on the other side of the river around the next bend, and there the Moreton Bay figs are tall and lush and green yet still people stand here and sweat, and wait. So often these once-in-a-lifetime exhibits are anti-climactic: entombed warriors that look like they were poured in a concrete factory in Moorooka; some squinty masterpiece on tour from the Louvre.

The queue isn't moving. Caddie skipped breakfast but she's got a salad roll in the hessian bag over her shoulder. The tomato will be liquifying into pulp. She'd like to get back to her paperback, her index finger marking her place, except it feels disloyal to be reading another novel while waiting to see the fragments, as though the ghost of Inga Karlson will find her wanting.

She should have arrived earlier. She lay awake and watched the sky drift from pitch to pewter through her wide bedroom window as though she were eight and it was Christmas morning, but she didn't want to rush this. She wants to remember everything.

The fragments are here, locked behind steel and glass inside the new State Gallery. The fragments. Irreplaceable, priceless. Here, in Brisbane.

She threads her hair behind one ear, turns and catches the eye of the large man in the queue behind her. He takes this as an invitation.

'Single most important invention in the history of western civilisation? Go on, guess.'

Short sleeves; some kind of logo embroidered on the shirt pocket. Socks pulled high and pleated shorts kept up at his broadest point by a nylon belt. The inch-wide strips of visible knee are red and peeling and the strap of a bulky black bag drags one shoulder down. He moves the bag to the other shoulder and reveals damp circles under his arms.

The wheel? The compass? The printing press?

'Aircon,' he says. He might be forty. His shirt has been ironed with such determination that it's still unwrinkled. 'Think they'd of walked on the moon without aircon? Plus, murder rate through the roof, car accidents, productivity through the floor. That bloke, the aircon bloke, give him a medal.'

Caddie raises her eyebrows, indicating the length of the queue, their common goal.

'My word. Snow, even. Couldn't care less. Worth it, you reckon?'

Of course, she says.

'Me mum, asked her this morning, do you wanna come? Nah, she says. She's taped Ray. Bloody Ray. Doesn't get it. Me, I like books. And paintings. I'm a photographer meself. Professional.' He inclines his head towards the banner at the front that says *The Fragments*. 'Me uncle seen them in New York. Seven, eight years ago.'

Lucky him.

'Lucky as. He's in Sydney now, eh. You ever been?'

To Sydney? Once, for a cousin's wedding.

He laughs. He meant America. She shakes her head.

'Karlson, hey? One in a million, she was. The mafia done it, you know. Just like JFK.' The man puffs his chest, cleans one ear with his pinkie. 'You been here before? The gallery? It's world-class.'

To this, she can nod. It's been open four years already, this world-class brutalism. She remembers the land before it was cleared, the long construction, the hoarding that wrapped around the corner with *95% OF ARTISTS LEAVE BRISBANE. WHY DON'T YOU?* graffitied in large, bold letters.

'I love it here,' she says.

There is no breeze. A few of the women wear sunhats and a couple hold matching umbrellas the colour of peaches. Directly in front of Caddie an elderly woman adjusts her scarf, patterned with silky swirls of green and aqua, her neck swathed atop a ramrod back. Every so often she turns as though she'd like to join their conversation but then thinks better of it. Caddie steps forward with the queue. A child's voice carries: 'Can we have chips after?' A little more distant is a young woman's voice. 'How good is Kmart? So good.'

Soon Caddie is under the shade of the concrete portico that radiates heat like a living thing, and then she's inside. The air conditioning smacks her like diving into a pool. She buys her ticket. The cloakroom attendant stows the gay umbrellas of the girls and the soft butterscotch leather tote of the old woman with the green scarf. He picks up Caddie's hessian bag—thumb and pointer, like he's discarding a dead thing by the tail—and slides her ticket across the counter. The photographer is wiping his neck with a handkerchief and arguing with a different attendant about special access. He knows someone, he says.

Now, she will see them.

In a wide chamber off the foyer, heels click on the cement

floor and the guards' uniforms are crisp like the air.

She steps inside.

It is crowded, but not impossibly so. Straight ahead is a floor-to-ceiling poster of Inga Karlson in black and white. Inga seems both innocent and wise, with eyes wide and glimmering and her pale hair woven in a narrow braid. That gaze. It's as though she can see into Caddie's soul, as though Inga alone knows her.

On either side of the poster, metres apart, are two smaller photos: in one, Inga is in a restaurant, surrounded by smiling waitresses and waiters. In the other, she's at a rostrum accepting a prize. To Caddie's left a room full of display cases shows the world in 1935, when *All Has an End*, Inga's first novel, was published.

Caddie will go back to these cases later, and to the display on the right that tells the story of Inga Karlson's life. She will examine the photos of Inga's childhood home in the old forest before she migrated to the United States, a cottage of hand-hewn timber and local stone quarried by generations of Karlsons. Inside will be a chair with its arms worn smooth, an apron on a hook, a cast-iron pot, a ladle. An oil lamp with a knob of brass and a frayed wick that witnessed tiny Inga learning to read. Some crackling, accented voice recordings of people who knew her: she was *kind* and *impulsive* and *contrary*, she was *hot-tempered*. Village ructions when, at six, she broke a boy's nose for torturing a kitten. At nine, suspected of climbing through the windows of well-to-do strangers just to sit in their chairs and rearrange their possessions. There will be books from the teenage Inga's library, probably;

her clunky black typewriter with keys worn concave, diaries in her own hand. All so much set dressing. None of which Caddie has come to see.

Towards the centre of the room the crowd is tighter. There are three displays in front of Caddie now. She stops at the first, the largest in the exhibition, devoted to *All Has an End*. There is a rare signed first edition: a modest print run for a small novel by an unknown female immigrant. There is the manuscript itself, with sentences underlined in faded blue ink and Inga Karlson's squat, confident jottings in the margins. There are the three brusque publishers' rejections, the ones that give comfort to writers everywhere, then the newspaper clippings of the book's triumph as it builds, and photos of mobs in front of bookstores in London, New York and Sydney. There are letters from bookstore owners: 'In twenty years in this business, yours is the one I am proudest to sell.' There are some half-dozen letters from Inga to her publisher, becoming less legible as the years pass, including the famous posthumous one. Karlson's Pulitzer is there, and selected reviews, some condescending ('undeniably pleasant') and some obsequious. There are the threats and the complaints; the letters that call her 'a traitor to her own race', 'an accomplice to the Jews or perhaps a jew yourself', 'a spreader of poison, of lies, of propaganda'.

Caddie takes her time.

When she passes the next display, the one about the fire in 1939 with the various theories laid out by the various experts, Caddie turns her head and keeps going. She knows the famous melted necklace will be there, and the funeral photos and mementos and the obituary and the letters written to Inga Karlson by readers around the world after she died, letters they still write to her. Other people's books, claiming they've solved this cold, cold case—all blindly confident, each contradicting one another.

And then Caddie is before the fragments: all that remains of Inga Karlson's second novel. She approaches, penitent to altar. Stands her ground in the jostling crowd. There is a small sign that says 'Do Not Touch the Glass' and another that says 'No Flash Photography'.

The fragments are like shabby tombstones in a long case. She can see the page numbers printed on the seven of them, these random sheets saved from the fire. In order, they are 46, 53, 108, 117, 187, 200 and 238. They are all damaged, although 108 has suffered only charring down the right-hand side and a small oblong hole in the top right corner. Page 200 has one whole corner burnt away and other parts are crumbling, swallowing every third or fourth word. This is where the title appears—*The Days, the Minutes*—floating in the last sentence on what is left of the page.

Caddie can see the fragments, and seeing them makes her long for her father in a way she hasn't for years, an ache that spreads up her side and finishes behind her sternum, which is a bone she knows to be smooth in other people's chests but imagines laced with steely holes like a box grater in her own.

She stays for an hour or so, oblivious to the strangers milling around, travelling through her past in silence. When she returns to herself she's being nudged by the photographer, who is positioning his tripod. He doesn't seem to recognise her. Caddie blinks. The logo on his shirt looks like a yellow-rimmed eye, wide and staring.

She exits through the gift shop. Souvenir catalogues and copies of *All Has an End* at every price point, from calf-leather bound with gilt lettering to shoddy paperbacks that Caddie's boss Christine would never allow in the bookshop. There are novels by others inspired by the fragments, reconstructing the story as fantasy, verse, crime and the rest. She passes all these by. The exhibition is here for a while. She needn't be greedy.

Outside, in the oven air, she blinks. Two smiling young people in red *Inga* T-shirts are at the top of the steps leading to the grass, handing out flyers advertising tomorrow night's lecture on the life, work and death of Inga Karlson. 'All welcome,' the boy says. Caddie takes a flyer and shoves it in her bag.

The sun is blazing now and she's struck by a smell of wet earth from nowhere obvious. The hum of the traffic mixes with the fountain in the river to make a buzzy white noise. Her eyelids are heavy. She can smell the frangipanis from here, both the flowers and the long dark leaves: tropical and fruity versus earthen and waxy. Frangipanis are green and lush and restful now, in summer, and bony like skeletal arms reaching skyward in winter to let the sun through. She imagines mist from the fountain on her skin and her stomach turns at the thought of her decomposing lunch.

'They remind one of a particular variety of Mormon,' a woman's voice says.

Caddie turns and recognises the scarf. The voice belongs to the elderly woman, the one who was in the queue. She's fanning herself with the flyer gripped in a gloved hand. She looks out of place against the cement and the blue sky.

'The Karlson fanatics,' the woman continues.

'They could take a tip from the Mormons,' Caddie says. 'If someone knocked on my door and said, "Can you spare a sec to talk about literature?" I would let them in. I would make them a cup of tea.'

'I saw you inside.' The woman raises an eyebrow. 'Were you also having a religious experience?'

Her voice is pleasant. She looks young despite the wrinkles. Her hair is white and soft. She wears no makeup other than a maroon lipstick, and her long-sleeved cream pea coat is linen. Her skirt is also linen and peacock green. Her gold and pearl brooch matches her stud earrings. She smiles.

Caddie must have seemed like an idiot standing there, thinking of Inga Karlson and her dad. 'I was miles away.'

'Entranced, were you?' the woman says, from behind pale, hooded eyes.

Caddie makes a face and flattens one hand over her heart. 'Guilty. I stand before you an unreconstructed fan. I think Inga Karlson was one of the best people who ever lived.'

The woman laughs, like an iron bell. 'Dying young was quite the career move, wasn't it? Especially for a one-book wonder. Who would remember her if she'd grown old and dull?'

A gracious person would smile and shrug and *agree to disagree*, but that's the kind of sensible thought that strikes

Caddie hours after the conversation's ended. She feels prickles rise but she can't stop them. 'The number of books doesn't matter. How she died—that was tragic, but irrelevant. Inga inspired people. She saw them. That's no small thing.'

The woman sniffs and waves in the general direction of the exhibition. 'People are sentimental fools, in general. All that fuss for a few charred sheets from a book no one's ever read. Most people would queue up to see a potato if someone wrote about it in the newspaper.'

'You don't believe books can change the world? The Bible? Ayn Rand?'

'I believe most of the people queuing to see those mouldy bits of paper hadn't heard of Inga Karlson before this week.' She pauses to move her handbag to her other arm. 'Had you?'

'I read *All Has an End* once a year, at least. My dad. He read it to me when I was little. And…well. My name is Cadence, actually. You can't be more invested that that.'

When she was younger, Caddie sometimes pretended she had another name, Sandy or Evelyn, but that was years ago. Her father chose her name and to deny it is a kind of disrespect. The briefest thought of him reminds her of warm flannelette sheets taken from a sun-baked clothesline; of slivers of apple from her lunchbox, tinged with the metallic tang of his knife.

'This rotten heat,' the woman says, and before Caddie's eyes her knees sag and the skin on her face seems to fall as though it's threaded with invisible wire pulling it down. She extends her gloved hand behind her but there's nothing to rest on.

Caddie leaps forward to take her elbow, bird bones under

the linen sleeve, and guides her to the stairs to sit. 'I'll get you some water.'

The woman grips her wrist with claw fingers. 'Don't you dare. I loathe fuss. Fuss and bother. Can't abide it.' Her voice is cut with sharp inhalations.

'I'm talking about a glass of water,' says Caddie, 'not a fleet of ambulances.'

'Keep talking. Talk, talk. It'll pass in a minute. Tell me, is that really your name? What a burden for you.'

'Not a bit. Everyone calls me Caddie, though. Maybe we should get out of the sun.'

'I should, you mean. No. I like the sun. Everything grows like weeds here. I'm old, that's all. Besides'—the woman smiles and drops her gaze to a silver bracelet watch on her bony wrist—'I ordered a taxi for half an hour ago. This town, honestly. I love it, but it's half-asleep.'

On the other side of the river the white expressway glints as it threads under the bridge—because that's what the river is for here: freeways and warehouses and industry. A wide highway for barges and dredges and scows.

The woman narrows her eyes and tilts her head, bird-like. Definitely not a dove. 'If you think those rubbishy old scraps are so important, I'm sure you remember the words written on them. Which ones do you think are the most…profound?'

'That's easy,' Caddie says, though of course it isn't. She loves all the fragments. 'Everyone likes the iconic line from page 46, but for me the best bit is from page 200. *And in the end, all we have are the hours and the days, the minutes and the way we bear them.*'

13

The woman juts her chin. 'Why? Why do you like that one best?'

Caddie thinks. 'It's the word "bear". You know some mornings when you wake up and wish you hadn't? You'd give anything not to have to face the day? You just want to shut your eyes and roll over. Inga understood exactly what that felt like. Yet she kept going. She makes us all want to keep going.'

'Oh, lord. How maudlin. I have never felt that way in my entire life.'

There's a toot. A yellow cab has pulled into the drive-way. The driver leans out the window and waves. 'Taxi for Rachel?'

The woman settles her bag in the crook of her elbow and stands. She turns towards the cab, steady on her feet now, as Caddie opens the back door. Almost as an afterthought, the woman stops.

'That fellow's wrong about the mafia. It wasn't them.'

'What?'

'Not that it matters. She's long gone.' Then the woman clasps her hands behind her back like a child reciting. 'Here's a puzzle for you, Caddie. That line of yours. It's my favourite too, as it happens. *And in the end, all we have are the hours and the days, the minutes and the way we bear them, the seconds spent on this earth and the number of them that truly mattered.* What fun it's been to meet you.'

The woman sits, the door shuts. The taxi makes an illegal three-point turn and vanishes around the corner. Caddie sits on the concrete. Something is wrong. It's the heat, perhaps, or the strange woman. That quote. Surely not. She is making an error. The air swims around her and she becomes conscious of her heart banging into the underside of her ribs. She grabs her bag and flies back up the stairs to the entrance, past the ticket counter to the door of the exhibition, where a guard sticks out his arm.

'Whoa. Hop on the end of the line, that's the girl,' he says.

'But I've been here already.' She's shaking.

The guard puts one hand on his walkie-talkie and asks for her ticket, which she finds by turning out every pocket.

'OK.' He thumbs behind her. 'But no bag. Cloakroom's back there.'

She drops the bag at his feet and darts through the crowd. There is a tangle of schoolchildren in front of page 200 now, laughing and shoving each other. Some are sketching the fragments in notebooks, but she can see over and between them. There it is, her line, her father's favourite line.

She reads it. She reads it again.

Caddie's legs are frozen but her hands move of their own accord. She pats down each pocket of her jeans. Her stuff is in her bag, on the floor outside. She prays to a god she doesn't believe in: don't let that sentence fall from her mind. She turns to a spotty boy in a blue-checked uniform, conscientiously sketching.

'Please. A pencil and a piece of paper.'

He looks around for a teacher but then, despite the wild in her eyes, he tears a sheet from his sketchpad and hands her his pencil. Caddie folds the paper over; with sweaty hands, she tries to write. The lead punctures the sheet.

'Here,' the boy says, and he flips his sketchbook closed and holds it out to her.

This boy. Kindness, where she would not expect it. She takes the sketchbook with both hands and, moving her lips with the words, she records the woman's phrasing in block letters, four lines across the page. When she's finished she reads it aloud, tapping each word with the pencil. She thanks the boy and returns his things.

He moves away. The fragment is sleeping inside its glass case as if it were a piece of Inga herself, suspended and waxen, waiting to be woken by—whom? By Caddie? Why not? Caddie understands waiting.

The sentence in the glass case reads: *And in the end, all we have are the hours and the days, the minutes and the way we bear them*

There is nothing else.

Nowhere can she read *the seconds spent on this earth and the number of them that truly mattered.* There is only the black-rimmed space burnt by the fire that killed Inga Karlson and destroyed every copy of *The Days, The Minutes*, her long-awaited second novel, almost fifty years ago.

2

Outside Allentown, Pennsylvania, 1928

On the morning they're due to leave the farm, Rachel slips from her bed and dresses in the cool dark in her best gingham plaid smock and apron, white collar and stockings, church shoes. She reaches under her pillow for her copy of *The Magical Land of Noom* and tucks it under one arm. Everything else she owns is already packed in the suitcases at the end of the hall. She's quiet because George is asleep in his cot across the room, one knee drawn up almost to his soft chin, thumb in his rosebud mouth. A tiny whistle as he breathes out. He'd want to come, if he woke. He always wants to come with Rachel, teetering on his white jelly legs, gripping her around the thighs.

Down the hall now, past the lurking, hateful suitcases. The oldest case, brought from New York: her mother's from when she first came here to marry Rachel's father, is tan leather with fat straps and buckles and shiny clasps and corners. The next is thinner, sturdy but worn in spots and bearing someone else's initials in chipped gold. A respectable case, passed from her Lehrer grandfather to her father and, in the years to come, to George. The last two cases, holding Rachel's clothes and George's and the spare blankets and tablecloths and towels, are cardboard with tarnished clasps that won't close, tied with string.

Through the kitchen, and a dozen times she wants to stop. She feels eyes looking at her from everywhere. She wants to vomit. She knows where to place her feet on the wooden boards and where to push the screen door so it doesn't squeak. She grips the book tighter.

Outside a cloud of bats darkens the night sky and she can hear peepers in the stream at the other end of the field. There's an owl in the elm beside the barn, squatting plain as day between the ropes that hold the swing. He swivels his heart face straight at her but she doesn't stop, she crosses the small yard and dodges the washing-line poles and a rake they won't be taking with them to the new house in town. Past the apple tree that will soon be alive with bees, until there it is in front of her, glowing in the late moonlight. A swaying sea of corn.

This is her only chance. By first light it'll be too late. There is a hint of softening in the sky now, and she pauses on the edge of the vast green and takes a breath. She steps in. The field closes behind her. The ears, smallish but forming perfectly, are above her head. She smells the soil moist with dew and the last of the corn pollen. The parchment leaves rustle as she passes, brush her from crown to ankle. The corn will miss her, she knows. It'll miss her father and the way he tends it. Her father speaks the language of growing things. Soil in his cupped hand, held to his nose. The early soft leaves folded between his fingertips. To see the last of the stars vanishing, she tilts her head all the way back because in every other direction she can see only stalks and leaves and ears tightly wrapped.

After walking a little way, she stops and sits. Her book is hugged to her chest. The stalks are dense around her. There's no one here but her and she's tired now. She's done all that she can. Now, it's up to chance.

She wakes to the tickle of a ladybird crawling across the back of her hand and the grainy feel of dirt on her temple. Her feet ache. The sliver of sky above her is the palest blue and as she watches, a flock of blackbirds swing across it. She's thirsty. At first she thinks it's the crickets that have woken her but then she becomes aware of a larger rustling, coming closer. The leaves near her begin swooshing and swirling as if they anticipate what's coming. She prays it's a buck from the forest behind the farm but then, before she can see him, she knows it's her father.

She says nothing. She wraps her arms around her knees and shuts her eyes and imagines herself smaller than a cricket but she can feel the air change as the corn in front of her opens. Then everything stops. The leaves, the insects.

'Up,' he says.

She doesn't move. She can't. If she only keeps her eyes closed. Tight. Tighter.

'Up, I said.'

She opens her eyes when his rough hand takes her wrist and jerks her to her feet. Others might get lost in fields the size of this but her father knows each plant, every breeze, the gentlest rise and fall of his family's land, and he strides back toward the house, unwavering, hauling her stumbling behind him, his fingertips pressing the flesh of one arm as she clutches her book tight in the other hand.

Out into the clear of the yard and Mr Debrees is there with the horses and wagon loaded with their furniture strapped down, the four cases and mattresses on the top. The black farm horses, pawing the ground and tossing their heads. Her mother, with George wriggling on her hip.

'This morning of all mornings,' her mother says. 'What's gotten into you? And the sight of your dress. You're nearly ten years old now. You should know better.' She lets George slide to the ground and takes Rachel's other wrist and jerks her free of her father. 'Mr Debrees, waiting all this time. Your father, up on the roof in his Sunday clothes. No help with George, no help whatsoever. As if I don't have enough to do, worrying about you. And dragging that book through the dirt! Treat it like that and I'll tell Aunt Vera you're never to have another.' She slaps the dirt from Rachel's skirt and sleeves with the flat of her hand, then spits on her own sleeve and rubs Rachel's cheek.

Her father still beside her, hands on his belt buckle, brooding like a storm.

Her mother raises her head as if she's forgotten he's there. 'On the seat beside Mr Debrees,' she says. 'Quick, Rachel. Take George. *Now*, I said.'

'Girl needs teaching,' her father says.

Rachel knows better than to move.

'She's an angel most of the time,' says her mother.

'Most of the time isn't all of the time,' says her father.

'Well,' says Mr Debrees. He's older than her father, rounder, with pale blue eyes and a brood of grandchildren on his own farm on the other side of the field. That's where Butter and her calf are now, and Lolly, Birdie and Minnie and their laying boxes. 'Most likely wanted to say goodbye to the corn, didn't you, Rachel? No harm done, Walter. No need to make a fuss.'

Her father, not moving. Rangy and sun-gold, skin like dried leaves.

'A day like this,' Mr Debrees says. 'Hard on everyone.'

Her father takes hold of the end of his leather belt and hitches it back. 'Not doing her any favours if she doesn't learn.'

'Later, then,' says Mr Debrees. 'I need to drop you folks off then get back.'

Her blood, ice in her veins.

Her father releases his belt, rethreads it through the loop and nods. 'Later, then. Rachel, in the back with me.'

Her mother and Mr Debrees look at each other, but her mother kneels beside her and ties her bonnet under her chin, then turns to climb aboard with George on the high front seat next to Mr Debrees.

'Horses,' says George, as he settles beside her mother. 'This one's Robin and this one's Dooley.'

'A good eye for horseflesh, this lad,' says Mr Debrees. 'Never you fear, Georgie. There's horses in town too, and plenty of 'em.'

At the back of the wagon, her father lifts her and they sit side by side with their legs dangling: her father's, long in black; hers in the damp and dirty pinafore. Her book is safe beside her. There's a jerk and the wagon begins to move. Rachel can feel the power of the horses, their great muscles and straining necks. They pass the house, their old house that Lehrers have lived in as long as anyone can recall. They pass along the side of the field, down the drive. The corn sways and waves to her.

Her father pushes his hat further down his brow. 'You ever pull that again,' he says, 'and I'll tan your hide so you won't sit for a week.'

'Yes, Papa.'

He slides a hand into the pocket of his coat and pulls out his closed fist. Opens it before her. It's a miniature ear of corn the length of his hand, wrapped in its papery skin. He peels it, leaf after leaf, and then he pulls back the tendrils of silk until it is revealed: tiny, golden, plump, shining in the morning sun.

He takes a bite then passes it to Rachel. She holds it, one small hand at each end, and feels the balance, the weight of it. She bites too. It's raw and crisp, warm and milky.

'You'll never taste the likes of that again,' her father says. 'Just picked, from your own land. Nothing like it.'

At the end of the drive the wagon turns along the long straight road that leads toward their new home, near her father's new job and away from this field, this house, the whole of her world. On the hill in the middle distance under two oak trees are the graves of all the blood on her father's side, sprinkled with white daisies. On the white of her arm near the wrist, the red marks left by her father's fingers will soon ripen to a dark purple. As the wagon sways, Rachel eats the rest of the ear. Every sweet, fading bite.

3

Inga Karlson was the stars and the light and the true north in the history of the twentieth century. She was beautiful, and that helped, people being what they are. She wrote from her feelings for all of humanity, a kind of herd empathy that only wanted the best for us. In that tiny forest cottage in the mountains of Austria, she sat up at three months, held a knife-sharpened pencil at six months, said 'I see bird' to her illiterate farmworker parents when barely a year old. When she was eight, the village took up a collection to send her away to school. She was marked from the beginning. Chosen.

Caddie Walker is not marked or chosen. She is twenty-eight years old, the same age as Inga Karlson when she died. Everyone expected Caddie would go to university and she did, for a while, but everything unravelled and her father was sick and then, when she was twenty-one, he died and everything stayed unravelled. The girls from school are all mothers now, or nurses or teachers, and every couple of years the part-timers at River City Reader lift off for Barcelona or London or Milan, where they intern at literary agencies or open sangria bars, and a new group, younger than before, bursts through the doors and Caddie trains them too, tolerating their airy confidence that they are meant for grander things. Sometimes she passes women on the street—suits and court shoes and briefcases—and she wonders what it is that they know and she doesn't. Sometimes she wakes convinced she is in her room at home and the window is on her right and the ridges on her pink hobnail bedspread are soft fur under her chin and if she keeps her eyes squeezed tight her father will come in to open the blind and kiss her forehead. She brushes her teeth and washes her face every morning and every night. She is not afraid of effort but she is afraid of reward. She is thin and that's fine with her: she's suspicious of the soft, the obvious, the cosy, the comfortable, as though taking the easy road even once would lull her to death.

It is after four when she lets herself in. Soon the sun will set red and gold behind the television towers on Mount Coottha. Caddie is sticky and gritty-eyed. Her forearms are glowing pink and there is a new blister on her heel. On the bus on the way home she kept opening her bag to check the sheet of sketchpad paper.

As she opens the door a dense fug of sour air wafts past. She yells hello up the hall; Pretty and Terese hello back. She leaves her shoes at the top of the hall, lined up with the others.

She shares a house with Pretty and Terese but it's not a *share house*. Those years are behind them: marijuana plants on windowsills and lounges scavenged on hard waste day and cigarette holes in everything and that peculiar smell of pepper and spaghetti that infests worker's cottages teetering on their stumps in West End and Highgate Hill and Dutton Park. They live in Auchenflower now, in a house that barely leans at all. Pretty and Terese have the two smaller rooms on the left so they can sleep in one and use the other for their clothes and sports equipment and desks.

Caddie's is the large room on the right, with wide boards and high ceilings, with a box window overlooking the sliver of garden and the mandatory jacaranda, a mass of purple on the footpath in spring. Against the wall is a heavy oak wardrobe—the kind with engraved panels and a centre mirror—that was her parents'. Books are piled in corners and double stacked on the bricks-and-boards shelves along the far wall, but fewer than you might expect—there is a grace to libraries that appeals to her. Next to her bed is her father's copy of *All Has an End*, and also *A Study in Scarlet* and *The Memoirs of Sherlock Holmes*.

There is less dust than might be found in the room of a single woman in her twenties and a strange collection of found trinkets among the practical bits and pieces on her dresser: some foreign coins that seem too light for their size; a shiny black pendant of a domino she found in the street; a dozen tiny white bones, soothing to tumble through her fingers at night; and a perfect green glass marble that is always cold regardless of the weather.

She drops her bag beside the bed, retrieves the precious sheet from inside it and pins it to the corkboard. Later, she'll transcribe it twice: in the purple-covered notebook she keeps in her bag and on a separate page to hide in her bedside drawer.

Now, though, she removes the salad roll, unrecognisable as food, from her hessian bag and takes it down the wide jungle hall past the white metal tiered stands and upended fruit crates and rusty stools on which sit a forest of plastic pots of anthuriums and ferns and peace lilies and snake plants, all with damp leaves like they've just been misted. The lounge/dining/kitchen is a thin open space. On the other side of the dining table there's an oscillating fan on a tall plastic stand, humming like an insect and shaking its head in vague disapproval.

Pretty is lying on the couch, watching television with the sound off. He's still wearing his basketball clothes and the deep neckline and long armholes show his ribbed chest. Caddie bumps his feet with her hip until he moves them.

'Good day?' he says to her, eyes on the screen. 'Sell lots of books?'

'Day off.'

'Lucky for some.'

Terese is in the kitchen stirring a dented aluminium pot that can only contain chilli lentil soup. She's wearing Pretty's jeans cinched at the waist with a too-long belt and a tentish blouse.

'This is my last dinner for the month, you both know that, right?' says Terese. 'I have a huge project due.'

'Got it,' says Pretty.

'And I don't mean springing for a pizza. We made an agreement. Vegetables. Saving money. Caddie?'

But Caddie is outside the gallery, listening to the woman—Rachel—quoting from the fragments.

'Earth to Caddie,' Terese says.

Caddie Walker and Terese Xanthidi, the last two names called for every school list and test and roll. Eighteen years ago, on the way home from the symphony at the City Hall—the sole music education day at their overwrought, under-resourced state school—one bench on the charter bus was missing its seat entirely. Mrs Powell faced a dilemma: keep the whole class waiting for another bus or trust Terese and Caddie to wait for an hour until she could return and collect them. Sure enough, in an hour's time they were sitting exactly where they'd been left—Terese with a sprained ankle, Caddie drenched and smelling like moss and pigeon shit and neither able to stop giggling. They formed an unbreakable, soul-sibling bond that lasted through separate high schools, various boyfriends, Terese meeting Pretty and Pretty moving in. Terese's mother Olympia still invites Caddie to Christmas lunch and plans something busy for them all to do on Father's Day.

'Hey,' Pretty says to her. 'Wake up, Australia.'

'I just heard something that isn't possible.'

'If it happened, it's possible,' Terese says. 'By definition.'

Caddie heads to the kitchen where she bins the roll, fills a glass from a passata bottle of water in the fridge and rests it against her forehead before draining it. She walks to the other side of the dining room and turns up the fan. In front of the whip of air she lifts her hair at the back and feels her neck damp and clammy. The buzzing of the fan vibrates under her skin. She feels like she's seen a ghost.

'Are you crazy? Don't do that, you'll get a stiff neck,' says Terese, tapping the spoon against the side of the pot. 'Another half-hour.'

'What's in it?' says Pretty.

'This and that. Recipes are for drones. So. What is this impossible thing that happened?'

'I met this old woman. She recited a line from a book no one's ever read. Well, two people read it back in the thirties but they're dead now. There are no copies of the book in existence. Only a few burnt sheets.'

'Inga Whatever book, that famous lost one?' says Pretty. 'Don't make that face. I'm an engineer, not a labrador—we read *All Has an End* at school. And *To Kill a Mockingbird*, and *Romeo and Juliet*. I can read. It was OK, actually. And everyone loves a good unsolved murder. Her picture was in yesterday's paper. Intense. Like a scary sexy nun.'

'She was just making it up. The woman,' Caddie went on. 'She must've been. Making it up.'

'Come and taste this, one of you.' Terese, with an airplane spoon cleared for take-off.

Pretty shakes his head. 'Don't want to spoil the surprise.'

'"It wasn't them."'

'What wasn't who?'

'The mafia. That killed her, I guess. She said that. And the line. There was something in the way she said it, like she knew it was going to drive me crazy.'

The woman's face, Caddie realises, was a magician's in the seconds before turning over the card you'd memorised. A fractional smile of expectation and control.

29

'Forget about it, Cads. Sometimes people say things just to spin your wheels,' says Pretty.

'But say she wasn't. How could she possibly have known the line? The only two people who read that book are dead. That's what everyone thinks. But what if that's wrong?'

'Cads. I bleed maroon, you know that. But—when did Karlson die? Before the war?—if some old lady read that book in America in 1930-something, I don't think she'd be living in Brissie.' Pretty switches off the set and ambles to the kitchen, gingerly, toes raised like he's picking his way across a lawn of bindis. He stands behind Terese and wraps his arms around her and takes the spoon and stirs. He is six foot three, she is five foot two. Terese smiles as he envelops her.

Caddie finds their relationship inspiring and depressing at the same time.

'Why not?' says Caddie. 'Why wouldn't she live here?' Brisbane, her father used to say, was like a member of your family: you yourself could call it out for anything and everything, but heaven help anyone else who cast aspersions.

'God, *all* of you stinks,' says Terese cheerfully. 'Shower.'

Pretty sniffs theatrically at his armpit, kisses Terese on the cheek and heads down the hall. 'Your little old lady was a stirrer, Cads. A senior practical joker.'

'Probably,' says Caddie.

'Definitely,' says Terese.

Now that the couch has been abandoned, Caddie lies down full stretch and hugs a cushion to her waist. 'I went back to the exhibition and spoke to the cloakroom man and the security guards. No one remembered her.'

'You're not weird at all.'

'Her first name was Rachel.'

'Too many novels. All those made-up stories. You should read more biographies. Or a story about convicts, that's just as good. Although the art gallery would've been a great place to be today. Cool as. Basketball, he must be mental. I went to the movies with Lisa.'

The possibilities of it. The endless branching scenarios, all competing in Caddie's imagination.

'What if someone found a Shakespeare play we didn't know about? Or if Harper Lee had written another novel and someone read it and remembered it?'

'But she didn't.'

'But what if she had? Just imagine.'

'It doesn't taste exactly like I expected,' says Terese, spoon to her lips. 'Maybe I should have measured the chilli.'

'"The seconds spent on this earth and the number of them that truly mattered",' Caddie says.

'You and books, heh?' says Terese. 'I suppose everyone's stupid about something.'

During dinner, as Caddie chokes down compulsory lentil soup, Pretty and Terese talk about this year's election and whether Joh can hold on (Terese: yes; Pretty: no) and whether the Mentals are the best Australian band ever (Terese: yes; Pretty: no). The conversation floats around Caddie like mist.

Afterwards, as Pretty washes and she dries, determination sprouts gossamer roots. Later as she shampoos her hair it burrows deeper; it reaches its tendrils into her imagination and takes hold. By bedtime Caddie knows she is committed. It is clear to her in a way that nothing else has ever been.

She is going to find the woman with the scarf.

Bursts of clarity like this are rare in anyone's life. She's read this chosen-one story in a hundred books and now, she thinks with a thrill, it has come to her. The nameless thing she's been waiting for. She imagines Inga Karlson herself willing her on: Inga Karlson, whose killer was never brought to justice, who whispers to her in her father's voice. Who speaks to everyone, yet makes you feel that she is speaking only to you.

At midnight Caddie is lying alone in bed as the ceiling fan sways and rattles and the bulb burns above her. As soon as she switches the light off, a mosquito dive-bombs her ear drum; as soon as she switches the light on, it vanishes.

'Do your job,' she says to the gecko in the corner of the ceiling, and it wipes its eye with its tongue.

4

Allentown, Pennsylvania, 1933–6

Rachel turns ten, twelve, fourteen in the house in town. It's a small house in the middle of a row and everything is hard and solid like bricks and road and nothing is green or yellow or swaying like corn when the breeze changes. There are people everywhere. Rachel hears them breathing on the other side of the wall, or pissing in a pot, or coughing. On their side, they all sleep in the same room, Rachel's parents Walter and Mary and her and George. Their debts are cleared from the sale of the farm so sleep comes easier, at first.

Her mother makes biscuits and beans and the best vinegar pie in Pennsylvania because, despite where they live, they are still country people. Her father takes them on picnics to the river and Rachel learns it forwards and backwards: the depths of it, the shallows. He takes them to singalongs at the church. The neighbours on either side work in the mines but Walter is lucky: on account of his skill with farm machinery he is well paid as a fixer in a silk mill. One of the few men among a workforce of females. He works hard and asks for little and, for a time, his belt stays in the loops of his trousers. For a time, Rachel's parents hold back the world for her. Her mother stays home with George and sews, and Rachel stays in school, the crowded one that smells of feet, on the other side of the factory. She is third in silent reading and oral reading and fourth in spelling, but can barely keep her eyes open in arithmetic and history and needlework. On her way home she snips cuttings from any rare thing she spies growing—a creeper on a crumbling wall; a miraculous broad-leafed wild-flower in a pavement crack—and plants them in eggshells filled with soil and then, if they survive, in rusty cans foraged from trash piles. They line the windowsills and aim toward the light. They tickle her palm when she brushes her hand over them.

Rachel turns fifteen. She hasn't seen the farm for years and is accustomed to the smells of the city, the wood smoke and rot. One silk mill closes, and then another. Walter keeps his job but his salary drops by three-quarters. Mary must work also and again they are lucky: she finds work as a silk hand in the same mill as Walter. Half the state is unemployed by now. People are hungry. There are marches in the streets; there is the Baby Strike, child workers picket-ing for a shorter week than the usual fifty-four hours and a minimum wage, and an end to the teaching charge they must pay before they're hired. On Sundays Rachel hoes the scrap of earth alongside the house and plants turnips and peas and tomatoes and potatoes. Other than the time she spends at the free library or with her nose in a book, she is happiest there with her fingers in soil. She coaxes this, gentles that. They speak to her.

Her father does not help. He smokes, standing above her as she kneels in the dirt, as though he's never grown a thing in his life.

She reads *Calico Bush* and knows that Maggie's burden is far worse than her own, she reads *The Good Earth* and hopes for the constancy and good sense of O-Lan. To spend her days reading and growing things: could there be any better life?

Then it happens that Rachel leaves school to look after George and the house. She already knows how to boil clothes and sweep before you mop and how to iron clothes smooth. She's known these things for a long time.

Rachel is almost eighteen when she's woken by Mary coughing. It's growing worse, this hack that began soon after she started at the mill. Months of festering illness have turned Mary's hair bone white and her constant wheeze has joined the soundtrack of their lives: the clank of the rail line behind the house, every roar and fart from the adjoining houses. Tonight the coughing goes on for hours. Rachel boils water for the steam and Walter paces as the edges of Mary's lips turn blue. It seems that every breath will be her last.

'Oh dear lord our God.' Walter rakes his scalp with his fingernails. 'She's a good woman.'

They pile all their coats on top of her and they rub her back and her feet. They make comfrey tea which she can barely sip. Walter has some whiskey in a flask, the source of countless fights between the two of them, but now he wets

Mary's lips with it and she shows no resistance. Somehow George sleeps through the worst of it in a corner of the bed he and Rachel share. That gasping. Like watching someone drown in air. Rachel would give anything to see her mother well again. She thinks the dawn will never come.

It does, though. Mary has survived the night and is asleep now. Her hair is damp and her breath still whistles but it's a solid sleep. Rachel and her father haven't slept at all.

'Get dressed,' he says to her. 'Outside clothes.'

She does. She makes oatmeal, leaves some covered in a bowl for her mother and George and then she sets out with Walter in the crisp dawn in her mother's coat and boots.

They arrive at the mill a little before seven. They walk along endless rows of looms, some already clanking, some starting up, all run by women who give neither of them a glance. Rachel has never imagined sound like this, filling every space within her head and without, but the windows are high and the space is tolerably warm. How kind these bosses are, she thinks. It takes her a few days to understand that cold fingers make errors and that light is necessary to see flaws and weakened spots in thread. This room and all its comforts are for the benefit of the silk.

The foreman, Mr Dimley, is at the end of a row near the windows and her father takes her by the wrist and leads her over.

'And who's this?' Mr Dimley yells over the machines. His shirt is almost white and he wears a coat, unlike the other men on the floor, who are mostly fixers like her father.

'Rachel, my eldest. Here in place of Mrs Lehrer.' Her father's voice reminds her of the day they left the farm.

Mr Dimley steps back and looks her up and down. 'In place of? Does this look like a charity? I have a list of women waiting as long as my arm.'

'There's no need for that. My wife's a good worker. She'll be back tomorrow.'

Mr Dimley sucks his teeth. 'Hands.'

Rachel can't imagine what he means.

'Show Mr Dimley your hands, Rachel. Quick now.'

She brings both up in front of her and Mr Dimley takes them. He turns them over and scrapes his rough thumbs across her palms and along the length of her fingers and then, with a sharp, hard jolt that takes her unawares, shoves his knuckles in the tender space where her fingers join without once taking his eyes from hers. She gives a sharp inhale but keeps her hands in his. They are hot and fleshy, like raw meat.

'Too soft,' he says. 'Useless. Never done a proper day's in her life.'

'She's finished her schooling so she'll be quick and clean.'

'No use in the world for a girl with schooling. You've done her no favours there.'

'That might be so for most girls but not Rachel. She's a good worker, Mr Dimley,' her father says. 'Does what she's told.'

'Well,' Mr Dimley says. 'I can always use a girl who does what she's told. Turn.'

She spins in a slow circle.

'She's tall for fifteen, mind,' he says.

'Mr Dimley,' her father says. 'Her mother's on a grown woman's wage. Rachel is eighteen, near enough.'

'Shame. I need a fifteen-year-old to hold your wife's place. Otherwise it's the next woman on my list. Let's ask your girlie, shall we? How old are you, Rachel?'

Rachel looks at her father. 'Fifteen, sir.'

'Schooling's good for something, then. Annie!' Mr Dimley calls to a younger girl with a scarf covering her head. She's flushed from darting between the machines, skirts bunched in one hand and an empty bobbin in the other. She comes toward them.

'Take young Rachel and show her your work. Look sharp.'

Annie jerks her head. 'Come on then,' she says.

Mary does not come back to the mill the next day. She can't take a dozen gasping steps without the world spinning. The frame of her ribs shudders and compresses with each breath, so every morning Rachel joins the girls walking to the mill with their hair in nets and their aprons in cloth bags. Silk is soft as the inside of a cheek and strong as wire. Rachel starts as a bobbin carrier working twelve-hour shifts and a half day on Saturday, zipping between the machines. Fibres become strands and strands become yarns and yarns are rolled into skeins and skeins are cleaned and dried again and shipped to be dyed, then shipped again to be woven into stockings and fabric. The weather turns colder every day. At home, she falls asleep as soon as she's eaten, after she's soaked her feet in a bucket of water.

'You're not speaking to those common girls at the mill, are

you?' Mary says to Rachel one night at supper, in her slow, heaving way. 'Just turn your head if they speak to you. They'll soon learn.'

'If she carried on like that she'd last two minutes,' her father says.

'We're not really factory people.'

'We're factory people now,' Walter says.

Mary reaches over to flatten the curl in Rachel's collar. 'Your father's people owned land in this valley. You keep yourself nice, better things will come.'

Walter stands, an eruption of force, and his chair tips over to the floor behind him. Snorts once through his nose. Picks up his plate scraped clean and hurls it at the wall.

George yelps. The plate has broken into three. The divot and crumbled plaster fall like snow.

'That's what we are now,' he says. 'Factory people. One more word, Mary. One more, so help me.'

He collects his coat and is out the door.

In the factory, Rachel sees her father anew. On the farm he was up with the sun, alone with the corn, planting or tending or driving the tractor as it pulled the harvester. He barely saw his children before nodding in his supper soup. Now, as she runs between the rows delivering fresh bobbins, she sees him work the floor maintaining each machine. She sees him drop small parts and tools so a girl will bend to pick them up. The smiles that he and Mr Dimley share across the expanse of the floor as though the two of them speak a language the girls do not. At home he rarely strings more than a dozen words together but at the mill he chats to everyone, he tells jokes, he commands the workroom. To the new girls, her father is a one-man welcome wagon. *You're from Cleveland! Well I'll be! My Uncle Frank's from Cleveland! I've spent lots of time there, what a town. I bet you were the prettiest girl there.*

After the first week, he no longer walks home with her. Longer hours mean more money, he tells her. *Get along with you.* One night, on an errand to a friend of her mother's in town to pick up a tonic, Rachel passes a tavern and, through the window, sees her father at the bar, arms wide, mid-story. Mr Dimley beside him, roaring with his head thrown back. She walks home alone with the little bottle clutched in her cold fist.

Later that night she's woken by her parents arguing in the kitchen. 'I only know that woman to pass the time of day with,' she hears her father say, 'whatever you think you saw.'

5

Brisbane, Queensland, 1986

Along the streets Caddie cycles on Monday morning on her way to River City Reader, the signs of change are obvious. Queensland's 'elected' officials yearn for their town to become a grown-up city: taller, shinier. *World-class*. Buildings are vanishing, replaced by car parks and deep pits and phallic towers covered in reflecting glass. They make the city even hotter and Brisbanites soon learn to lower their eyes.

At the end of the seventies the Bellevue Hotel, which had stood for close to a hundred years, was bulldozed illegally by its owners, the Queensland Government, its exquisite iron lacework sold for scrap. Cloudland Dance Hall, where Buddy Holly and Johnny O'Keefe and Midnight Oil and The Saints all played, had a roof arch nearly eighteen metres high, lit by dozens of tiny lights, and was linked to the city by an open-air funicular. Four years ago a wrecking ball ripped through it at four o'clock in the morning.

Caddie arrives at the bookshop ten minutes before the

doors are due to open and carries her bike through to its space under the back stairs. Her bag contains a thermos and an apple and her keys are on a string around her neck. She feels radioactive—pedalling fast along Milton Road seemed cooler in her mind than being wedged on the bus with the office workers, but now she regrets it. She takes a handful of misshapen ice cubes from the small office fridge, wraps them in a tea towel and holds it to her throat.

Before she turns on the lights and brings out the vacuum, she stands between the two 'specials' tables with her eyes closed, arms outstretched. Fiction runs along the wall on her right, biography and travel along her left. All these stories, real and imagined. If she could only read more, she thinks. Books are time travel and space travel and mood-altering drugs. They are mind-melds and telepathy and past-life regression. How people can stand here and not sense the magic in them—it's inconceivable to her.

The front door slides open: Christine, arms loaded with parcels and juggling keys and a lunch box. She's wearing a tweed skirt, which she does regardless of the weather, a T-shirt, a cotton cardigan and a look of benign exasperation. Caddie has never seen Christine outdoors yet she has a Queensland décolletage: distinct, jostling white and brown spots overlaid on angry red, like an aerial photo of a dry river system.

Christine sees Caddie, arms outstretched, palms raised. 'You look like you're about to conduct Beethoven's fifth.'

'I'm communing with nature,' Caddie says to her. 'Just a sec.'

Caddie has worked for Christine on and off since she was fifteen. Back then, Christine was over seventy. Now that Caddie is older, Christine is about fifty. She owns reading glasses in a variety of strengths and chooses them depending on the tiredness of her eyes. She eats Red Tulip After Dinner Mints straight from the box all day and leaves the empty crinkly pockets scattered over the floor of the shop to be crunched underfoot by the unsuspecting. When Caddie lost her father, Christine was businesslike and poker-faced and made everything better by not pitying her. When Caddie first knew her, she was convinced that Christine had read every book that had ever been printed in the English language, but now she's wiser about things like that. Ninety per cent, tops.

Caddie drops her arms, communing over. Christine comes up behind her and tucks the label of her top inside her collar.

'Well?' Christine says. 'The fragments. Did they live up to expectations?'

'And then some.'

While she switches on the fluorescent lights and they blink and buzz, Caddie tells Christine about the encounter at the exhibition. It seems even madder this time.

'Fancy that,' Christine says. 'Wouldn't read about it.'

Christine perches on her stool behind the counter to serve the few early-morning customers: regulars picking up special orders, window-shoppers killing time before dentist appointments. Caddie suspects that no one unpacked Friday afternoon's deliveries so she heads out the back to the storeroom and sure enough there they are, end on end in a corner, waiting. She doesn't mind. She's happy on her own, amid the boxes. There's a sagging armchair and a sink, there are mugs right-side up, filled with tea-leaf speckled dishwater and spoons, and assorted tea towels of dubious provenance. There are piles of orders waiting to be checked off. She has a lot to think about.

By midday, she can't stand it any longer.

'Do you need me this arvo?'

'You should have taken a long weekend. I'll call Dan, he needs the extra hours.' Christine's hand is already on the phone.

'Sure you don't mind?'

'Don't be ridiculous. You spend more time here than me. I only wish you were heading off on a date. Can't have everything, I guess.'

Caddie was burnt in love once, but that was long ago. Now she sometimes takes a half-hearted stab at dating, the occasional ritualised dinner with a friend of a well-meaning friend. Six months ago she soldiered through an excruciating one-night stand with a boy she knew from high school, clearer-skinned now, with better clothes, but the same bumptious boy. At not yet thirty, she can feel her life shrinking into the gentle sameness of her days and she knows she is pacing back and forth in a comfortable cage of her own construction. She needs someone to bump against, to disrupt things. She can't go on like this, she knows. She must resolve the tension between longing and fear.

But not right now. Right now, she has something else to occupy her. Caddie grabs her bag. Outside, the sky is pale and high and she legs it up to QUT at the far end of the city, sticking to the shade where she can.

The library isn't crowded. She's good at this and soon, in the reference section, in the *Concise Companion to American Literature*, she finds what she's looking for.

Karlson, Inga (Born 1910 Preitenegg, Austria; died 1939, New York City), American author of the Pulitzer Prize-winning *All Has an End* (1935) and the lost work *The Days, the Minutes* (1939). Karlson's work explores themes of tolerance, injustice and equality. Her surviving novel tells the story of Cadence Wells, an American girl of Austrian parents, who must protect her father from his past as totalitarian forces gather in Europe. Some scholars believe that Karlson's second lost novel was a sequel or even a prequel to her earlier work, on the basis of the letters 'Ca—' appearing in the much-studied remaining pages, or 'fragments'. 'The "Ca—" is clearly a reference to Cadence Wells,' writes Professor Milo Halloran. (For an opposing perspective, see *The Inventiveness Test: Redefining Inga Karlson's Literary Legacy* by Professor Maurry Klink.) The exact subject matter of *The Days, the Minutes* will likely never be known. In February 1939, following intense public interest and an attempted robbery of the plates of the novel, strict security was put in place. The only two people who had read the manuscript—Karlson herself and her publisher and editor, Charles Cleborn—perished in a tragic warehouse arson attack that destroyed all the finished copies of the novel, as well as the safe containing the printer's plates. The police investigation was inconclusive, though the role of Cleborn himself remains the subject of conjecture. A separate branch of Karlson scholarship has arisen examining the cause of the fire. (See *What Forensic Science Reveals about the Murder of Inga Karlson*,

45

by Virginia Kray, *Betrayal: The Death of an American Legend*, by Wallace Fillipi, and *Mob Assassinations: How the FBI failed JFK and Inga Karlson* by Skip Johanson, among others.)

This entry leads her to another, then another. They all say the same thing. There were two people who knew the contents of the novel. They both died. There was no one else.

It's well after lunch when she remembers her apple. She heads out to the lockers and, when she reaches her hand into her bag, finds a piece of paper, folded and scrunched, stained with tomato from yesterday's roll. It's the flyer for tonight's lecture on the life of Inga Karlson, to be given by the retired academic Dr James Ganivet. The leading Australian expert on the life and work of Karlson will speak, it says, in a rare public event. If the woman, Rachel, really did know a line from the missing novel, he's the one to ask about it.

Instead of cycling home later that afternoon, she rides to Dutton Park at twilight. She walks her bike down the creaking timber jetty and boards the ferry to Queensland University just as the black clouds of flying foxes arrive from their colony upstream at Indooroopilly Island. She's the only passenger. There's a breath of wind but the tide is strong and she hears the waves against the bow and sees the light glinting on the surface of the river. The river, the campus, the angle of the light. There is nowhere else like here in these lavender hours.

A million years ago she was a student here, while her father was alive. She remembers her exhilaration when she first saw the green acres of playing fields and the sandstone.

The disciplined neatness made her happy. No other lawns were so pleasingly laid out or such a perfect green. In the whole world, no other shrubs had ever been so precisely clipped nor any fountains drilled so as to fall in such elegant sweeping arcs. In her class was a boy who looked Asian; she passed women in exotic headscarves in corridors. On Friday nights at the Rec Club she watched people her own age drink Bundy and Coke and laugh and talk as if born to it. She felt like she had a passport to a bigger world. Now the gardens seem tortured, each stunted plant the misshapen foot of an ancient Chinese maiden. This campus: it has a force field. She almost turns around and goes home.

Instead she finds the lecture room and chains her bike at the front. It's full, but not with student types—semester doesn't start for another week or so. She's lucky to find a seat at the back near the door. The seating angles downwards towards the rostrum and the art gallery's director of exhibits, Malcolm Kirby, is already there. He's a jolly man, or he does a good impression of one. He talks about the fragments, the years of planning to bring them here, the insurance hurdles, the logistical nightmare, the sleepless night when they were in the air. The fragments had their own seat in business class, he says, though they made poor use of the complimentary champagne. All this effort—and there's a touch of the shoulder-chipped genius, a disrespected Sinatra about to break into 'My Way'—has been vindicated by the response. The queues, Kirby says, the queues and the press. At last, he introduces the retired expert. Bachelor majoring in English literature, honours thesis on 'Romantic Pacifism: ethics, politics and tolerance in the novel of Inga Karlson', master's on 'Moral Storytelling and its Role in Community: global implications of *All Has an End*'; PhD on 'Imagined Heroes and the Danger of Projection: the nature of identity in the life and work of Inga Karlson'. He post-doc'd at Harvard, published widely. His loss to academia is the private sector's gain. His name is Dr Jamie Ganivet.

It occurs to her now she's heard the name before. Ganivet Rare Books on Charlotte Street.

Dr Ganivet climbs to the rostrum from his seat in the front row. His 'retirement', she realises, is from academia rather than the workforce: he's not yet thirty-five, despite his too-long pepper-and-salt hair. It falls foppishly across his face. He's a solid man, fleshy in his jeans and jowly in his open-necked shirt. The captain of the debating club gone to early seed. At the rostrum he takes off his glasses and cleans them on his untucked shirt before positioning them again. He moves his face too close to the microphone.

'Um,' he says. 'Hello.'

Sharp feedback. Everyone winces.

'Sorry. Is that better? Can everyone hear me?'

The audience is asleep, or dead. He uncurls a sheaf of papers and they slide from the rostrum to the floor. Everyone else is unmoving while he drops to his knees, collects them. Reorders, clears his throat, begins again.

'Um. Inga Karlson,' he reads, 'is not much of a correspondent. Like Santa Claus and Juliet Capulet, she receives hundreds of letters every year and never replies.'

Caddie cringes for him but as he progresses, his delivery

becomes more fluent and he seems to forget the audience, so involved does he become in telling Inga's story. She remembers the rockstar professors from her university days, the clever, witty ones, with their dry remarks about academic rivals and theorists. Jamie Ganivet has none of this. His sincerity is almost painful. He loves Inga too, Caddie can sense it.

She already knows about Inga's ancestors and parents and childhood, her home, her village. But soon he moves on to textual criticisms and points of literary theory, interwoven with trivia—the name of Inga's childhood pet (a cat: Muschi); her early work (an attempt at acting in the pioneering talkie days and a screenplay, sold but not produced) and some rumoured past lovers (a renowned surgeon-to-the-stars; the silent matinee idol Conrad Nagel). He quotes from letters and diaries of literary intellectuals at the time, either rude, dismissive or lascivious on meeting Inga, and sexist in the discussion of her work.

The matter of her murder—this he skirts around. He's not a detective, he says, and this is not his area of interest. *There are many theories, most of them ridiculous and all of them unrelated to the legacy Karlson has left us.* He never raises his eyes from his notes.

It's more than she'd hoped for. His words are heavy with feeling. She could listen to him all night. There are, however, no hints towards a solution to her puzzle.

She's startled by a rustle of applause. A few concluding remarks from Malcolm Kirby and the whole thing packs up. People leave in dribs and drabs, though a few approach Ganivet for short chats. Caddie waits until last. While he's packing his papers into a leather satchel, she asks him if he has a moment.

He doesn't look up. 'A number, I expect,' he says. 'Though none of us can really know, can we?' He folds his satchel closed and clicks the latches.

'Right,' she says. 'I meant an actual moment, now.'

He looks up, eyebrows knitted. For the first time she can see his eyes: deep and clear, with lashes that could advertise mascara and rims that hint at kohl. Oh, my. How he would have been picked on at school by the footy boys.

'Look, sorry,' he says. 'I'm not really—'

'I'll be quick. Is there any chance—'

'No,' he says. 'I'm sorry to be blunt, but the fact is: no. There's no chance.'

She has a sense of déja vu. The memory hits her with full force: here in this very lecture theatre, asking the wrong questions to the disdain of the professor and titters from the other students. The expression on her lecturer's face, a kind of petulant withholding. He had knowledge, she lacked it. A different expression from the old woman's yesterday, outside the gallery, but the same effect.

'You don't know what I'm asking. It's important.'

'Let me guess,' he says, not unkindly. 'Inga Karlson changed your life. She opened your heart, you receive messages from the great beyond, she's a real presence to you. Or you're research-ing a book. Or a short film. Perhaps you've already sold your proposal and now you're on deadline. You think Inga is the way to make your fortune, or at least your fame, because you've been in love with her since you were a child.'

She feels her face bloom. 'Wow, incredible. Not just knowing my question before I ask it, but the uncanny prediction that you won't be able to answer it. You should be on the stage.'

'Well, yes. I am on the stage. Literally.' He looks at his watch, then walks to the edge of the platform and down the steps, Caddie following. The jolly Malcolm Kirby has been chatting to people also and is already halfway up the aisle. He turns, then he waves.

'That was great, Jamie, great. Well done, stellar effort,' he says. 'We could repeat it next week at the exhibition itself. "Once more unto the breach"?'

'"Or close the wall up with our English dead" is the next line, if you recall,' Jamie says. 'Once only, that was the deal. Now we're even.'

'Correctamundo. But if you change your mind, give me a tinkle, yes? Such a waste, you. The one that got away. Catch up soon?'

Kirby jogs to the door. Jamie stares after him: a man who's pelted for the last bus in the rain, to watch it pull away. They're alone. He stops and turns. Caddie comes up to his shoulder— his build camouflages his height. He ducks his head through the strap of his satchel, takes off his glasses and wipes them on his shirt. Without them, his eyes seem even softer. She feels the hairs on her arm stand on end. She moves to block his path.

'Look, sorry. You'll have to excuse me, please.' He steps around her.

'My name is Caddie,' she says, in a rush. 'That's actually my name.'

He turns. 'That's not your fault, unless you named yourself. But you're not Cadence Wells. Cadence Wells is a character in a book.'

'I met a woman who knows a missing line from the fragments. From page 200.'

He looks to the ceiling and reaches one hand to the back of his neck to rub the base of his hairline. 'See, here's the thing, Caddie. You can't know if this woman knew a line or if she didn't. No one can be sure, because no one knows what the missing lines are.'

A lost Christmas beetle bounces off the fluorescent light above them, once, twice.

'It sounded perfect.'

'What it sounds like is the kind of exercise they'd give in a creative writing class: take page 200 of the fragments and keep going until you have a short story. Your woman was probably a retired English teacher.'

'No,' she says.

'No?'

'That's crap. I've read and re-read every line Karlson wrote. I can practically recite her first novel. Anyone who's studied Inga, anyone who's serious about comparative literature, would spot it as a Karlson sentence.'

'Listen,' he says. 'Try to believe me: I'm doing you a favour. Inga Karlson. She's charming. The wonderful novel, the tragedy of her story. She has this seductive pull. She sucks you in.'

'Yes.' Caddie thinks: Jamie Ganivet understands.

But he continues. 'It's easy, when you're young and smart, to spend years falling into the life of another person, a dead person. You need to walk away now and live your own life. If you don't, Inga Karlson will take over and before you know it, years will be gone and you'll never get them back. Now excuse me.'

She says nothing and he turns and she is alone in the lecture theatre. Just Caddie and the rows of empty chairs.

For the next few days, it's hard to concentrate. She works as best she can, fielding the usual questions. *I'm looking for a book, you know the one, it's yellow* and *Why do authors use such bad language these days; can you guarantee there are no four-letter words in this?* and *Have you got* Fit for Life*, my friend Debbie lost seven pounds.*

A few of the casuals invite her to the Gold Coast for the weekend: the new casino has opened, just like Las Vegas. They want to see dancing girls sausaged into diamante body-stockings and balancing feather headdresses; they want to stand at the roulette wheel and put the rent on their birthday and watch it spin. Caddie's never been a punter. She declines, and all the while Rachel is a pebble in her shoe. Jamie Ganivet also, the way he delivered his bad news with his soft eyes.

On Wednesday after dinner, while Terese and Pretty study, she lies on her stomach on the couch and watches *Cheers* and *Moonlighting* and realises, when the credits roll, that she has no idea why Maddie was so mad at David and everyone was so mad at Sam.

Thursday night her dirty clothes are washed and hung under the house to dry.

Forget it, she tells herself.

Ganivet Rare Books is an antiquarian dealer and auction house in an old printer's warehouse near the pancake place with the giant chess set. Sometimes on school holidays Caddie's father would take her there for a short stack and they would play. She remembers the huge pawns and knights, almost as big as she was.

On the way to work on Friday she pays special attention to the window displays on Adelaide Street, noticing the angle of every dead-eyed mannequin. At the shop she brings out the plastic tackle box they use for tape measures and scissors and staplers and double-sided tape and, her favourite, the hot glue gun. A cookbook display, she thinks. Ice creams and salads and microwave cooking because it's too hot to switch the oven on. She finds posters and streamers. She cuts snowflakes from pastel sheets of cardboard and uses cotton balls to look like drifts. It's passable, she supposes. She's never seen snow.

She's up and down the ladder in the window between rushes of customers and deliveries for most of the day. Christine is pleased.

At 4 p.m. Caddie finds herself standing out the front of Ganivet Rare Books.

6

Allentown, Pennsylvania, 1938

In some ways the mill isn't so different from school. Arrive early, do your best, keep your head down. Some of the girls started at fourteen and are already weavers or quillers. They are hardy girls used to cold winters, the daughters of miners. Girls who contribute much to their family's keep but will be *girls* until they marry. If they marry. In the mill, there are girls in their sixties. Men cannot do this work: slender fingers coaxing the slightest of knots in the finest of gossamer threads.

'Working in a factory,' Mary says from her chair as Rachel rushes to make dinner. 'My mother would be turning in her grave. My aunt, I'll never be able to tell her.'

'It's good for girls. Keeps them busy. Stops them turning into harlots,' her father says. 'Course, it's too late for some.'

The *some* he speaks of work the machines at the back. Ruth, Helen, Lidia. Others that come and go. They call to the fixers as they pass, they laugh among themselves. The bottoms of their petticoats show below their skirts. Some days, when the weather isn't too bitter, they eat their lunch in the small courtyard between the factory's wings: standing, because Mr Dimley disapproves of sitting on their breaks. It encourages idleness. So they lean against the cold brick with their lunch baskets in one hand and chat as best they can above the machines clanking on the other side of the wall.

'Yoo-hoo. Come stand with us,' says Helen, during Rachel's second week, when she's standing on the other side of the courtyard with Annie. Annie shoots out a hand to grab her forearm. Rachel feels Annie's hot palm first and wonders at it, before she realises Helen's call is directed at her. Annie shakes her head, a tiny movement.

'Come on then, Miss Nose-in-a-book,' says Ruth. 'Don't listen to bug-eyed Betty there, it's none of her beeswax. We don't bite.'

There is nothing for it. Rachel moves toward the other girls. Annie watches her go, arms folded.

'Isn't this nice? All friends together,' says Ruth.

'Mr Lehrer is your father, can that be right?' Helen says to Rachel.

Rachel nods.

'We never seen you at the dance hall,' says Lidia. 'Too much of a prude to dance, are you?'

'If you want a boy to ask you, you'll need to be more encouraging,' says Ruth. 'You don't even smile at them right. You tilt your chin down, see? And give them something from your lunch pail to show what a good little cook you are.'

'A sweet thing. A piece of pie, not a tunafish popover,' says Lidia.

'Let the kid alone,' says Helen. 'The boys around here, who'd bother?'

'I don't know how to dance,' says Rachel.

'You need a man to teach you,' Ruth says. 'A grown man.'

'A grown man can teach you other things besides,' says Helen. She puts one arm out in front, around the neck of an invisible dance partner, and rests the other where his hand would be and sways, before breaking into a one-girl Lindy Hop.

They dissolve in giggles, all except for Rachel. Rachel can't take her eyes from Helen, the way her body moves. She's like a snake. It's wrong even to look at Helen dance that way, she's sure of it. These girls are three or four years older at most but they seem another type altogether: accustomed to hard work and not surprised that they're the ones to do it. Turning their meagre wages over to mothers with big broods of baby siblings and carrying the water to wash their fathers' clothes.

Ruth slaps her knee and looks sideways at Helen, a pantomime of disapproval underlaid with admiration.

'What?' says Helen. She lifts her skirt to the level of her knees before dropping it again. 'Bad enough that life's short. Shouldn't have to be dull too.'

These girls are common, Rachel knows, and for the first time she thinks that might have some things to recommend it. On her long walk home she imagines dance-hall music, the swishing of skirts, those warm girls laughing with their arms around each other, and her among them.

The next morning, she's packing her lunch basket and her father's pail when he emerges from the yard, straightening his shirt. She almost doesn't recognise him. His hair is black with brilliantine, slicked. She's failed to notice he's grown a thin and debonair moustache, like Clark Gable's. It's as if he'd never spent month after endless month tending corn. If he wasn't her father, he could be a movie star.

Inside, her mother is sitting at the table. George has already left for school; he meets with a herd of boys from down the street, no doubt for mischief, on the way.

'What in heaven's name do you call that?' Mary says when she sees her husband.

The silence is thick like bread on Rachel's tongue. Her father's head pivots. The turning of a mighty ship.

'Who is it you're speaking to? Is it me?' her father says.

'Is there anyone else here?' Mary says.

Rachel. Rachel is also here, but she knows what her mother means. She feels like a ghost in this house, like a cloud of gas you could walk right through. Her hand could not grasp her father by the arm or cup itself tight over her mother's mouth even if she tried.

Her father puts one foot on the seat of a chair as though he's never in his life been told not to do that, and he polishes the top of his shoe with his sleeve. Looks at it this way and that. Spits and shines it again. 'I thought perhaps you were speaking to the furniture, that tone,' he says. 'Not to the man who puts food on your table.'

'There'd be more food if you spent less on making yourself ridiculous,' Mary says.

Rachel is near the window on the other side of the world and she watches her father stand upright. His gleaming foot lifts from the chair and rests on the floor, without a sound. She wants to stop things now. She wants to press on the clock hands with her fingers because there is only one way this is headed and she's amazed her mother can't see it. She needs to say something, smash something, puncture the air but she's only a spirit herself.

Her father raises his right arm across his body in a gentle arc until his hand is above his head and there it pauses, a pendulum at the top of its swing. Nothing will change the coming of the weather, there is nothing to say. His arm swoops down and his body pivots and the gliding hand connects with the side of her mother's face in a slap Rachel feels in her stomach. The arm continues its swing with smooth grace and her mother is lifted from the chair, which falls on its side. She hits the wall—*thud*—and there she slumps.

Everything is still. Rachel cannot move for trying. It takes some time but even as Mary holds one hand over her mouth, dark blood begins to seep between her fingers. Her father walks over to where her mother lies. He squats beside her and observes, head cocked to one side. She gives a small gurgle.

'Look what you made me do,' he says, soft in her ear.

Mary rolls to her hands and knees, then he stands again and kicks her in the stomach, the sound of a heavy rug thumped with a rattan beater. She drops.

'Respect, Mary,' he says. 'It's not too much to ask. And do something with your hair. Sticking up like that. You look like a coloured woman.'

Mary's rolled up in a ball now, tight and groaning. She

coughs and a white sliver of tooth tumbles into the pool of blackish red.

'As for you,' her father says, and Rachel is surprised that he knows she's there. She raises her hand and turns it, front and back. It's true, she is visible. Or perhaps he can hear the thudding of her heart.

'If you're late to your shift don't expect me to save you,' he says. 'And don't be slow today. A one-legged girl could move faster than you.'

He picks up his pail and he leaves. Rachel sits up most of that night and the next, listening for his key. He doesn't come home for two days.

7

Brisbane, Queensland, 1986

Caddie pushes open the heavy door of Ganivet Rare Books. In front of her is a narrow foyer with cracked leather couches in a U-shape and glass display cases scattered like pillars. Behind them is a trestle table fronted by half-a-dozen plastic garden chairs on which men are sitting: middle-aged men with beards and with glasses; one with a walking stick leaning against his thigh. She's amazed. At the bookstore where she works, women customers outnumber men ten to one.

The men are looking down at books open in front of them. They turn pages and run their fingers along the lines and make notes in small pads and not one pays any attention to the opening of the door or to Caddie. She is invisible: a spectre.

On the other side of the table are shelves of books and three young people, student types, replacing and finding leather-clad volumes and laying them in front of the perusing men in a hushed ballet of stretching and bending. Further back, the room expands into a wider space: more plastic chairs arranged in rows in front of a rostrum; walls lined with overflowing bookshelves.

She hovers, clutching her handbag. No one approaches. No one says anything, so she stands in front of a glass case, trying to appear absorbed. She sees a *1984*, author and title in white cursive script on a rust-coloured dust jacket; two volumes of *The Ingenious Nobleman Mister Quixote of La Mancha*, an English translation, in dark green leather with with the title in gilt; and Evelyn Waugh's *A Handful of Dust*, the Chapman and Hall edition with *7/6 Net* printed on the spine of the dust jacket. All arranged on perspex stands behind glass: exhibited as decoration.

Caddie thinks of the men and women who used to own them. She wonders who they are, these people, unaware their possessions are here abutting the books of people they've never met, linking them with strangers. There's something heart-breaking about secondhand bookstores. All those stories, bought because they were once wanted and then discarded like rubbish or hocked for cash.

A voice behind her asks if she'd like a catalogue.

She turns. It's him, Jamie Ganivet, in a white business shirt and grey suit trousers. He looks like he's slept in them.

'Hi again.' She raises her palm.

The door jangles opens and they both turn. The man who enters is fifty-something, grizzled and bearded with motor-cycle leathers and huge hands, and a black helmet under one arm. He looks as though he eats his meat off the bone, Flintstone-style.

'Ganivet,' he says, as he passes. 'Has that Akhmatova come in?'

'Any day now, Simon. I'll call you.'

Simon strolls towards the back, swinging his helmet like a bowling ball.

Caddie is expert at finding pleasure in small things that belong only to her. Even in the bookshop, none of the casuals would have read Akhmatova. Only one or two would have recognised the name. She smiles. She sees that Jamie Ganivet is also smiling.

'Mad Max, beyond thunder poem,' she says.

'Conan the librarian,' he says.

Something crackles between them and is gone.

'Caddie, is it? I told you already, I can't help you.'

'This is a bookshop. I want to buy a book. How much is that one?' She points to the Cervantes.

'It's four thousand five hundred dollars. Will that be cheque or card?'

She picks at the plastic strap of her bag. 'What's the point of books like that anyway? You can't read them. It's like they're in prison.' She taps her fingernail on the glass, as if to get the books' attention.

'I prefer to think of it as a zoo, preserving endangered species for the benefit of future generations. Look, I'm flat out. I work for a living. I'm not an academic, I'm a bookseller.'

'You're not a bookseller,' she says. 'I'm a bookseller. Booksellers are professional reading consultants who sell books that normal people can afford to people who want to read them.'

He reaches into his trouser pocket and pulls out a collection of keys, on a ring. 'Hold out your hands,' he says.

She blinks, but does as he says. He takes a step to the glass cabinet, unlocks it and takes out one volume of the Cervantes. Rests it in her hands.

The weight of it surprises her. 'Don't I need gloves?'

'You can't feel it through gloves,' he says. 'This was printed in 1742. It has engraved plates, see here...' He opens it with only the tips of his fingers, to show her. 'This isn't just a story. This is...a way to understand the world, passed down from person to person, and changing each one on the way. It's the smell, the touch. Books are art that talks to us.'

This glorious thing, heavy in her hands. Cadence Walker, the last link in a chain spanning centuries. She sees that space and time are not always linear but are sometimes folded into pleats. She imagines all the people who've held this book. Everyone walking in the footsteps of others.

She holds it out towards him. He tucks it back in its case.

'Inga Karlson,' she says. 'Please.'

He says nothing.

'Look. I have to know. I won't stop until I know.'

'Is this for a thesis? Some kind of work?'

No, she says. She tells him again. She spoke to a woman outside an art gallery. That's all. She can't remember the last time she's felt so ridiculous, or when she's felt this excited about anything, about a possibility. She thinks of her workmates, packing for their trip to the casino. Perhaps she is a punter after all. Chasing the long odds, the million-to-one.

'I'm not normally like this,' she says.

He's quiet again. He opens his mouth and closes it. Then he says, 'I've had offers for that Cervantes. I've never sold it. It was the first book I bought when I took over the business. It was my favourite novel as a teenager—not that edition, obviously. I love that mad old bastard,' he says. 'Wait here.'

He disappears into a small office and comes back with a wallet in his hand.

'Marika, I'm grabbing a tea,' he says, to one of the young people filing books. 'Won't be long.'

In the pancake place a few doors up they sit in a gloomy booth in front of the chess set. There's not much light from the tall stained-glass windows but she can see that several pieces are worn and the edges of one black knight are chipped. She remembers her little hands, post–short stack, leaving butter smudges on the narrow waists of the pawns when she rocked them to pivot forward. She was terrible at chess. Seeing half-a-dozen moves into the future? Weighing up possibilities before acting? It's not her.

The ponytailed waitress knows Jamie drinks English Breakfast. Caddie orders one too, though the woman doesn't look at her. The building was once a cathedral and the ceilings are dark timber and high and raked. It's cool in here, a kind of crypt. There's a full-size suit of armour guarding the hall to the toilets. Caddie has no idea why.

Jamie rests his elbows on the table and joins his fingertips together. Tilts to look at her over his glasses. 'Convince me,' he says.

She takes her notebook from her bag, opens it to the page

where she transcribed the line and slides it across the table.

He reads it and shrugs. 'That doesn't prove anything. Anyone who's studied Inga's style could have written that line. Even if she's the right age—what sort of accent did this woman have? Just say, by some miracle, she's read the manuscript. What on earth is she doing here?'

He's right; it's a problem. But not one she's prepared to face now.

'No one else read this novel back in the thirties, that's the story, right? How is that even possible?'

'Inga Karlson had always been reclusive, even before the huge success of the first book. She hated interviews, hated parties. In her Hollywood years she was well known for showing up at functions only to vanish halfway through. Introverted almost to the point of agoraphobia. No close friends. No relatives in the US. Didn't trust anyone, not even banks. And she only worked with Charles.'

Caddie asks how they met, although she knows.

'Complete coincidence. When she first moved to New York from Los Angeles—she was trying to break into movies and failing—she worked as a babysitter through an agency. She ended up looking after his kids. He wasn't famous yet but he was a smart young publisher with family money, and he was going places. Man about town, in that martini-drinking New York way. Everyone he met thrust a manuscript at him.'

Something has changed about his face. Something has awoken. His eyes are fiercely lit now, his speech is animated.

'Including Inga,' Caddie says.

'She was smart. She didn't say a word. Just left it on the

coffee table one night before she went home. The whole house was covered in half-read manuscripts, he left them lying around all the time. Everyone thought it was something he was working on. The next night after his wife goes to bed, he pours himself a drink and he sees the thing right where Inga left it. He reads the first page. Next thing he knows, the maid is letting herself in. It's six a.m.'

Caddie imagines that morning: Charles Cleborn, blinking, in a worn leather chair with an empty whisky glass and a full ashtray beside him, surprised by the sound of the door and the light peeking in the windows to the east. The thrill of knowing he has discovered something miraculous, a chink of time when a masterpiece belonged only to him.

'Even now I can't think about it without my hair standing up.' Jamie rubs the back of his neck.

'And there was no one else. No one called Rachel. You're sure?'

The tea comes and he pours. His nails are short, clean. The steam looks like it belongs here, in this old church for this conversation, like incense from a thurible.

'I'm sure. The whole world is sure. Inga is one of the most studied writers of the twentieth century. We know the names of everyone in her very small circle. If there was someone else and I knew about it, I wouldn't be auctioning books. I'd be living it up on the proceeds of my bestseller.'

'There must have been an editor?'

He shakes his head. 'Charles edited it himself. It wasn't uncommon back then, to be both publisher and editor when the firm was small.'

'Who else would read a book normally before it was published?'

'A jacket designer—but not in this case. The printer reported it was plain red cloth, with her name and the title embossed in gold. A typesetter, but Charles did that himself. No proofreader, she wouldn't allow it.'

'The typesetting. Isn't that weird, the publisher doing it?'

He nods. 'It was the only way she'd agree to publishing another book. She was pretty paranoid by that time. After the first book came out and was such a smash, photo-graphers lay in wait for her, people would rifle through her bins. She found all the attention really unsettling. One day, she received sixty-two letters, all handwritten, all begging for a reply. Most people loved her first book but lots didn't. She had death threats, a number of them. There's a letter from Nabokov to his wife, funnily enough, in late '36, recounting how he ran into Inga somewhere and she said she wanted to move far away from New York and live somewhere where no one knew who she was.'

'How can you be sure? About the typesetting?'

He tilts his head and frowns at her. 'Why does this matter?'

How can she explain? She is one of those people for whom things matter. She's surrounded by people who skate above the surface of the world. The *she'll be right mate* and *close enough is good enough* people who promise customers they'll order something and never do, who misfile things, who open cartons with a Stanley knife and put the damaged books on the shelf anyway. It's as if she lacks the same skin as other

68

people. There's something uncool about caring. The very word 'cool' implies a chilly indifference.

Finally: 'It just does.'

He nods sharply, as if she's given reason enough. 'The typesetting bit is in the posthumous letter to Charles. The famous one. It's here in Brisbane right now, it's in the exhibition. It arrived after they were both dead. She must have mailed it on the day of the fire, this rushed kind of note, you can tell she's under the pump. It says: "…and all the trouble you've gone to, to master those horrible little letters just for me. Typesetting it yourself was the greatest kindness, Charles, I shan't forget it."'

He too is the kind of person who knows sentences off by heart.

'It seems like an enormous effort.'

'It was extraordinary, but he was dedicated. You have to remember, Inga's first book was hugely successful. Publishing is rife with these stories. Maxwell Perkins edited Tom Wolfe so…'—he searches for a word—'so *aggressively* that researchers argue about where Wolfe ends and Perkins begins. Back then, they did what had to be done.'

'So there's no chance of anyone else.'

He leans forward and joins his hands, fingers threaded together. His mouth is turned up at one corner, but his eyes are kinder.

'If there was, someone would have found them by now. It was a big deal at the time, as you could imagine. Inga, dead? She'd sold the film rights to *All Has an End* for twelve thousand dollars, almost a quarter of a million in today's money, at the tail end of the Depression. She'd won every book prize going and sold maybe two million copies in the first year, over fourteen reprints. The fire was front-page news. The whole building gutted, two firemen badly injured.'

'How do you think the fire started?'

'That's not my area.'

'You must have an opinion.'

'My opinion is that people should stop theorising without the facts. Yes, they found traces of an accelerant. Yes, Charles had the only key to the warehouse. That doesn't mean he did it. It's easy to blame him, he can't defend himself.' His cup rattles when he replaces it on the saucer.

'But he died too.'

'People say he somehow stuffed it up. The book was terrible, that's the theory, and he decided to torch every copy to keep the Inga mystique and boost sales of her first book. So not only is he a murderer, he was also incompetent.'

'But you don't believe that.'

'I think the so-called accelerant was the bottles of booze he stored out the back going up like rockets. Charles liked a drink. Prohibition only ended a few years before and I'd guess he was still sitting on a stash, just in case.'

'And the bodies? They were positively identified?'

He nods. 'Inga sent Charles a telegram asking him to meet her at the warehouse; it was found in his pocket. Charles wasn't burnt as badly as Inga. Smoke inhalation. Her body was in a terrible state, except for one arm. Positive ID. They matched her fingerprints to a copy of her will, which was lucky enough to have an ink smudge on it. And the case has been revisited with cutting-edge forensics as well—fingerprints have been taken now from a number of letters she'd sent to fans. Everything matches. Dying that way…it seems kind of exotic now but safety standards back then were rubbish. The Cocoanut Grove fire was only a few years later—almost five hundred people incinerated in a few minutes from one match. Did you see the necklace? The glass one?'

No, she didn't. It was in the exhibition all right, in the display about the fire. The one she turned away from. Caddie shakes her head.

'Green glass, with bees on it. She was never without it. It melted in the fire but it was recognisable as hers. All those books, all that paper. It was an inferno. The warehouse had bars on the windows—the firefighters reported there was no way either of them could get out.'

She's treading the path already worn by much smarter people than her. Of course there's nothing left to discover. 'Charles must have been devoted to her, to have gone to all that trouble of doing the typesetting.'

'He was, but not like that. There was nothing between them in that way. He had a reputation as a ladies' man, of course—flamboyant, hard-drinking, loved a party. Hats and cravats. But she had a kind of purity that was impossible to resist,' he says. 'By all accounts, she was the sort of person who inspired devotion.'

'The exhibition's fabulous.' She's descended into platitude, she knows, but she doesn't want the conversation to end. 'It's wonderful so much of her legacy's been preserved.'

He smiles at her. He's amused.

'Most of that was sheer luck. There was a great outpouring of grief at the time of her death, of course, but later that year Hitler was invading Poland and then the world had other things to think about. Most of Inga's stuff was moved into a storage unit. Charles had a widow and children. His publishing company was wound up. One daughter kept all his papers in boxes under the bed. By the time the war was over, *All Has an End* was exactly what people needed to read—the Inga craze took off from the post-war reissue.'

'And you?'

'And me, what? Your turn now. The woman—your old lady.'

She describes the queue, the chatty photographer with the yellow eye on his shirt, and the woman's manner. The mysterious Rachel. It feels vague and minuscule, like describing the way the hairs on your forearm register the sun going behind a cloud. What was she thinking, wasting this man's time?

'Thin,' he says.

'I know. Wishful thinking.' It's been a long time since she wished for anything. This very act of longing has made her happy, she sees now. It's a vital, pulsing thing, the energy that comes from yearning.

'Most people spend their whole lives wishing for things,' he says.

'How did you become interested in Inga in the first place?'

He finishes his tea and fiddles with the cup. 'It started as a tiny project in the first year of my arts degree, a ten-minute presentation on Charles Cleborn. I was a terrible student. I cribbed a page of notes, aiming for a solid pass so I could get to the pub, and then for some unknown reason I kept reading. I was young and naive. She seemed exactly what I was looking for. I found myself falling in love with Inga.'

This she could understand. 'So you're a Charles expert as well?'

A little shrug. 'There's not a lot about him in the record. It's a shame. Inga was magic, of course, but there was something special about Charles. His firm seems old-fashioned and a bit eccentric to us now; little style quirks—even diaereses, for heaven's sake. You know? Like an umlaut? Only the *New Yorker* does that now, but at the time he was avant-garde. He was a war veteran who'd been injured in France and people used to say his list had a European slant. What else? Rich, of course. His grandparents were in banking so he didn't have to work much at all. And famously impatient with all his other authors but he did whatever Inga wanted. He'd be forgotten now, except for his connection with her. I can't help wondering what he would have done with his life if he hadn't died so young.'

There it was again, the pinpoint deflection. He answered her question about him by talking about Charles instead. It was elegantly done. Most people wouldn't have noticed.

'And your passion for Inga?'

'A thing of the past. I sell old books now. Books destined to be unread, as you've remarked.' He shuffles to the end of the booth. 'I'll fix up the bill on the way out. Take your time, Caddie.'

*

Two nights after tea with Jamie Ganivet, Caddie wakes in the early hours, sweating and tangled in sheet, to the sound of hail pounding the corrugated-iron roof. These heavy summer storms are common in Brisbane but more usual in the afternoon. You glance out the window to find the air suspiciously still. If you drive anywhere with any regularity, to an office or a factory or school, you carry with you a mental map of all the undercover parking places along your route: bridges, overpasses, the awning of an abandoned petrol station. Some days the clouds have a greenish, bruised tinge and when the skies are like that the hail can come down without warning. An oval becomes a sea of white, birds are struck dead on the branch. Holes drill through windows like a straight drive down a fairway, divots as deep as your first knuckle appear on car bonnets. Then the wind picks up, then the rain. Turmoil, like being trapped inside a washing machine. The price to be paid for all those days of endless blue.

She could get up to see the sky lit by zigzag bolts. But she has no obligations in this brooding hour—no car, and as for the condition of the roof, there's not much she can do about it now. She thinks about her dream instead: a hot-weather dream, dense and muddled. Her small self sitting on the floor of the garage in her school uniform with her father bent in concentration over a watch.

Her father repaired watches. Breitling and Omega, IWC and Rolex. Fobs, sometimes, but wrists for preference. He loved their mix of elegance and utility. He'd begun his working life as a jeweller because it seemed a way to combine his eye for fine detail and his obsession with art deco. During his apprenticeship, his heroes were the great jewellers of the twenties and thirties—Després, Lalique, Boucheron—but as he grew into the work he loved them all: precious things that worked hard at a purpose. It's not the nature of the job that matters, he sometimes said when she was small. What matters is the way you do the job, any job. That's what shows the world your character.

He kept an old desk in the garage, each drawer wedged full of tattered cardboard boxes without lids. Some contained movements sorted by size and maker; others, backs of different metals, or lenses. Along the front were stoppered plastic pill bottles of tiny screws and pins and dials and hands and buckle tongues and free loops, all sorted by size and colour and sometimes model. He had half-a-dozen magnifying glasses, though one was his favourite, and tweezers and razor blades and plastic bags and spools of thread. He had case bands and bezels in every colour hanging on nails on the top of the desk alongside watches, mid-repair, suspended by the buckles.

She liked to check on him while he worked. Often she'd go to Terese's after school, where Olympia cut them orange wedges to eat in front of the television, but once home she headed straight to the garage to check her father's desk light was on and make him tea. She was a bossy child. She'd stand with her weight on one leg and her hands on her hips, telling him off if she found his lunchtime sandwich uneaten with the bread curling at four in the afternoon. On weekends she would sit cross-legged on the floor reading her book, looking up to see him hunched at his desk before his wall of torn-out photographs of precious jewels. The concentration, the patience. Half the time he didn't even notice she was there. Sometimes even now if she glimpses a lovely watch, an old, special one, on the wrist of a customer, she imagines his long fingers bent in its service.

In her dream, it was just like that. He doesn't know she's there, watching. She sees the tanned back of his neck, his trimmed sideburn. The watch hands are moving as he works on it. Tick, tick. The ticking grows louder until it morphs into the hail on the roof, but her father doesn't react. Nothing will hurry him. She sees his focus, his quiet diligence.

Charles Cleborn had money. He was 'famously impatient' with all his other authors—when it came to Inga, though, he did anything she wanted. She sees her father, surrounded by his ragged jewelled pages and all those tiny watch parts, perfectly sorted.

She doesn't know the first thing about typesetting but she knows the kind of man who can devote himself to the exquisite order of things. Her father was not inclined towards business. He was employed in jewellery shops sometimes, but more often than not he drove bosses crazy: his perfectionism, his insistence on painstaking care. He would come home, unexpected, with a cardboard box of stained tea mugs and his tools, his expression sheepish but unsurprised. *Let go*, is how they said it. *We have to let you go*. That's why he worked in the garage for private clients—people who found him by word of mouth and would send their heirlooms, present and future, for repair by courier from Melbourne and Sydney.

Caddie sits up in her bed and punches her pillow. There'll be no more sleep tonight. She doesn't know how books were made back then but she pictures a desk like her father's, except instead of watch parts it has tiny individual *a*s and *t*s and *w*s in cardboard boxes wedged in a drawer. Would Charles Cleborn—injured war veteran, wealthy businessman—have loved Inga's *horrible little letters* enough to take responsibility for an entire book? She must find out.

8

Allentown, Pennsylvania, 1938

The Sunday morning of that week, Rachel wakes early. George
is like a starfish in their bed, dead to the world. In the bed
opposite her father lies, cradling her mother from behind. In
sleep her mother has nestled into him; his arm reaches over the
top of her. In recent days they've been tender. Walter cutting
Mary's food into small pieces or producing a banana from the
pocket of his coat like a magician. Mary, coquette eyes, giggling
behind her hankie. Both of them laughing at Rachel for not
having a beau. You'd think they were honeymooners if not for
the mulberry cloud along the line of her mother's jaw.

Rachel wraps herself in the gown that hangs behind
the door, wrestles her feet into boots that were reserved for
outdoors when they lived on the farm. Everything is rough
on her skin: the coarse weave of the gown, the splintering
timber of the dresser, the jagged finish on the floor. Back on
the farm, beauty was all around her and so common it was
never remarked upon. It's taken a while but she's begun to see

tiny hints of beauty here in town, and not just in the silks. The girls, their strong arms pulling the spools, their proud necks, corn hair as it frames their faces.

She lights the still-warm stove to boil water for the oats. She opens the front curtain to a late frost: a dusting on the bottom corner of each pane and, up close, a lattice of crisp white ferns creeping across the glass. Beauty everywhere, even in this town, she thinks, provided you don't touch anything.

Then she glimpses a girl standing across the street, leaning on the black railing of the apartment building opposite. She's wrapped in a good coat, arms deep in the pockets. One leg is bent for a foot to rest on the step behind her and the boot that's visible is yellow against the last dirty snow. A heavy dark scarf all but covers her face. She's picked an odd place to wait for someone, Rachel thinks.

Later, Walter, George and Rachel are leaving for church. Her mother isn't feeling well, she says, as though it's her asthma that's kept her indoors this last week and not the great bruise on her face. Rachel notices the girl is still there, standing with the other foot raised this time, wrapped like an owl on a branch. Now that Rachel is outside and closer, there is something about the girl that is familiar.

'Can that be Helen over there?' she says to her father.

'Who?'

'Helen. From the mill.'

He doesn't so much as glance. 'How should I know?' he says. 'Am I in charge of every loony girl in the neighbourhood?'

Rachel takes George's hand. He wriggles it free.

'Yeah, Rach,' he says. 'Is Pop in charge of every loony girl?'

They're on time for church, for a change, though they walk fast in the brisk air. George chats all the way. *How much does a bicycle cost, Pop? I'm going to get myself a paper route soon, aren't I? When I get a bicycle. And then I'm going to save up for a car, and when I get a car, I'm going to take you and Mama for drives on Sundays and we'll have ice cream. Rachel can come. I guess. If she says please.* He dances along, half in the gutter, tightrope walking the edge of the kerb.

At the door of the church, Walter stops. 'I've been good in the eyes of the lord this week,' he says. 'The two of you go on.'

'But Pop,' George says.

'Go on now. The good lord will understand.'

'What will he understand, Pop?' says George.

'That a man needs one blessed day with no damn questions,' he says. He guides George inside, steers Rachel with his hand in the small of her back. This close to him, she can smell his lathering soap.

'We'll wait for you after the service, Pop,' she says.

'No,' he says, and he takes off his hat and holds it in his hands. 'You're a grown woman. You can find your own goddamn way home.'

They do. It's not far, but Rachel and George dawdle because if there's one thing that's rare in their lives, it's time that's unaccounted for. They play I-spy as they walk. By the time they reach their own street, it's late. Their mother greets them at the door in Walter's bathrobe.

'Where is he?' Mary says at once.

She's let the stove burn low and Rachel goes to feed it.

'Someplace where there's no damn questions,' George says.

Rachel sets the table for four with forks and knives and ironed napkins, and they eat their dinner, and they sleep. In the morning there is no Walter but they find his key on the dresser next to an empty French cameo glass atomiser that was a gift from Mary's Aunt Vera. Rachel goes to work and George to school. Walter is not at the mill. Only a little way into her shift Rachel notices an empty machine in the back row. Helen is also missing.

At lunchtime, Rachel plucks up all the courage she has and asks Mr Dimley if, beg your pardon, she might have a word about her father.

He blinks and he focuses, as if she's materialised from the air in front of him. 'And who are you, when you're at home?'

Rachel Lehrer, she reminds him. The daughter of Walter.

And then she is bawled out for her trouble, for the inconstancy of people, their lack of appreciation for a good turn. As if it were Rachel who worked there first and vouched for her father instead of the other way around.

'I should fire you while I have the chance,' he says to her. 'Bad blood.'

Instead, he pays her what she should always have earnt: a grown woman's wage.

In that first week without Walter, Mary's bruises grow richer and deeper and George asks *When is Papa coming home*, it seems to Rachel, on the hour.

In the second week new bruises which Rachel has no memory of seeing inflicted bloom from deep within her mother's flesh where they've been waiting their turn.

There are no more questions from George. The air is heavy, a shoe waiting to drop.

One night Mary wakes from a dream screaming, covering her face with her hands and Rachel crawls into her bed and holds her until she falls back to sleep. In the front room, there's a flyer on the table that Helen's brothers handed to everyone at the mill at the end of yesterday's shift: *Missing Girl*, it says, above a grainy photo of Helen with her hair flattened by a woollen cap, squinting into the sun. *Reward offered*. They made every worker take one, or more. Their faces, gruff and set. Gritted teeth.

'I don't suppose you know the whereabouts of your father,' the elder one says to her, standing too close. 'We'd like a word.'

Rachel shakes her head.

By the third week they are short of money, with only Rachel's salary, but George picks up some hours after school, cleaning barrows at a foundry. He stops gripping her in the night, his skinny fingers no longer squeezing her wrists. Mary takes in some mending. They eat corned beef and beans and crackers. In the fourth week, Rachel's mother's skin mellows into its own colour—warm prairie wheat. Rachel is nineteen now, her mother thirty-four. They would have looked like sisters if not for her mother's missing teeth. On Sundays they sleep late if they choose. As the weather gets a little warmer there are Rachel's vegetables: new potatoes, parsnips, green onions. They trade the surplus for eggs and a little salt pork and eat cold pork and eggs fried in butter with their fingers, sitting on the back porch. They have what they want.

Here is the fact: Walter ate a lot, and he drank. Men require walking-around money—they feel belittled without the tinkle of coins in their pocket—so the three of them have more than they would have guessed. Rachel even manages to save a little money that she keeps wrapped in a handkerchief in the bakelite canister with the flour. She sleeps all night through because small sounds no longer wake her; there is nothing to check on, no vigilance is required.

One day Rachel comes home from work to see Mary sitting up at the kitchen table shelling peas from her apron into a saucepan, and smiling. Mary does more, cleans more. It seems to Rachel that she wants to see the house shine because it's theirs, not because of the trouble that would otherwise rain down upon them. Before bed, she sits behind Rachel and brushes her hair with a hundred strokes. George is the man of the house, he is growing into it. Rachel hides her father's key at the back of a drawer in the dresser.

'I don't want him back,' Mary says, one night at supper.

Rachel passes George the beans.

'I want you both to know,' Mary says. 'It's not his temper. That's part and parcel of being a wife. It's the shame of it, this missing girl. The way folk look at you in the street. I don't want him back.'

In the beginning of the tenth week, when Rachel rises to light the stove there is a strange smell in the front room. Faint, but clear: tobacco. She feels her mouth fill with saliva. She creeps to the small window beside the front door and teases open the curtain an inch. There is a dishevelled man asleep in the corner of the porch, collar pulled high, hat pulled low, coat spread like a blanket. He's thin as a hickory stick but she can tell by the jut of the shoulders that it's her father.

9

Brisbane, Queensland, 1986

Another day off, and Caddie finds herself again on the ferry approaching the university, but this time it's mid-morning. It's only been a week since she was last here. The campus is deserted this early in February, flat and baking despite the sprinklers on the playing fields twirling hypnotically. She changed her mind a dozen times last night. She can barely believe she's here. She might have gone to all this trouble for nothing but she couldn't bring herself to ring first. The premeditation of it, the acknowledgment of her own intent: she would have lost her nerve.

From the river it's a fair walk up through the bowels of the student union complex, past the Refec. The complex is gloomy inside and the doors to the Student Legal Service and the hairdresser and the Womyn's Room are locked. There's no one sitting on the bench seats and tables out the front, no market stalls of incense or tie-dye T-shirts and no Hare Krishnas giving away rice and dhal.

Inside the Great Court, she waits under the cloister just outside the Forgan Smith, leaning on the sandstone. She knows where the office is, the one she's come to visit, but she needs to compose herself before climbing those stairs. She waits. She breathes; she calms her racing heart. The grotesques leer at her. This morning she couldn't force the muesli past her lips so she left the house with two baby cheese wheels in her pockets, like creamy erasers wrapped in softening red wax. She's scoffed one already and rolled the wax into tiny bullets. She imagines watching her younger self strolling by and flicking the wax at her. She wonders what she would say to herself in warning.

Christ, Caddie, she thinks. She must want to unravel the puzzle pretty badly. This is nature's way of telling you to fix your life. Find something to care about. Ten-pin bowling; line dancing.

The man she's waiting for is not the kind of person who changes his habits so it doesn't take long. He appears through the open door, walking with a young woman towards Caddie. The woman—girl, really—is in a denim skirt and thongs and an electric blue singlet. Her black hair is pulled into a high ponytail and her face is fresh, scrubbed. She's holding a pile of books to her chest and she has a black backpack over one shoulder and she's walking fast to keep up with Philip. She's a student of his, Caddie guesses. He's talking, gesturing with his free hands, animated and *present*: right here. The girl is nodding, rushing after him. He stops mid-sentence when he sees Caddie and the girl pulls up too. There's a softening before his mouth tightens. Her heart thumps.

He raises one eyebrow, like an actor. His eyes are chips of blue ice, his hair is straw. He's wearing a short-sleeved blue linen shirt and pleated camel cords and boat shoes. He's even more handsome than Pretty, whose real name is Jon. That's saying something.

He clenches his jaw and folds his arms across his chest: a fighting stance, a makeshift shield.

'Well, well,' he says. 'The prodigal student returns.'

All she can say is hello, in a voice somewhat similar to her own.

'Jo, be a dear and start without me, won't you? I shouldn't be long,' he says, without taking his gaze from Caddie.

'Sure,' the girl says. 'I'll just get your usual, shall I?'

He nods. The girl, Jo, walks on along the cloister, ponytail swinging.

Philip leans against the sandstone.

'It's been a while,' Caddie says.

'Your gift for understatement is intact, I see. Have you been well? You're thinner, I think.'

Yes, she tells him. She's been very well.

'And your father? He's well too, I trust.'

Yes, she says without a pause. He's fine.

Longing, that's how she felt about Philip at the beginning. She was eighteen years old and destroyed by wanting. Sometimes she thought she would die. No one had warned her that love would strike that way, like a disease. She sees it clearly now, the progress of her downfall. Her exuberant, giddy falling; his reserve in reaction; her devastation. His pragmatism as he unveiled her naivety—she was *immature to think this was love.* She *didn't understand how the world worked.* She was *too impulsive.* Is, still.

Those first few weeks after it ended with Philip, every bit of her ached. Her eyelids, her toenails, the pads of her fingers. It was hard to move and impossible to eat. The years since have passed in a flash, like when you come out of an afternoon movie and all at once it's night. When she looks at him now, though, her body remembers; it's ingrained in every cell. Her pulse speeds up, she's conscious of the way her tongue sits in her mouth. A moment passes. Philip was good at silences, she remembers. Manufacturing holes for you to step in. His face is just the same. Even more handsome, if that's possible. A little greyer and more confident.

'Your small talk hasn't improved much.'

'No,' she says, and she recognises her voice again. 'I need you to tell me about the mechanics of book publishing in the US in the late 1930s.'

Ten minutes later, they're in his office. Philip behind his carved desk, swaying in his executive chair with one ankle resting on his knee. Caddie in front of it, in an armchair reserved for visitors. The door is open. The window behind him looks west to the wide sky, towards the playing fields. His office is bigger: a wall has been removed and now it incorporates the room next door. This is a good sign, in university semiotics, as is the tiny futuristic computer on his desk. Its beige screen—roughly cuboid, but with angled, sloping sides—is sitting on top of a box no bigger than a Betamax, with a floppy disc drive in front. He's come up in the world. There's even a spare desk in the corner—for a research assistant, she guesses. There are still stacks of papers overflowing everywhere and the cracked old tan leather couch that was always a bit dodgy now has one leg missing and is propped up on books. He's forgotten all about Jo, waiting somewhere with his cold cappuccino. Caddie doesn't remind him.

'So, how have you been, Philip?' he says. 'I'm deeply sorry I haven't been in touch. Tell me, Philip, what you've been up to over the last six years?'

'How rude of me. I should have asked. I'm sorry. How are you, Philip?'

He waves a dismissive hand. 'Muddling along. Working on another book, though it's a wee bit over deadline and my agent is ripping out her hair. But never mind that. I admire the way you get down to business. Let me follow your lead. I don't remember you being particularly interested in history or publishing when you were here,' he says. 'Romantic poets were your thing, weren't they? And Inga Karlson.'

'History of the Book was an elective,' she says. 'I was busy with other things, if you remember.'

'Oh, I remember.' He smiles lazily, looking into the middle distance. 'I don't know how much *you* remember, but it wasn't my subject. Jamieson taught that. It doesn't exist anymore. They cut it.'

His desk is covered in books and papers, purposefully ordered. There's a stickytape dispenser and a fountain pen in a case next to the phone. There's nothing in this whole room that seems specifically his except a poster for *Raging Bull* on the wall beside the door. De Niro, battered and shirtless:

sweaty, brutal and brutalised yet defiant, focused on his fate. Caddie tries to imagine Philip bedraggled and bloody, squaring up to his opponent. The battles of tenure and office size and first years and sabbaticals are a glancing, sideways business. Shake hands and slap backs and slide a thin blade between the enemy's ribs.

Philip reaches for a handful of coloured paperclips from a glazed pottery bowl on his desk and begins idly to straighten them. He knows enough to help her, she is sure of it. In the years before she met him, one of his major successes was a paper on *All Has an End*. His interest in Inga had come from nowhere and soon faded but it earned him hundreds of citations and helped with his promotion to associate professor.

'But you know about that stuff, right? The history of publishing?' she says.

'I covered for Jamieson the year of his sabbatical. He should have retired by then but—tenure, what can you do? If a man wants to occupy an office and go to seed in public and eventually drop at his desk while reading Yeats, who's to stop him?' He rips off a few small pieces of stickytape and wraps them around the ends of particular straightened paper clips.

She clears her throat. 'How difficult would it have been to learn typesetting in New York in 1938?'

'As I said, it wasn't my subject and the university dropped it anyway. The book is dead, Cads. People like Jamieson should be decomposing in the zoology department somewhere between the dinosaur footprint guy and the nerds working on continental drift. Or they should make him take all the first years. God, first years. Talk about delusions of grammar.'

He rolls his eyes. '*Ta da.*' He holds up the paperclips. 'What's this? Guess.'

He's unfolded and woven them together into a flat grid with the outside made of two straightened yellow clips reinforced by a couple of green ones along the bottom half, and a blue and a black one threaded vertically and a red, horizontally.

'I can't imagine.'

'Come on, make an effort. It's genius.'

He waves it in the space between them in line with her eyes, pinching the yellow ones together between thumb and forefinger. 'It's the London Underground map, obviously. See? The red one's the Central Line.'

'Of course. London. Silly me.'

He throws it in the bin beside his desk like a frisbee, then he leans forward conspiratorially. 'It's becoming a jungle around here. The politics. If I didn't have tenure I'd tell them where to stick it. There's a uni in Vancouver looking for a reader in Commonwealth literature. I'm seriously considering it. That'll wake them up.'

If the department is truly becoming a jungle, she has no doubt who's at the top of the food chain. Philip is Machiavelli in a tweed jacket.

'Please, Philip.'

'Pretty please,' he says. 'With sugar on top.'

'I'd really appreciate it. You'd be doing me a huge favour.'

He waves his hand at her, which she takes to mean *continue*.

'Was it difficult, typesetting a book in the late 1930s?'

'Very. Operating a linotype was extremely skilled work.'

She doesn't know what a linotype is. She's never heard of it.

He shakes his head and leans back in his chair. 'If you'd stuck it out, you'd know all this. You'd have your PhD by now. Maybe I should show you, what do they call it—tough love? Force you to come back to the department. I'm sure I could find room for you on my team.'

She folds her hands in her lap. She waits. She looks calm, she thinks, and that's what matters.

'A linotype is a machine, kind of like a typewriter attached to a hot metal casting apparatus. That's how type was set for books back then. The operators were very well paid, highly sought after. People were apprenticed at it, it wasn't easy to learn. Huge concentration required. The keyboard had ninety characters. It was hot and dirty and if the machine jammed, a great chunk of hot lead would squirt out and land on your leg. And there was a lot of pressure. Every mistake meant a rubbish slug, straight in the bin. Linotype operators were the highest paid people in a publishing company. Sometimes they earned more than the editor.'

'How did it work?'

'Ingenious, really. The operator would sit in front of it and type, and then the machine made a line out of moulds of the letters. Then they were cast as a single piece for each line, in metal. A slug. The lines slid together to make a page.'

'A single line, in one piece?'

'That's what I said.' He moves towards a grey metal filing cabinet behind the door, the last in a set of three, squats with his knees wide and rifles through some hanging folders. 'Here.' He hands her a sheet.

It's a photo of a huge black machine with a small keyboard, and an apparatus behind it with many levers and arms. At the top, there's a sloping screen and some kind of roller. It's hulking and vaguely malevolent. It's not what she imagined at all.

'Do you think that machine could be described as using "horrible little letters"?'

He shrugs. 'That sounds more like a description of setting type by hand. That's when you manually pick up each individual letter, called a sort, and slide it into a composing stick. When did you say, '38? Hand composition was long gone by then, except for things like headlines and specific design effects. Linotypes were introduced in the 1880s. By the 1910s, they were everywhere.'

In an instant, two separate truths occur to Caddie. One: Inga didn't know how books were typeset. She didn't know about linotypes. She'd never seen one. She'd had the same image in her head that Caddie had, of Charles Cleborn picking up each letter individually and setting it in a frame. And two: Charles, with his New York townhouse, his money and cravats, his famous impatience, wasn't the kind of man to apply himself to that noisy, dirty machine. Charles had lied to Inga. He hadn't typeset *The Days, the Minutes* himself. There was someone else who had read the book.

'Hello?' says Philip. 'Anyone home?'

'Were they always men, on the linotypes? Were there any women?'

'Not that I've ever heard of. Christ, is this some feminist thing? Have you gone off men, Caddie? Jumped the fence?'

He's only half-joking. He wants her to say yes. He wants a reason she hasn't called him in all these years. She has a flash of memory: his bathtub, an old claw-foot type that took forever to fill. The white peaks of their knees the tips of waves on a tumultuous sea. His house, flat-roofed sixties style surrounded by bush in the numbered avenues in St Lucia, and his spare Danish furniture, the bare timber and lack of ornamentation that spoke to her of straitened circumstances. The key under the potted cactus by the back door where no one could see her comings and goings. He kept his good whisky lined up on the top of his dresser in the bedroom—it was cooler. The taste of it, from cold, heavy crystal and from his warm mouth. His tanned skin against her pale flesh. The simultaneous feeling that she's the luckiest girl in the world to be there with him and the equal certainty he's picked her out of the class because he knows she's the weakest, like a leopard eyeing an antelope on *Wild Kingdom*. She feels a red heat spread up her throat, her face. Coming here was a mistake, she sees it now.

'If you typeset a book, using one of these machines—is it the same as reading it? I mean, could you absorb the text that way?'

He rests his chin on his threaded fingers. 'I guess you could, if you focused. Mostly, operators didn't pay any attention to the words they were typesetting. It was difficult enough just working the machine.'

'If there were any female linotype operators back then, how could I find out?'

'A boyfriend? You must have a boyfriend. Put me out of

94

my misery, Caddie. The idea of you, lovely you, all alone will keep me awake at night. Tell me he's treating you right.'

She flutters her eyelids. 'I'm holding out for a particular kind of man. One who can tell me if there were any female linotype operators in New York in 1938—or even which operators worked for which publishing houses.'

Philip laughs. 'You're joking. About a quarter of all people working in publishing in the US back then lived in New York. Maybe forty thousand people. There were hundreds of men on linotypes, more if you count apprentices. Maybe thousands. Finding a woman among all of them? And besides, they weren't the kind of people who went down in the historical record.'

This isn't the end of the road. It can't be. 'There must be some way of finding out.'

He leans forward across the desk. 'Why? What's going on?' His eyes narrow. 'What are you not telling me?'

She opens her mouth to tell him about the woman, but his eyes are narrowed and gleaming. 'It's nothing,' she says instead. 'A puzzle. How can I find out?'

'Caddie. Sweetie. It was nearly fifty years ago, on another continent. If a woman was enough of a novelty—maybe the *New York Times* might have mentioned it? There's a vast collection here in the library. Maybe they'd have interviewed somebody or featured something. But you'd have to spend days in front of the microfiche. Weeks, more like it. And it's highly doubtful you'd find a thing. Drone work for dull people, and a long shot. I'm sure you could think of much more rewarding things to do with your time.'

'Would anyone else know more about this? Anyone at all.'

He sweeps his arm. 'I'm not sure if you're aware, but this, my Caddie, is Queensland. The inter-war American publishing industry is not exactly our specialisation. If you wanted to know about thoroughbred blood proteins or cattle-breeding programs? World leaders, *mate*. You could talk to Jamieson, if you can keep him awake. I used to know a mad Karlson groupie who was the apple of the dean's eye until he dropped out in a cloud of angst to become some kind of bric-a-brac dealer but I haven't seen him in years. Some people have all the luck in the world and still throw everything away.'

This 'Karlson groupie'. Jamie, surely? Were he and Philip close, prior to a falling-out? The speed with which this thought comes to her: Jamie Ganivet has been burning at the edges of her mind all day while she tried to focus on other things. The heft of him, in contrast to Philip's angles. She hesitates.

'Leave me your contact details and I'll let you know if anything else occurs to me,' he says. 'I don't bite. Normally. Only on special request.'

He hands her a pen and paper, and she writes down her home address but not her phone number. He folds the paper and slips it in his pocket.

'Are you going to tell me what's behind this little flight of fancy? A research project?' he says.

If things had worked out differently, she might have her own PhD now. She'd be working here, perhaps, as a tutor or junior lecturer. She'd have the office next door. But—and this is hard for her to admit, even to herself—the thing she'd wanted

96

when she was so, so young, was to marry him. She'd wanted to make a home with him, to cook him dinner at the end of the day. Fill a page with 'Caddie Carmichael' in cursive script.

'I don't research anything. I work in a bookshop.' She stands. He's a busy man, she knows. She should be grateful for his time, his attention, *little flight of fancy* or not. 'Thanks anyway. I appreciate it.'

'Don't be like that,' he says, and he really is very attractive, with his jawline and his lovely eyes, and he knows it. For years she's been moving through the days alone. Cold at night, calm when she wakes. Never late, heart always steady, clean and tidy.

He leans forward across the desk. 'You're older now. You're no longer a student here. I miss you. We could go to the Kookaburra, have a quiet dinner.'

There's a noise behind her: she turns and in the doorway is Jo, holding a styrofoam cup. 'Excuse me, professor. I thought…'

'And an excellent thought it was too,' Philip says to her, 'Ms Walker and I were just finishing up.' And then, to Caddie: 'You have everything you need now, yes? If there's anything else I can do, you'll get in touch? I mean it, Caddie. Anything at all.'

'Yes,' Caddie says. 'Yes, I will.'

Her legs feel somehow unwound at the hips, but she walks to the door, passing Jo, who hands the coffee to Philip. The girl is beautiful: lean and glowing. Caddie feels a wild surge of energy as she passes her in the doorway. That girl would kick her in the shins given half a chance.

*

97

A few days later, Caddie sees a punk sitting on the carpet in the furthest corner of the bookstore reading Burroughs' *The Wild Boys*. Her crown of hair spikes is a good handspan in height and only the top three are crimson to match her eyeshadow and her lips and the tartan of her tights, visible between her black skirt and massive buckled boots. She must be boiling, thinks Caddie, and that jacket covered in buttons and studs surely weighs a tonne.

The girl doesn't look troubled. Her legs are crossed despite the boots. Christine is indulgent towards the store readers. It's better than if they shoplift, she says, because at least we have a chance of selling the book. Caddie feels the same and besides, she's fond of the punks. She likes the trouble they take. She leaves the girl alone, although she is doubtful about Burroughs. Maybe she should recommend Lessing?

Christine comes up behind her and taps her on the shoulder. 'Normally I wouldn't say anything.'

'Right,' says Caddie. 'You've always been the kind of person who keeps her opinions to herself.'

'You're not applying for jobs, are you? Or starting your own business, or something? Not that I'd blame you. But you've definitely been weird. Not normal.'

'I was normal before?' says Caddie. 'Jeez, Chrissie, you might have said something.'

Christine folds her arms. 'Phone.' She jerks her head towards the office. 'A man. Of the male persuasion.'

In the back room, Caddie picks up the receiver and says hello.

'Finally. I've rung four bookstores looking for a Caddie.'

Jamie Ganivet.

'I didn't expect to hear from you. I was pretty sure you'd be glad to see the back of me.'

'I didn't expect to be calling. But I had a visit this morning from an old colleague. Professor Philip Carmichael of Queensland Uni.'

Caddie remembers Philip's hooded eyes, his fingertips lightly touching, his gentle condescension—cover for his ultra-competitive brain, ticking away. 'What does this have to do with me?'

'I'm not sure. He asked about the Karlson exhibition, if anyone had been in contact with me looking for inform-ation about a typesetter. The same question you asked: could anyone else have read the book and remembered it. A woman. He also asked if I knew who Charles's usual linotype opera-tors were. He thought someone might approach me.'

She should have expected this. 'Is that all?'

'Only that if someone should contact me, he'd appreciate a call. *One scholar to another.* And here's the thing: he bought a nice first edition Rilke I've had for a while. *Letters to a Young Poet.* Hardback. Light sunning and the spine is cocked and a bit loose, but very nice. I'm dropping it in to him when it gets back from the binders.'

'So he bought a book.'

'Last time I saw him we didn't part on the best of terms. Today, he couldn't have been more charming. He even bought something without trying to bargain me down. Which means he wants something.'

'You don't like him,' Caddie says.

'I wouldn't say that. He's very likeable. I just think he's a prick.'

Silence stretches between them.

'I went to see him last week,' Caddie says. 'To ask about typesetters. I know him. A bit. From years ago. When I was a student.'

'Do you,' says Jamie.

The plastic receiver seems all at once heavier in her hand.

'I didn't say anything about the Karlson exhibition. He couldn't have possibly known about that.'

'Did you mention 1938, specifically?'

She did. She had to be specific, to find out what she needed to know.

'You show up, asking those kinds of questions while the whole city is talking about the fragments? He's not stupid.'

She winds her fingers in the phone cord. Philip must have guessed how difficult it was for her to ask for his help. He could only conclude that there was an important reason for her behaviour, one that would be worth his while to discover.

'What did you tell him?'

'If you mean: did I tell him about you, and who you're looking for—this Rachel—then no. I told him that I had no patience with Inga conspiracy theories, and zero tolerance for people wasting my time. He knows me well enough to know that's true. But, Caddie, I know him pretty well too. He won't give in if he thinks there's something to find.'

She uncurls her fingers from the phone cord. 'But there's nothing to find. You were right—there's no way of knowing if the woman knew the line or was making it up. It's a dead end.'

He pauses. She can hear a vague clunking and sliding. It's a familiar sound—a box of books being delivered? Until then she hadn't considered the similarities of their work, only the differences. Caddie can hear him breathe. She can almost feel it against the pink of her ear. Through the crack in the door she sees the punk girl look around, then slip the Burroughs into her bag.

'Sharks can pick up one drop of blood in a million drops of water,' he says.

'What?'

'My father used to sail. That was one of his sayings. He knew about stuff like that, fishing and sharks and what you should do if you fall overboard. He used to check my backpack before we left to make sure I wasn't trying to smuggle a novel on board.'

'He sounds fun.'

'Oh, he was. Up at six for callisthenics, then reef the jib. My knot-tying skills are world class.'

'I don't think Charles typeset the book,' she says. 'I'm sure he didn't. So maybe the woman was the typesetter.' She tells him about her father's temperament, the little letters, her misunderstanding.

'Not exactly conclusive,' he says. 'What do you want to do now?'

'Does this mean you believe me?'

'I wouldn't go that far. But I suspect there's a possibility of giving Philip the absolute shits and that's very appealing.' He sighs, into her ear. 'Or maybe after all these years, I'm still a little in love with Inga.'

'The university library has the *New York Times* from the late thirties. Philip suggested that if there's any evidence of a female typesetter working in New York back then it might be there. But it's too big a job.'

'Too big a job for one person, maybe,' Jamie says. 'Not for two.'

10

Allentown, Pennsylvania, 1938

Rachel does not make a sound. She creeps to the kitchen and back again, nudges her ear against the door and hears nothing but guttural breathing from outside. The room becomes very clear around her: the green tin light shade above her head; the three lace-fronted shelves above the low dresser; the chipped blue enamel milk jug and matching coffee pot and two shiny saucepans hanging on hooks. A Goodrich calendar with sailing boats at harbour in front of a dawning sky. Time passes; she doesn't know how long but a patch of sun appears on the floor. Then she hears a voice so like her father's that her stomach turns over.

'I'm hungry, Rach, light the stove.'

It's George, barefoot and rubbing his eyes. He's close to twelve now, a little man.

She puts her finger to her lips. George waits and soon they both hear it. A shuffling on the porch, a scrape of arm and boot sole on timber. Fabric rustling like the shake of a damp dog. Then Rachel hears the knock of a single knuckle on the door.

'Mary, my love.' Walter clears his throat. 'I seem to have misplaced my key.'

Rachel and George stand stock-still.

Another few knocks, a jaunty rat-a-tat-tat.

'Georgie boy, there's a good lad. Are you there? A man could freeze to death out here.'

Mary appears in the hall in her nightgown and a blanket, hair soft and loose around her shoulders. She cannot take her eyes off the door. Hand to her mouth, ghost face.

Now the whomp of a flat of a hand against the door. Now the side of a fist and a forearm.

George starts toward the door, stops.

'I'm asking nice for the last time,' Walter says. 'Open this door or there'll be hell to pay.'

Rachel feels a thousand insects crawling under her skin. 'Papa?' she says. 'Is that you? Where've you been all this time?'

'Rachel, there's my good girl,' Walter says. 'Open up now.'

'It's been months, Papa,' Rachel says. 'Whatever became of you? We thought you'd passed over.'

A throaty sound that might have been a laugh. 'No, no, Rachel. I'm sound and well, praise the lord, though not for want of effort from some people in the world.'

Mary staggers to a chair and folds into it. George drops to his heels as though his legs can no longer bear his weight.

'Everyone's been looking for Helen, Papa.'

'There is evil in the world, Rachel. There are black depths in the soul of mankind.'

'Do you know where Helen is?'

'Ah, well.' She hears a scratch and the tinny sound of a match flaring. A pause for him to light a cigarette. 'I'm sorry to say that I was badly deceived by that young woman. But that's not a matter to be talking about through a door, nor is it for children's ears.'

'Everyone's been worried about you both.'

'She preyed on my kindness, Rachel. She was alone in the world in her condition and in an act of Christian charity I gave her my protection even at the expense of my own family. But I'm home now, the lord be praised.'

No, Rachel, Mary mouths.

'I knew if I turned my back on that girl in her hour of need I could never look your mother in the face, not ever again. Your mother is a saint on this earth.'

Mary stands and starts toward the door. 'Where is she, Walter? Where's the girl?'

'Is that you, my darling wife? Open the door, there's my sweetheart.' Then, when none of them moves, a thump and then a kick. 'Open it, I say. I was deceived, that's what happened. She was revealed to me as the worst kind of loose woman. As if I can't count to nine, as if I'm some kind of fool. She took advantage of me to cover for her actions with another man. A trolley-load of other men, most likely.'

Mary shuts her eyes. George sits back on his bottom and wraps his arms around his shins, kneecaps in the hollow of his sockets.

Rachel draws air deep to the bottom of her lungs. 'Go away, Papa.'

'It's not your house. It's nothing to do with you. I'm staying here until I hear from my Mary.' His words are warm and sweet like treacle. 'If she has truly forsaken me, I'll go, of course I'll go. But I know my Mary. My Mary wouldn't cast me out because of the wicked character of some whore.'

'Rachel,' Mary whispers. 'I don't know.'

But Rachel knows. This, she knows.

'Go away, Papa,' she says. 'Mr Dimley's given Pat McClure your job and we've become accustomed to things. Best you make a fresh start somewhere else.'

There's a mighty smack, a strong shoulder against the door. A run up, and then another. The three of them flinch, but the door holds.

'Let me in, Rachel or you better pray to god to stay my hand.'

The back door is locked and solid, Rachel knows. The windows too. They are two women alone with only a boy; Rachel took the precautions herself.

'If you stay out there making a spectacle, someone will tell Helen's brothers and they'll come for you, Papa. They're worried sick, and they're angry and things might not go so well for you. Best you be gone now.'

Another slam. Another kick.

'I need to lay down before I faint,' Mary says.

George does not go to her, nor Rachel. Mary stands on legs of water. She teeters down the hall with a hand on each wall.

'Papa,' Rachel says. 'Papa, we don't wish you any ill. But you need to go, with all our blessings. Please, Papa.'

There is silence outside for a minute. George raises his

head and looks at Rachel. She creeps toward the window and pulls the curtain aside. The porch is empty: nothing but a crumpled Lucky Strike pack and the core of an apple. She pulls the curtain wider and looks toward the street. Nothing, up or down. Her father will be fine, she tells herself. It's warmer now, he won't freeze. He'll find work as a miner in Luzerne County and everything will be well.

Then a noise so loud the house seems to shake on its foundations. The taste of acid in her mouth, a mad desire in her legs. *Run, run, run*, they say.

They're still saying it as the back door slams.

11

Brisbane, Queensland, 1986

When Caddie was ten, she fell in with some neighbouring children from a subsection of Christianity that disapproved of grandeur. One Sunday afternoon she went with them on a scavenger hunt around their church, a peeling weatherboard hall in the middle of a dusty park.

The minister who'd organised it, a bearded and bejeaned type with a tie-dyed shirt, handed them the first clue in a used envelope that had once held a gas bill. It said: 'Find your direction in Isaiah 38:8', which meant nothing to Caddie but was understood at once by the other kids. Off they ran in their ironed jeans, jostling and giggling with not a little un-Christian tripping. Caddie followed. They found another note hidden at the back of the church, under the tenth step from the top, and on it went. It should have been fun but the competitive desperation seemed out of proportion to the ultimate prize, which was a pop-up book of David and Goliath.

This excursion feels just like that. What would evidence of a female typesetter prove, even if they could find it? She tells herself to be sensible, and then she thinks about Philip and his breath on her neck. She knows what she is running from, even if her goal remains a mystery. Philip has research assistants, graduate students, undergrads. Caddie knows, better than anyone, that he has a way of organising people to do what he wants and making them feel like it was their idea in the first place.

Saturday morning, and she meets Jamie out the front of the undergrad library. He is in a white shirt this time, jeans and Wayfarers. The wind is picking up. There are students milling on the stone stairs and the grass, smoking, waiting. They all look similar—big tousled hair, baggy pale jeans, polos in various shades of blue or checked flannel shirts—except for one or two mature-age students who could be dentists and a solitary Boy George fan who must have woken at dawn to apply his makeup. When the doors open they all leave their bags in the racks and pass through the turnstiles.

Caddie and Jamie stride with a sense of purpose. They might be one of those TV detective pairings: Laura Holt and Remington Steele or the Hart to Harts. It feels like a road trip. She should have brought a bag of snakes.

Since she was last here black card-catalogue cabinets have sprung up, squat as beehives, in every conceivable space. Smoking is banned now so there are no pinprick flares among the gloom of the stacks as they pass but dancing milky sunbeams still weave from the high windows to the floor. It is always crowded, this library: built when it seemed impossible that there was anything more to discover. More than fifty years of ad-hoc extensions and mezzanine additions and compactus shelving—so much wallpaper over inadequate timber. Caddie has always felt welcome here. This is a place for people who want to find things out. She has always been a person like that.

The library hush settles on them like a quilt. That smell—mouldering cellulose with a touch of cut grass and vanilla—calms and focuses her. The carrels fill quickly but they find a table that's almost empty close to the microfiche readers. Jamie tackles the catalogue while she assembles notepads and pens to keep track of their efforts.

'Here,' he says, returning with an armful of cardboard boxes. Inside are reels of black film, rolled tight. 'Where do you want to start?'

A small current runs through her. Her muscles feel alive beneath her skin, she can feel them twinge and sparkle. She hopes she isn't coming down with something.

'1935,' she says, without really knowing why.

The challenge was to not be distracted. In the 1930s the *New York Times* had advertisements for alligator bags and Safari Alaska Sealskin coats and ermine and stories about exotic and impossible crimes. Eight thousand dollars' worth of jewels recovered by the cops in a 'tedious search' of a storm sewer after they were lost by Princess Mdivani on her way home from the Navy–Yale game at New Haven. Caddie didn't know which seemed less likely: a) a princess living in your city, b) a princess going to the football, c) while wearing her jewels, or d) the police searching a sewer to recover them. In 1980s Queensland, if you own something worth stealing, the last people you'd tell would be the police.

She reads the public notices: *New Jersey Building Loan Shares*; *College Graduate Will Purchase Salesman's routs*; *Must Sacrifice Complete Kitchen*. She reads the weddings and radio guides and obituaries. She reads the employment: *Dependable married man sought*; *Canvassers (4) experienced in selling newspaper subscriptions*; *Be a fashion model, Empire Mannequin school*. If only she could do this for a living. Every day, the thrill of this mental hunting and gathering.

Two hours later, though, she no longer feels like a television detective. She's skimming, as she's sure Jamie is on the machine beside her. When she shuts her eyes the light box is still there, busy with black type, etched on her retina. There's also something existential going on. Pages and pages of things that mattered so much at the time, that kept people awake, frantic, devastated, ecstatic; all of it worth nothing now. No one cares that those jewels went missing, or that the princess got them back. We are specks in time, Caddie realises, and it's liberating. There's nothing to worry about, not really. The best part of five decades makes an excellent filter for the dimensions of her preoccupations.

When the words start to dance before her eyes, she concentrates on scanning for the word *typesetter*. She finds a story about workers striking at a newspaper in Illinois because the publishers refused to assign a union member to operate their new 'teletypesetter' machine (whatever that was); an obituary for a former editor of the *Chattanooga Times* who began his career as a typesetter; and a tiny piece about a 'Negro' typesetter who is unable to read or write but still produces perfect copy by matching the shape of each character with the typewritten pages he's given. She finds nothing about a woman.

As if he can hear her thoughts, Jamie pushes his glasses up on his forehead and rests his hands flat on the small of his back. 'This is some kind of mediaeval torture device.'

She nods. 'You can stop any time.'

'I volunteered,' he says. 'I have only myself to blame.'

'Perhaps if we look at the article about the fire. Just for interest.'

After some rifling, he finds the film they need. He pulls out the tray and places the new film on the spindle and threads it under the glass and into the take-up reel. He winds the reel then fast-forwards to the first image.

He finds the fire quickly enough: it's a huge piece on the right of the front page, surrounded by articles about the arms race with Japan and Republicans urging Democrats to cross the floor against Roosevelt's higher taxes for business. She stands behind him to read his screen. She bends forward. His neck is tanned. She finds this strange in such a bookish sort.

NOVELIST INGA KARLSON MISSING AFTER WAREHOUSE FIRE
Tributes flow for Pulitzer-winning writer and her publisher
The body of a woman in her twenties of slight build and a man were found yesterday severely burned at the Cleborn Publishing warehouse in Division Street, following a huge fire. The bodies match the descriptions

of Miss Inga Karlson and her publisher, Charles Cleborn, neither of whom have been seen since Tuesday afternoon. The personal effects, found on the bodies, have reportedly been identified. Police are also said to be in possession of a telegram from Mr. Cleborn to Miss Karlson requesting her attendance at the warehouse at the time of the fire. Police are expected to formally identify the bodies today. The warehouse contained over $100,000 of books and paper, staff at the Cleborn Company said.

The fire was discovered at 7 p.m. by a passer-by and, after a desperate battle, was brought under control by the four engines attending by 2.30 a.m. There was initial concern that a neighboring tenement was at risk from the flames, which shot through the roof. Three firemen of Searchlight Company 1 were injured by falling glass. Two required transportation to hospital where they underwent stitching and the other was treated at the scene and remained on duty. A thorough search of the ruins has failed to find evidence of any further victims. The cause of the fire was undetermined.

The story went on to give details of Inga's life and career, as well as a brief profile of Charles. Inga, it said, 'has no living relatives in this country. Efforts are currently underway to determine if she is survived by any family in her native Austria'. Charles was survived by his wife, Madeleine, two daughters and a young son. There was expected to be an outpouring of grief worldwide at the loss of Inga. Funeral details to be announced.

They skip forward two days.

ARSON EXPERTS AID KARLSON INQUIRY

As widespread mourning grips the city following the identification of the body of novelist Inga Karlson, three arson experts from the New York City Police Department arrived at the Division Street warehouse to aid local officials in determining the cause of the fire. The officers declined to comment on the direction the investigation might take but said that more than thirty persons had been questioned in an effort to uncover the person or persons behind the fire. They also refused to comment on allegations that officers had been seen removing boxes of documents from the offices and home of Charles Cleborn, Inga Karlson's publisher, who also died in the fire. Mr. Cleborn's widow has also declined to comment, except to say that any rumors about the identity of the arsonist are wholly unsubstantiated.

'It's a lovely day outside,' Caddie says. 'It's unfair to keep you.'

They're a long way from the windows. It is a lovely day, despite the wind, but she doesn't need to look outside to know this. Where they live, it's always a lovely day.

'I told you, I volunteered.'

From the far end of the long table, a man in trackpants looks up with the intensity of a brain surgeon interrupted mid-cortex and shushes them, then rearranges his perspex ruler, row of ballpoint pens, three coloured highlighters and bottle of liquid paper.

Caddie sits down again and pulls her seat closer to Jamie's. She leans closer, so she can speak softer. 'How long have you known Philip?' she says.

'Long enough. He was my tutor through my undergrad

degree. He often…hung out with students.' He blinks and looks back at the screen. 'How long have you known him?'

She feels her face prickle and she picks up a pen and begins to twirl it. He's not looking at her, and she's grateful but she wishes that she were as tiny as the letters on the acetate film in front of her. If people needed a special machine to view her, that would be fine. She would be safe from everyone except those prepared to make an effort.

'It feels like a very long time,' she says.

He nods.

'Why didn't you tell him what I was looking for? The woman, outside the gallery?'

'It wasn't my story to tell.'

She nods. 'So we keep going.'

'Right,' he says. 'We keep going.'

They go back to 1937 in their magic time machine. They begin again. They take it slowly.

It's almost time for the library to close when she finds it. It's not what she imagined: it has nothing to do with a woman typesetter. It's barely an inch long, published three days after the fire.

LOCAL MAN KILLED IN MUGGING
Stabbed in struggle with suspected thief
Samuel Fischer, 45, a typesetter of Perry Avenue, the Bronx, was stabbed and killed in a suspected mugging near his home on Sunday evening. Some men passing came to Fischer's aid and medical assistance was swiftly obtained but there was nothing that could be done for

the victim. The assailant, described by witnesses as wearing a tan trench coat that flapped loosely about him, fled on foot. Police say the wound was deep. The bloody murder weapon was recovered by police at the scene. Residents have been increasingly concerned by an upsurge in violent crime in that part of the city.

One paragraph isn't much for a man's life, she thinks, and reads it again, and the black ink on film forms images in her mind. He's here in front of her. Samuel Fischer. He's a jolly fellow; he hasn't always been prosperous, but typesetting is a fine trade for a man. He looks fine, too, in his grey suit and hat and best shoes. She can see this Fischer walking down a darkening street. He's not coming home from work; he's too spruce for that. Too jaunty, with a little skip in his stride. Dinner, perhaps, or a movie with a lady. There is a change in the air. Wind blows. Papers whip along the street. He passes brownstones and telephone boxes and a small bodega. He passes a hot-dog seller, who feels the atmosphere change and packs up his cart. Men scurry past with umbrellas unfurled, ready. The sky is a steel grey.

Fischer turns a sharp corner into Perry Avenue—in her mind, a narrow, tree-lined street of apartment buildings with steps in the front and faded red awnings—and he almost collides with a man in a tan trench coat. This man does not step back. He continues to stand too close. Fischer does step back and to the side and the man follows him in a kind of dance. Fischer looks up to make that awkward grimace of strangers who unwittingly block each other on the sidewalk but then he feels the press of something sharp through his suit coat, through his shirt, through his singlet. He feels a needly point against his ribs.

Oh, he thinks. This is something else altogether.

He is startled but this, Fischer thinks, is the price of living in the most exciting city in the world. He's grown up in these streets. This is a straightforward transaction, not unusual in these difficult days. He knows no one has to get hurt. It is a simple matter of handing over his wallet and perhaps his watch, that is all.

Yet somehow that is not what transpires.

Fischer drops to his knees. His tight fists clasp the man's coat as he falls then—he's surprised—his hands unclench of their own accord and the coat slips through his fingers and he finds himself on the sidewalk. This is a bad idea, he thinks. His trousers will be filthy. And then he feels the liquid pooling beneath him, running into the gutter, a red ribbon winding along the channels between the cobblestones on the road.

The man in the trench bends over him and extracts a wallet and slips the watch from his wrist, then he kneels and wipes his knife on Fischer's trousers. He lifts his lapels and lowers his brim before hurrying away but there is no one on the street to notice. By the time a passer-by finds Fischer, the red liquid has formed a pattern between the cobblestones like the ink between rows of type.

Caddie feels her heart thump. 'Here,' she says to Jamie.

He stands behind her, reads over her shoulder.

'A weird coincidence, so soon after the fire,' she says, but that's not what she believes. Her pulse is telling her something else. She feels an urge to downplay it because if anyone is going to point out that this article has nothing to do with their search—the word 'typesetter' only, and the date—she'd rather it was her.

Jamie rubs his hand along his jaw. 'Perhaps. Coincidences do happen. Surely there were plenty of stabbings in New York back then, and plenty of typesetters. Except. That name. Fischer. I've heard it before.'

12

The walls are inches from her now: the house has shrunk to the size of a matchbox. After the door slams she hears his footsteps approaching and she thinks of the silkworms that make the thread that clacks on the looms. Every worker in every mill, their families, the shops in town, the movie theatre—everything rests on the filaments of their labour, and they themselves resting snug in their cocoons. They know of no other world until the instant they are plunged into the boiling vat.

He is before her, rolling up his sleeves. He takes up more space in this house than the three of them together. She knows him. Part of her comes from him. There is greying stubble on his cheeks and a red, raised, two-inch scratch that runs from the side of his throat to the base. She has never seen that shirt or jacket before. He has a pocket square, of all things, too large and too violet. The smell of cigarettes hangs off him. When she was learning to walk, back on the farm, she'd toddle toward him. How could that have been possible?

'Lock me out of my own home,' he says. 'That's the welcome I get?' He makes and remakes his fists and she sees the blue veins lift on his arms. George is nowhere to be seen.

Her mother is standing behind Walter with her arms folded. 'I'm surprised at you, Rachel,' she says. 'Honour your father and mother, the commandment says. There is no sin greater.'

Rachel knows she is solid by the shivering of her flesh. The first swing knocks her to the floor.

In that turning mix of dark and light, her skin opens up to become her new world. Every part of her body is connected by a web of paths previously unimagined: her little finger and her hipbone, the inside of her knee and her clavicle. This world is cold and hot, radiating, stabbing. Did she ever feel invisible? Ethereal, like mist? She cannot recall it. She is alive, she is an animal. She is earth and clay and blood. She is conscious of her cheekbone, the space above her belly button, her shin. She tastes iron and she smells it. She is newborn, slicked and writhing. Time passes.

She raises herself to her elbow to vomit and her mother is there to catch it in a basin.

'A week or two, trust me,' she says. 'The ribs, maybe a little longer. If your water's still pink by Friday we'll get the doctor, but it won't be.'

Rachel lies back down but there's nothing in the world soft enough. It's as if sharp stones in the middle of her are grinding against each other. One eye won't open but with the other she sees Mary dip a cloth in cool water. She wipes Rachel's brow, her arms and the top of her chest, then swishes the cloth in a jug and wrings the pink away.

'That storm was coming and it was either you or it would have been me and your brother too and that's the facts of it. One is better than three. Otherwise who would look after us?'

The joints in Rachel's wrists click and sigh. Every breath is the scraping of a thin shale across river sand. There is language here. Her body is speaking to her and she could hear it if only the wailing would stop. That infernal moaning, like a torrent through a cutting.

'Quiet now,' her mother says. 'It's over, no need for all that fuss and carry-on. They don't like it brought to mind after it's over. Men, I mean. They calm down at the end of it, it takes the sting right out of them. That's something you'll learn. Anything you want, you ask for afterwards while it still shows.'

There is an answer to this somewhere but there is no space in Rachel's mouth to form it.

'Best stay inside for a week or so. Do it right and no one'll ever know. Even people under the same roof don't always know. A woman's life is pain, that's all there is to it. Pain and blood. When I had you I thought I'd die from the pain. I imagine my mother thought the same thing, and her mother. You'll think it as well when it's your turn.'

Soon the ceiling blurs and Rachel sleeps and wakes and sleeps again in a strange world of scarlet and rose and magenta and shade and light swirling together and the whispering of her bones lulling her to sleep. What is her body saying to her? She focuses, she listens as best she can. It's a murmur, a hush. She tosses and turns and every movement sends new sparks through her. There is a message here, if only she could understand it.

When she wakes again, she is lying in bed with the sun lancing across her. The house is quiet. She places her hand in the middle of her chest and feels it rise and fall despite the pain. She is here. She has always been here.

She staggers to her feet. Her limbs don't fit together right but there's a pleasing kind of agony when she moves. She checks the bedroom, the street through the window. George must be at school, but her parents? Who knows.

She uses the pot under the bed and sees that her mother was right: there is no longer any trace of pink in her water and her stream is strong and fast. Later, on the way to the outhouse to empty it, she feels the blue sky pressing on her skin, every breeze, every ray of sun. On the fence a robin tilts its head and looks straight at her. It seems she's missed more than a day. Summer is upon them. She has never felt the earth so solid beneath her feet before.

She drags a chair from the kitchen to the bedroom wardrobe by taking a few steps at a time then resting. She worries her knee will give way but she stands on the chair to reach the suitcases they brought from the farm all those years ago. She empties her drawer into the best one. Tunics, smalls, stockings. Her coat, folded. The first book she ever owned, *The Magical Land of Noom*, and two others she picked up from street stalls: *Goodbye, Mr Chips* and *All Has an End*. A lace tablecloth that was the beginning of her hope chest. Her best hat—red wool—from the hook behind the bedroom door and her Sunday dress—cotton—from its hanger. All those months gentling fibres of silk into being and she doesn't own a thread of it.

She pulls, too early, a spindly ghost hand of orange carrots from the windowsill and wraps them in an apron and they go into the case as well: dirt, feathery tops and all. She takes the money in the handkerchief in the flour canister and rips out the page of her mother's notebook with Aunt Vera's address in New York City. Rachel has a body now, she does not intend to waste it. She leaves the chair in the bedroom and her key on the dresser where her father left his those weeks ago.

13

Her bike is in the back of Jamie's car with the front wheel removed—he is amazed that she doesn't own a car. Brisbane is a hilly city. His car is a daggy white Holden that once belonged to a sales rep. It has a few dings but the inside is tidy. Before setting off, they opened all the doors and ran the aircon for a couple of minutes but the steering wheel, she knows, must still be blistering. His radio is on; he turns it down. Jamie drives in silence, one hand on the wheel.

'You live in Bulimba,' she says, as they get closer. It is the other side of the city from Auchenflower.

'Born and raised.'

Bulimba is tucked in a curve of the river, hilly and laced with small creeks like veins, most of which have been built over. It is close to Morningside, where she was born, where she lived with her father. Morningside was like a small town inside a small town and she knew every inch of it. Her father told her stories of the people: the Jensens and the McKenzies, and the Lees who lived in the big house on Wynnum Road, and the famous Holland boys who swam in the quarry when it flooded and trained by towing half-full four-gallon kero tins behind them. The Rossiters who owned the tannery and the Whites who lost their youngest when he tightened a belt around his neck while playing at being a puppy and that boy who melted three toes clean off playing on hot tar when he was a toddler. Even now, she doesn't know how many of her father's stories were true. Packing up and moving across the river to Auchenflower when her father died was her great act of separation, as significant in her small world as moving to New York or London.

They drive into Bulimba and the mid-afternoon light is coming in, low and sparkling. It carries chirping cicadas with it. The air has cooled to the temperature of blood. They pull up in a sloping street.

'Wow,' she says.

Queenslanders are usually simple worker's cottages on sixteen perches, wobbling on their stilts with a choko vine growing on the outdoor dunny next to the concrete path that leads to the incinerator. Jamie's house, though, is three times wider than a normal block with verandahs that wrap all the way around and front stairs that descend to a landing and butterfly left and right to the ground. She's lived in this town her whole life and never met anyone who lived in a house like this.

He opens the door and looks at the keys in his hand. His eyelashes flutter. 'Like many things,' he says, 'it's a disappointment when you look a bit closer.'

When she unpeels herself from the vinyl seat and steps out, she sees the garden at the front is dense and dark, studded with gums, dangerous with oleander, spattered with sprinkles of light filtered through monstera leaves the size of umbrellas. As they walk the narrow path from the street, strange pods crunch underfoot. In one corner is a broad stand of bananas with a single immature green hand and a hanging purple flower, and in the other is a huge mango tree: a Bowen, not a stringy. Every second house has trees like this but they belong in the back garden, not the front, which should be the preserve of roses and hibiscus. Perhaps a frangipani on one side.

This house is backwards, she thinks. It cheers her. She loves mango trees: the smell of the bark and the small hard bubbles of sap that form like jewels on the limbs. The memory of childish suspension, hanging from branches with waterfall hair. As they near the house on the concrete path, things with hooks catch Caddie's clothes, lattice webs cling to her like caul. She stops and tries to untangle herself. Jamie stops also, and turns.

'Sorry.' He moves his hand to touch her hair, hesitates in mid-air before pinching out something she cannot see. 'Good intentions, but it gets away from me. I like it this way, I guess. It's a garden that doesn't let anyone tell it what to do.'

From the road, the house appeared to float on a cushion of green with its windows glinting. Now she can see that the stumps are wedged with odd bits of timber and the paint is flaking, brittle as parchment. The front steps have no rails.

'Careful,' he says, as he climbs the stairs, jangling his keys.

He takes a large stride over a tread that looks splintered and moist. 'That one's a bit iffy. Here.'

He holds out his hand. 'Big step,' he says.

His hand is warm and dry. She feels giddy, as though she's about to enter some other world.

'OK?' he says.

She holds his hand tighter and steps where he steps. At the top, she turns and looks down towards the river. She'd forgotten that the south side smells different: the noxious pet food factory and the bacon factory and the rendering plant and the fertiliser works, the mangroves and their mud and, when the wind is from the east, as it is now, the faintest hint of decaying fish washed up on Colmslie Reach.

The front door opens into a long dark hall with closed doors leading off it. The pine boards are polished but there is no hall stand, no paintings or rugs. He flicks a switch that lights a naked bulb. Halfway down, the space opens up on the right but the house is almost empty except for lumps of furniture under old sheets. There's a ladder against one wall and tins of paint on the floor. The cottage arch above their heads has been stripped back to pine and so has the one that divides the two rooms. It's stuffy—paint and solvents and windows closed tight on this hot afternoon.

The kitchen is half-finished and cupboards, empty boxes really, are part-installed without the benchtops. The drawers are in a concertinaed pile in the corner. There's a microwave oven on a wooden stool in the other corner and on top of it, a torch. There'll be another torch in the bedroom, she knows without looking, and one in the bathroom. Everyone knows that the power could go out at any time.

'Maid's day off,' Jamie says. He opens all the windows along the back, which overlooks another verandah. As she comes closer, she sees the glass is dimpled and thicker at the bottom than the top.

She sees faint horizontal lines on one of the doorjambs: alternating faded scribble near them that would be easy to miss if there was anything else to look at. Old height markers, for two growing children. 'All these original features. You're keeping them?'

He nods. 'It's masochistic. By the time it's finished, I'll be too old to climb the stairs.'

She runs her finger over the bumps and ridges of the pane and thinks of the generations of people who've done just that before her. 'This bubbly glass.'

'I grew up here,' he says. 'When I was little I used to look through the glass, then through the open window, back and forth. The world looked weird. People on the street seemed sturdier and broader in the legs. It always made me think other people stood more securely on the earth than we did.'

'Your family home,' she says. 'You must love it, to have stayed.'

'I didn't stay. I went away, then I came back.'

It's an important distinction, she understands. Everyone loves Queensland, but very few have anything to compare it to.

He heads across the hall and opens a door to a room crammed with furniture. 'My filing cabinets are in here.' He squeezes through a gap to reach the far corner, where he pulls off a sheet and reveals a four-drawer filing cabinet made from some dark hardwood. He opens the top drawer and rummages, then closes it and does the same at the bottom.

'Eureka,' he says at last. When he turns, he's brandishing a tattered manila folder.

The sheets have been removed from the dining table and from two unmatched chairs. Caddie and Jamie sit together, almost touching, the manila folder open in front of them. It's had a hard life: the spine is reinforced with yellowing tape and the tab has been labelled and relabelled with different coloured markers. Caddie can make out *Reviews, Karlson and 30s lit, general* and *Oz Lit, general*.

Manila folders cost what, a few cents? It's so much easier to toss a used one and grab another. Philip's study at home could be a newsagent's, all of it nicked from the department's stationery cupboard. Someone who reuses folders—especially if they own a house like this—is a particular kind of person.

Inside the folder is a fat pile of letters: a mix of fine paper and coarse, of varying faded inky blues, alarming reds, disconcerting browns. Some are handwritten and others typed. Some are neat, margined, crisp; others are grubby and crumpled like they've been retrieved from the bin. They all have envelopes stapled to the top left-hand corner addressed with varying degrees of legibility and abbreviation: *Dr James Ganivet, University of Queensland*.

'My fans. Ten years' worth of correspondence. Here is where conspiracy theories go to die.'

Jamie moves the stack closer and begins to leaf through it, turning each letter over to form a new pile as he scans down the page, focused and thorough. Caddie picks a few at random as he finishes with them.

I NEED YOUR HELP! If the TRUE FACTS are brought to the attention of the AMERICAN PEOPLE, INGA CARSON will be revealed as the world's most norotious PLAGIARIST!!! The true author of her books is JOHN STEINBECK who is an american HERO and he is the one who deserves the credit...

I really hope this doesn't sound like I'm some Elvis crazy but the truth is I know for a fact that Inga Karlson is alive. She used to come into our nursery all the time and buy plants and I got to know her over a number of years...

It is a little known fact that the Karlson books were really written by Louis Bromfield. I know this to be true because he was my grandmother's cousin and we as children spent time at his house and he told me so himself and I saw his jornals, all of which contained the books as claimed. It was a pact. They did it together and it was the Marxists set the fire because she owed them money. I hereby offer you 50 per cent of the royalties if you write the book revealing the truth. I will provide all documents on receit of your check...

'I know it's here somewhere,' Jamie says.

A typed sheet, near the top, says:

Are you working for our enemies? Inga Karlson was a Russian spy and COMMUNIST who was executed by the CIA as a threat to America. The Cold War will be won by us and then the proof will be revealed. Stop promoting the work of this traitor!

Caddie feels faintly ill.

'Ah,' he says. 'Here.'

He takes a letter from the pile and places it on the table between them. It appears ordinary enough: normal A4 paper, unremarkable typing.

September 17, 1981

Dear Sir,

My name is Martin Fischer and I am writing concerning my father Samuel. He was murdered on Sunday February 12, 1939, when I was eight years old.

Time gets away from us all and I feel that I need to do my best for him as now I'm a grandfather myself and my grandkids are asking questions about who my pop was and what he did. He was a typesetter and the last job he did was for Charles Cleborn, it was Inga Karlson's lost book. Don't tell me he didn't because I know he did. He worked on it, all night sometimes, and he's been left out of history. It's not right.

Have you seen any reference to my father, Samuel Fischer, in any papers or documents relating to Inga Karlson? Any reference at all, to anyone named Samuel, or Sam, would give us all something to be proud of for a change, for the sake of my kids.

I remain yours faithfully,

Martin Fischer

Under this are an address in Williamsburg and a phone number.

'It was almost five years ago,' says Caddie. 'He could have moved house.'

'We won't know unless we phone.' Jamie looks at his watch. 'But not now. Now, it's three a.m. in New York. We need to fill in the time.'

She knows what those words would mean if Philip had said them—but Jamie is reaching for the phone.

'Pizza?'

The sun is heavy in the western sky. Tomorrow is Sunday so they agree to phone at midnight Brisbane time, 9 a.m. over there. It's an easy decision for two single, childless people but once it's made, there's a change in the air. Jamie has no television in his empty house. They can't make the usual vacuous conversation about furnishings and curios because there aren't any. No photos in frames, no fruit in bowls, no curtains, no cushions.

Jamie has half a camembert in the fridge and a packet of Jatz, but the pizza comes quickly, delivered by a tired middle-aged woman in an old Ford. Half margherita for Caddie, half vegetarian with chilli for him. She finds her purse in her bag but he waves it away. The kitchen cupboards are missing their doors and the crockery is packed in cartons under the house so they eat straight from the box with paper towel for plates. Jamie spots a corkscrew on the window ledge and produces from the front room a dusty bottle of red wine. When he opened the door to fetch it, she spied a mattress on the floor and, suspended above it, the stark white veil of a mosquito net open like a parachute. He shut the door behind him.

In the kitchen, he rinses two paper cups and pours. Rips another two sheets of paper towel from the roll and hands one to her. He lays the other across his lap as though it's fine linen.

'It might surprise you to learn I don't have a lot of visitors,' Jamie says.

She tells him it's fine. She wishes she knew something—anything—about wine. Her father never drank it. When she was a child, only winos did; everyone else drank XXXX, or Bundy and Coke. Jamie's red tastes metallic to her, and faintly soapy. She takes delicate sips to guard against a winey clown-smile and says nothing at all. She lifts a sagging slice from the oil-shadowed box, leaning over the paper towels. It smells magnificent. Tiny bites, mouth closed. There's something about the house that demands it. Unlike every other home owner of her acquaintance, Jamie doesn't talk about his renovation, for which she says a silent prayer of thanksgiving. She's known people who can make the pulling-up of the kitchen lino last longer than *Out of Africa*.

'Help yourself to the phone,' he says, 'if you need to let anyone know where you are.'

He looks weary. She bets he wishes they'd never begun. She wonders how people lived in a time before television without dying of embarrassment. Dust motes dance in the valiant last sunbeams. Distant traffic. An itch behind her ear, another on her wrist. The old house creaks and groans.

'Are you hot?' he says. 'There's a fan in one of the boxes under the house. I could get it.'

'It's fine. They were made for heat, these houses.'

'True,' he says. Then: 'How about Scrabble? I have a set around here somewhere.'

*

She loses the first couple of games, can't seem to put words together for anything. English seems impossibly limited, so few words for so many things, and tonight she can only recall the gaps. Is this really my first language? she thinks. They sit across from each other, as far apart as the table will permit. Outside, the garden settles in to its own hours. She hears a possum clambering across the roof. Jamie doesn't seem to notice. The Scrabble set is old and the dark red box pristine. Caddie orders her tiles along the rack, in possibilities. Jamie leaves them where he places them. No fiddling. When he moves the tiles, it's deliberate. He aligns them on the board with the tip of his index finger.

Then she relaxes and starts to win.

'She's on a streak,' Jamie says.

'Care to make a small wager? I'm sure this is just a temporary reversal of fortune.'

'No fear,' he says. 'I think you were foxing at the beginning. Though we can try something else, if you'd like? Monopoly?'

'"Try something else"—is that Bulimbian for chicken?' She feels a bead of sweat run down her back. A persistent moth headbutts the light bulb.

'I'm merely being a good host,' he says. 'Ganivets never shy away from a challenge.'

'Then we stick with this. I like this game,' she says, 'I like the rules. You get what you get. No selling or buying; no chucking out. You might be blessed with wonderful tiles or cursed with *x*s and *j*s. It's up to you to make the best of it.'

'A person who likes a challenge,' he says.

'I like…' She thinks. 'Making things move. Going from one thing to something else.'

'So what is it you like about Inga?'

'Everything. Raised in a tiny village, parents had no education, and she writes this book that changes lives.'

'So the story of the author matters. It's not just about her work.'

She frowns. 'It's the whole picture. A person's work is the extension of themselves. Plus, it's the impossibility of it. The near impossibility.'

'"In order to attain the impossible, one must attempt the absurd."'

'You do know your Quixote.'

'I told you, I love that book. I do take books off the shelf, you know. Occasionally I even open them and turn the pages.'

His hands are still as they play but his gaze flicks over his tiles, dancing between them, ordering and reordering in his head. He makes different sounds with the tiles as he lays them down, like punctuation: one he settles edge first and then clacks it down, for emphasis; he slides another with one finger, a smooth swoosh like a child with a toy car. There's a language here, she thinks. You could speak it, if you knew the rules.

They play until almost midnight and it's only when he takes off his watch (they've decided to try speed Scrabble, against the clock for variety) that they realise the time has passed.

'Time to ring,' he says. 'I imagine you're dying to get home.'

'Yes,' she says. 'Dying.'

The phone rings a dozen times, no answer. She's about to suggest they try again in another hour when his face changes: someone has picked up. He's holding the receiver because it's his phone (and his phone bill, she thinks: international long distance). He turns the receiver slightly away from his face and she brings the side of her face to its other side. His knuckles, tight around the receiver, brush against her cheek before she corrects it.

'I'm not sure if I have the right number. I'm looking for Martin Fischer,' he says.

There's a faint crackle on the line like paper being screwed into a ball.

'This is Marty.'

Jamie gestures towards her with the receiver, offering it. She shakes her head.

'Mr Fischer, my name is Jamie Ganivet, from Brisbane. Australia. I'm calling regarding a letter you wrote me five years ago.'

He won't remember, she thinks. It's been too long. They live on opposite sides of the world, in two cities that couldn't be more different. She can't think of anything that could link them. It's absurd. If Brisbane and New York are somehow connected, then the world must be a markedly smaller place than she has always believed.

'It's Marty. Australia, did you say?'

Yes, Jamie says. Brisbane. Australia.

The wonder of it. Marty Fischer whistles loud enough for

Jamie to pull his ear away. 'I remember, of course I remember. Well, fancy that. One of the Karlson guys, the down under one. You took your sweet time.'

'I wasn't in a position,' Jamie begins. 'I couldn't help you back then.'

'But now?'

Jamie angles his head to catch Caddie's eye. 'Now I have a lot of questions.'

'Funny, now I have no questions and even less interest. Hang on.' There's a clunk as the phone is laid down somewhere, on a laminate kitchen table, Caddie imagines, and then a stream of fast, distant talking. She can only pick up every third word but the others are easy to guess: *you kids, eating in front of the television, just this once, bit of peace* and *don't spill anything or so help me.* The family breakfast she hears so faintly could hardly be further from her and Jamie, alone in this hot house in the middle of the quiet night. They are like two lost astronauts connected to civilisation by a spiral cord.

'OK. The grandkids, they're watching cartoons. The house could burn down, they don't notice,' Marty says, when he comes back.

'Marty,' Jamie says, 'I'm going to put you on to my colleague, Caddie Walker.'

She's mouthing *no* but Jamie hands her the receiver and she takes it, steels herself. Introduces herself to this distant voice, this orphaned son.

'Why did you send that letter, Marty?'

A sigh escapes down the line. 'Look, I don't know. I was grabbing at straws back then. I knew the old man was a typesetter. I knew the last job he did was that missing Karlson book, the burnt one. I got it in my head to find out what it was…what people say about my old man in all the books about it, and it turns out they don't say anything. And then… like I said, I'm not interested anymore.'

'Well, everybody—Karlson scholars, academics, historians—they know your father didn't typeset that book. Charles Cleborn, he was Inga's publisher—'

'No kidding,' Marty says.

'You must know about the posthumous letter from Inga, thanking Charles for doing the typesetting himself.'

'Inga never wrote that letter. She couldn't've. She was dead by then. Look, the letter arrives two days after the fire and everyone thinks it's from her. Inga. But two days for a mail delivery? In 1939? Now, maybe. Now, it'd take them a week, the bums. Not then. Not on your life.'

Jamie and Caddie look at each other. Jamie takes back the phone. Caddie comes a little closer, then closer still. She wants to hear. She wants, beyond reason, to be closer.

'The provenance of the letter's been established,' Jamie says. 'Her stationery. The handwriting, it's been shown to be Inga's, compared with examples from several sources. There were heavy snow falls around then and the letter was delayed, that's the theory.'

'I don't know anything about handwriting but no, no way. It's faked or something. That stuff about the weather: convenient, but garbage. Listen carefully. Inga never wrote the letter because she was dead by then. And also because my old man typeset that book.'

Caddie brings her palm to her mouth.

'The old man was no angel. He had a temper, he was mean when he drank. He had…certain political beliefs. He bitched about that job every time he came home. Even tried to resign once and Cleborn offered him a bonus if he stuck with it. He promised me a Buck Rogers rocket pistol, which I never got, by the way. Then, a few weeks after he finishes and three days after the fire, he's dead. It stunk to high heaven.'

'You suspect there's more to it?'

'I don't suspect, buddy, I know there's more to it. I was only a kid, but everyone knew. Stabbed, around the corner from our place? Where he'd spent his whole life? Not in a zillion years.'

'Your mother. She didn't say anything to anyone? To the police, maybe?'

'The police were no fans of my father so let's just say they were not motivated to work very hard on the case.'

In the pause that follows, Jamie says, 'It must've been hard on her. Your mother.'

'She never talked about it. I mean at first, the grief—said she shoulda told him the money didn't matter. She wished he never met Charles Cleborn, or Inga, or any of that crowd. But we did OK for a widow with three kids and no job, I guess. We still lived in the same shitty apartment. We got by.'

'Where did the money come from?'

'Who knows? I was a kid. Rent gets paid, food appears on the table. That kind of stuff doesn't mean much to kids.'

'People die in muggings,' Jamie says. 'All the time. Your

father's murder must have been a coincidence.'

Caddie hears a rasping noise: a man in his mid-fifties running a leathering hand over an unshaven face. Turning pale, thinking about his grandchildren eating in front of the television in the next room and praying he'll never have to leave them. No matter how many years have intervened, the death of a boy's father is never the past. Marty Fischer will hang up now, surely. They'll ring back and he won't answer and that will be the end of that.

'You ain't the first person to try to tell me that,' Marty says. There's a shrug in his voice. 'I could care less these days, frankly. I mean it used to make my blood boil—being treated like a fool or a liar by the kind of dumbass who believes in a coincidence like that. And I wanted to find out *why*, you know? Why we lost—' He clears his throat. 'Anyway, now I know the full story I don't really give a shit who offed him.'

'What full story?'

'We found out…it was when my mother died last August. There was a box of the old man's stuff among her things and…' He clears his throat again and lowers his voice. The kids in front of the TV, Caddie thinks.

'Look, you wanna know? My father was a Nazi. An actual, card-carrying, paid-up member of the German-American Bund.'

A world away, Marty Fischer sits in his kitchen, telling his story. All across Bulimba, all across this city, people are asleep beneath their cotton sheets, alone and together, spread wide and curled tight. In this room, in this half-empty house, Caddie and Jamie are still where they were ten seconds ago

140

under the naked bulb, possum still scrambling on the roof. They are not the same, though. Caddie looks at Jamie's face and knows it mirrors hers: a sharp intake of breath, a pallor. Horror and excitement; revulsion and the thrill of the chase. A Nazi who knew Inga, Charles and the missing book. Killed only three days after the fire. To cover it up? Almost five decades have passed. A clue to the mystery of who killed Inga Karlson: have they found it?

'Your father.' Jamie's other hand goes to his own throat. 'I don't know how to ask this, Marty.'

Down the line: 'I've always found that straight out is best.'

When Jamie speaks again his voice is softer than she's ever heard it. 'Was your father capable of violence?'

A short, harsh laugh. 'That's affirmative.'

'Marty,' Jamie says. 'We don't know anything yet, and there's lots of research to be done. Interviews with people who knew him, archival research on the ground. But if it turned out that your father was involved in the fire that killed Inga Karlson—how would you feel about that?'

There's a pause that makes Caddie feel sick to her stomach.

'I read that book—what's it called? *All Has an End?* After the war. My kids have all read it.'

'Marty,' Jamie says. 'This is really important. This is something the world will want to know.'

The squeak of a distant chair, the wheeze of a heavy man sitting. He was a small boy, Caddie reminds herself. If he wants to protect his father, that's something she understands. He'd be within his rights to hang up on them. She braces herself.

He says: 'These bums. Beating women and kids, terrorising half the goddamn world. He was a rotten father and a worse husband. Just tell the truth, that's all.'

'Are you sure?' Caddie says. 'Your grandchildren. This might be a big deal.'

'Understand this: if he had anything to do with that fire, I'd have killed him myself. If the kids and grandkids can't be proud of him then I'll damn well make them proud of me.'

'It's a horrible thought, we understand,' Jamie says.

'Let's just say I wouldn't put anything past him. Probably one of his Nazi pals killed him, that's what probably happened. I got distracted by the flowers for a while but if you lay down with dogs. Well. Fleas is the least of your worries.'

Caddie tilts the phone so that it's level between her and Jamie. 'What flowers, Marty?' she says.

'That's got nothing to do with anything.'

Caddie nods, even though she knows Marty can't see her. 'But you thought they did, at one time? Some flowers? Did your father send some flowers to someone?'

'Look. I'm pretty sure this is personal business, but what happened is this: at the old man's funeral, this big bunch of flowers came. Biggest you've ever seen. White lilies and chrysanthemums and you name it, four feet high.'

'Who sent them?'

'Someone my ma didn't care much for. She takes one look at it, she yanks the card from the flowers and reads it. Then she picks up the flowers by the brass stand and she walks back down the aisle, dragging them along the floor of the St John the Evangelist, screech screech, and she tosses them down the front stairs. Crash, it goes. And whaddaya know, she rips the card in half and throws it out the door too.'

'The card,' Jamie says. 'I don't suppose she told you what was on it?'

'She didn't say a word,' he says. 'Never mentioned it. It happened, though. Like it was yesterday. No one in the church knew where to look.'

'Oh,' Jamie says.

'Things like that, they drive kids crazy. The *loss* part hadn't sunk it yet. Later, sure. But at the funeral—I was curious. I mean, he used to buy me *Detective Picture Stories*, *Detective Comics*. Mostly after he belted the living Christ out of me, but I was a regular junior Ellery Queen. Anyway, I said I had to pee and snuck out the back, around to the front of the church. Someone cleaned up the flowers but they didn't see the ripped-up card in the snow. I found it, eight little bits, because I was looking for it.'

'And what did it say?'

'Short and sweet. With deepest sympathy, then it was signed. But this is nothing, and I don't want this blabbed everywhere. If the old man committed a crime and you can nail him—go right ahead. But private business should stay private. Probably he was having an affair, probably that was it. Why else was Ma so mad?'

'Who signed the card, Marty?'

Caddie knows what Marty Fischer is going to say before he says it.

'It was a woman's name. Rachel. Rachel Lehrer.'

Part 2

14

New York City, 1938

Rachel Lehrer is grateful. The black Schrafft's uniform is scratchy and the white collar and cuffs are stiff, and she wonders how many other bodies sweated in it before it was starched and folded and given to her, but she's grateful. Her hair, every mousy strand of it, is wedged up under the cap and the pins pull tight, digging in. The other girls won't talk to her. Won't even look at her. It's early, before the breakfast rush. Last week the east coast was hit by a biblical storm and here in Manhattan the drains are still clogged with trees and street signs and sheet roofing. It's September and the weather is cooling after a summer that seemed to bake the green from the trees and sent half the city scurrying out to Rockaway or Belle Harbour. This morning she rose in the dark and detoured around the flooded streets and it took her an hour and a half on foot from Hell's Kitchen all the way down here to West Thirteenth and Fifth Avenue, but she's grateful.

'Don't make me regret it now,' says Mrs O'Loughlin. Her folded arms make her bosom a fearsome promontory.

'No, Mrs O'Loughlin,' Rachel says.

'I take people as I find them,' Mrs O'Loughlin says, in her gull's voice. 'But I can be too kind-hearted. That's my weakness.'

Rachel doesn't trust her own face at this declaration. She stands straighter, flattens the corners of her mouth.

'You'll have your trial and sure as eggs if you can't work as hard as the other girls there'll be nothing for it. If you're not an ornament to this restaurant it won't matter who your mother's aunt is.'

Mrs O'Loughlin should play the trumpet in the New York Philharmonic, Rachel thinks. Breathing in through your nose without a break in your diatribe: that's a rare ability.

'Yes, Mrs O'Loughlin,' she says.

'Take Bridget here.' Mrs O'Loughlin inclines her head toward a stocky girl standing to the side of the main counter, neat in her black and white and cap, order book in her hand, weight even on her flat shoes. 'Heaven knows she's no beauty queen but you can't hold that against her, straight off the boat from County Cork. You ask her if she'd rather be here or back on the farm with her twelve sisters and brothers. She's in paradise, that's what she'd tell you. Never had it so good.'

Bridget's eyes narrow to slits.

Another *Yes, Mrs O'Loughlin*, tolls in Rachel's head, but she's not sure if she says this one aloud.

'You take the orders, when directed,' Mrs O'Loughlin says. 'The customers, they're your lord and lady for the day and if

148

you can't manage that, if you think you're too good for that missy, well your time here will be short make no mistake. You bring the people their egg salad and their cream cheese sandwich and their waffles and you always *always* use a tray. You say ma'am and you say sir. How do you hold the tray?'

'With straight arms, Mrs O'Loughlin.'

And on it goes. You do not speak to the men at the counter, even and especially if they speak to you. You do not speak to the soda boys. You do not speak to the girls behind the candy counter. Every morning before your shift you will be inspected because nothing kills the appetite so fast as a waitress with dirt under her nails fit to sprout potatoes. Coffee in the pot will be replaced after twenty minutes and if I see a pot with old coffee in it, there's the door.

'Are we clear?' says Mrs O'Loughlin.

We are clear. Her cheeks are burning, the other girls are smirking, but she nods. Rachel is grateful, so grateful.

When she first arrived at Great-Aunt Vera's house in Park Slope she was black and blue, and close to fainting from hunger. Vera fumed at the sight of her. She let her sleep on a camp bed in her pantry and fed her soup. That man was trouble, she'd told Mary over and over. Rachel, being half her father, was trouble too and that was plain to see. Vera had no time for trouble. She wasn't well herself. She'd help Rachel find work and a place to live but that was the end of it.

For the first few weeks, Rachel ironed in the laundry of the Methodist Episcopal Hospital close to where Vera lived. One of the mending girls had a cousin looking for a roommate in a tenement on Ninth Avenue. Carol was not quite five feet tall and stocky as a miner, blinking and fidgety, and the room was drafty and dank. The other laundry girls thought Rachel was crazy moving to Hell's Kitchen but in those early days in New York, Rachel seemed cured of any kind of fear. The city was laced with tiny treasures that she alone noticed: golden robed statues on top of traffic lights; patterns made by the morning sun reflecting on canyons of marble and granite. The power of this city. The arrogance of all that steel piercing the sky—and the men pulling handcarts stacked with lumber in Chinatown, like another country altogether.

Then Great-Aunt Vera found her this job, closer to her new home than the hospital. She's done her duty by Rachel, twice over. She isn't to bother her again.

Waitressing is a step up and Rachel doesn't intend to waste it. She spends the day with her head down. The other girls, mostly Irish like Bridget and more used to milking cows, don't speak to her, and it's not just because Rachel was born here in America or because her Great-Aunt Vera was the midwife who saw Mrs O'Loughlin's daughter through a difficult confinement. It's more than that.

Rachel has been here before, as a customer with her mother and Vera on a rare visit to the city when she was small, when the farm still seemed like an empire. That was the day she first saw a neon sign and an aeroplane floating in the clouds. Her mother ordered the blue plate special, which was eggs cooked in butter, and for Rachel, a crushed strawberry sundae. It tasted of all the things that were waiting for her in the future.

Now, all morning as she's waited tables, she's had the

sensation of being split in two—she's a girl sitting on a stool beside her mother, swirling red and pink through white, yet she's also the straight-armed, clean-nailed waitress who takes her order. Rachel looks up from the menu and sees Rachel standing there in cap and apron. Does she recognise herself? It's as if there's been another Rachel hidden inside her for all this time but she hasn't yet emerged, not really. She's still lunching Rachel—but costumed and acting, like in a play.

It's busy at Schrafft's and it makes the day go quicker. By the time the breakfast rush is over, Rachel has the hang of the trays and the way the orders are passed to the kitchen. A matronly customer yells 'Maid!' to attract her attention. By the end of lunch, she can feel blisters on her heels. She's been doing all right, she thinks: she knocked over a glass of water on seventeen but wiped it in a flash and the lady there only smiled. Maureen's been here for weeks and she dropped an ice cream soda on the counter and some dripped on a woman's shoe.

It's nearly three o'clock when the girl comes in: Rachel sees her right away near the door. Looking back, she can't put her finger on why she noticed her among the constant stream of customers. Was there something furtive about the way she stood? Schrafft's customers are mostly women from all levels of society but for all of them it's a treat, coming here. The shiny checkerboard floor, the polished chrome and dark wood and the long curving marble counters. The cocktails and fancy boxes of candy and uniformed staff. Women glide through those swooshing doors as if visiting an ancestral mansion, as if sitting on high stools and drinking fruit cocktails through a straw is a return to their rightful state.

From the moment Rachel sees her, though, she can tell that the girl doesn't feel this sense of homecoming.

Mrs O'Loughlin sits the girl in Rachel's section. The girl looks barely out of her teens but her eyes dart like someone older. She's slender like a birch from back home. Wears an oversized man's coat too light for this fall weather, cotton maybe but made from a black, white and grey twill that looks like fine patchwork. The girl keeps it on, the coat, instead of hanging it on the racks by the door and it pools around her as she sits. If not for her radiant face and her hair she'd look like a bum. Her hair. It's in a long plait and so blonde it's white; so blonde it hurts Rachel's eyes to look at it. You could cut yourself on her cheekbones from a distance of ten feet.

When Rachel greets her, the girl doesn't speak. Maybe she can't, Rachel thinks. Or not English, at least. It's not shyness. She looks right at Rachel with eyes that seem somehow too big for her face. She wears no makeup and there's a freshness to her skin that brings to mind dark fir trees and meadows and mountain lakes. She orders a hot chocolate with whipped cream by pointing to the menu. When Rachel brings it and places it in front of her, she wraps two china-white hands around it and bows her head.

'Sure and that's an odd one,' Bridget says, when Rachel returns to her place.

Rachel serves another table next, then another single, an older woman who orders a hot butterscotch sundae with vanilla ice cream and toasted almonds and after her two women who might be mother and daughter, who both have the chicken à la king. There's a boy with them in a peaked cap, younger than George, who decides after much deliberation on grilled cheese cut in triangles. She makes it clear on the docket, even draws the shape but the grilled cheese comes out in squares and must go back and then the boy doesn't want it anymore, he wants chocolate and maple fudge—no, chocolate with the marshmallow in the centre.

'That's not allowed,' one of the women tells him, eyes flicking to Rachel. 'It's against the rules. Isn't that so?'

'You have to eat your lunch before you're allowed dessert,' she says to him, and as soon as she sees his face she regrets being an accessory to this type of thinking. Eat the fudge, she wants to say to him instead. Eat the cherry patties and the thin mints and the peanut butter cups. Everything might change tomorrow. You might never be a customer here again.

By the time the grilled cheese has been restored and she looks up, she sees the woman with the plait heading to the cashier's desk, check in hand. There's a slide to her steps as though she's skating. She swerves toward the candy counter and trails her fingertips along the glass, dawdling over the cookies and cakes and trays of fudge as if she has all day.

Along the top of the counter are glistening jars of jams stacked in pyramids and velvet boxes of candy of various sizes and shiny tins, square and round, gold or silver or embossed with flowers and tied with ribbons and bows. The girl picks one up in a random browsing way, turns it to and fro to admire it, and replaces it. She chooses another, examines it, puts it back. Then she picks up a third, a small crimson chest of chocolate bon bons with a bright satin flower on the top, and drops it in her pocket.

Rachel feels the tiny action reverberate around the restaurant like a sonic wave. She looks around: no one else reacts. No one yells or runs toward the girl. Is Rachel really the only one who saw it? She thinks about her mother, the way she could see, yet somehow fail to register, her father's anger. It's as if an action has to fit with the observer's reality in order for it to happen. No one would ever contemplate that stealing chocolates in front of Mrs O'Loughlin was even a remote possibility, therefore it isn't.

All around Rachel, everything is normal. Busboys pass with heavy trays, clinking with crockery. People eat their sandwiches and their salads and their parfaits, they talk about their cousin's wedding and their plans for the afternoon. Waitresses thread between tables like swallows and the hostess watches everything from the door. Perhaps Rachel is mistaken.

The blonde girl doesn't hesitate. She continues walking to the cashier. Rachel is paralysed with the thought that the girl won't have any money at all, not even to pay for her hot chocolate, and she tastes acid in her mouth as if she is the one about to be hauled off in front of everyone. The tension vibrates in her skin and just as Rachel thinks she can't bear it another second, that she'll have to excuse herself and rush out to the back, the girl reaches in another of her pockets and pays casually with a note large enough to warrant smaller notes in the change. Then she leaves and no one stops her, and Rachel? She is welded there.

After the girl has left, Mrs O'Loughlin calls them all

together in a huddle at the door to the kitchen. 'That girlie in the coat,' she says. 'A coat like that, with those pockets and not wanting it hung up. If she comes in again, I'll thank someone to keep an eye on her.'

'I'll do that,' Rachel says.

When she reaches the top stair and lets herself into the tenement at the end of her first day, it's dark again. At Schrafft's, the shifts are shorter than most places and the waitresses don't rely on tips, but her feet don't know that. It'll get better, Rachel tells herself as she opens the door. This won't be forever. This is just for now.

She knows straight away that Carol isn't home—there's nowhere to hide in this tiny room. The two of them sleep head to tail in a pull-down bed that latches against the wall, the broad heat of Carol's shins pressing on Rachel's back. The couch was there when they arrived and there are two chairs and a rickety card table where Carol's half-written chain letters are stacked next to envelopes. No closet, even. All their dresses hang on nails. There's a thunking radiator under the window that makes more noise than heat and a galaxy of mould sprinkled across the ceiling, and there are the things that make the room hers: tiny plants lining the walls and ledges, growing in Mason jars and coffee tins and dried-milk canisters, and there's a pile of secondhand books in one corner. She has *Out of Africa* and *Of Mice and Men* now, as well as the ones she brought from home, and she's read them twice each. There's a cold-water sink in the kitchenette where they've both been known to wash when they've been too tired or disgusted to face the bathroom at the end of the hall. It's supposed to be women only, this floor, and maybe it is and maybe it isn't. Yet she's lucky, she knows that. On the floors below, families of six and eight live in two rooms and a tiny kitchen.

When she switches on the light, she sees the note from Carol on the table, weighted down with a Boston fern in a rusting K plum jam tin. *At Zoe's*, it says, *for a little party. Come if you like*.

Rachel doesn't like. The good news is that Mrs O'Loughlin said she could come back tomorrow. The bad news is that her back throbs and her arms quiver like jelly. She couldn't manage the walk home. The Fifth Avenue coach cost a dime, twice the cost of a normal bus, but she wanted something special to celebrate her first day. She shouldn't have spent it, she thinks now. She doesn't know how long this job will last. Instead of Zoe's party, she boils a saucepan and fills up their aluminium tub and drops a spoonful of lumpy seltzer in it.

The thrill she felt when she first stepped off the bus from Allentown: it's there still, somewhere under the blisters. The city was so swathed in fog that first day that she could barely make out the towers lancing the clouds. But this was the city that called to people around the world. Rachel knew she needed to be here.

She can't undress yet, or feed herself. She's not hungry anyway, not when the cooking smells that invade the hall are a whole league of nations clashing and bubbling in her throat. Her feet, they're what matter. The heat of the water uncurls her toes and softens her skin and drops her shoulders. She wonders if the girl in the coat is eating the box of bon bons right now, on a park bench somewhere or huddled in a tenement even shabbier than her own. Bread, she could understand. Stealing eggs or a hunk of pastrami or an apple. That girl took a hell of a risk for something so impractical. She swirls the bathwater with pointed toes. She's used to long days and knows she can manage it again tomorrow, and the next day and for as many days as necessary, provided she keeps her eyes on the horizon.

She sits with her feet in the water until the last trace of heat has gone. Rachel's dinner will be leftover liver loaf with mashed potato. She might even sit outside on the iron fire escape to eat it, if she can force herself to disturb the pigeons on the railings. There are barely any stars here. If she'd known this was the way of things, she'd have tried to memorise the ones at home. She'd thought the stars as constant as the sun.

If she had a radio, she'd listen to *The Hermit's Cave*. But there is no radio. She reaches for *All Has an End* and starts again from the beginning. The bravery of Cadence, the way she never gives up on her father. It brings tears to her eyes. These are the kinds of books she likes the most—of struggle and victory, or even honourable defeat. The tense wondering about what will happen next.

Before she goes to bed, she'll water her plants from the tub that holds her feet. She is too tired to sleep easily but when she does, she'll dream she's lying on a bed of whipped cream floating on a hot-chocolate sea while an ivory hand feeds her stolen bon bons that taste of chocolate and of woodsmoke and cloves, warm and smooth and sweet on her tongue.

15

Brisbane, Queensland, 1986

Caddie can think of nothing else. The possibilities. Jamie feels the same, she knows. It's almost 2 a.m. when they leave Bulimba and he drives the empty streets in silence, through South Brisbane and over the Grey Street bridge, opening his mouth and looking at her now and then as though about to speak before thinking better of it.

'Marty Fisher is an extraordinary man,' he says, finally.

She agrees. She wonders how many people that brave and that honest are wondering around unbeknown to her. If she's passed them on the street, never guessing she was inches from someone who was truly special. They—these special people—are easy to identify when they're faced with something dramatic. But how do you spot them in normal everyday life? The clues that reveal character, she thinks, can be easily obscured by a little wishful thinking.

They park in front of her house.

'No one's thought of this before?' she asks him. She keeps

her voice low on account of the neighbours, and Terese and Pretty in the front room. 'Inga and the Bund? Are you sure?'

He's focusing on extracting her bike from the back seat of his car.

'I reviewed everything before my lecture,' he says. 'There was nothing about the Bund when I was studying Inga and there's nothing now.'

'How can that be?'

The wheel catches in the doorhandle; he wriggles it back and forth to free it. He must be very tired but there's a patience to his actions that belies the hour. 'By the time Inga scholarship took off in the fifties, America was focused on the evil commies. And no one's questioned Charles being the typesetter until now. Until you did. And no one's spoken to Marty Fischer before. Good research is like that—creative, not formulaic. A spark of inspiration that combines two things no one's ever considered before.'

The bike, extracted, sits on the footpath between them.

'Thanks for the lift,' she says.

'Good night.'

She feels a little drunk; heady from surprise and possibility and knowing something no one else does. With both hands on the bike she rolls forward onto her toes, reaches up and across and kisses him on the cheek. Her smooth face lingers against his. She feels iron-filing prickles and a rough heat. She feels his cheek pressing back against hers.

When she rocks back to her feet, the look on his face. She laughs.

'Sorry.' She's giggling now.

His eyes are wide and blinking. 'God, don't be sorry. I just. I don't. Wasn't expecting that. Surprised. Extremely good surprise, wonderful surprise. You're absolutely.' He bites his top lip. 'This has been quite a night.'

His hands find hers on the frame of the bike. They're smoother than she'd imagined, and stronger. He intertwines his fingers with hers.

'Well, goodnight,' she says.

She leans up to kiss him again, and this time he's ready. He bends his head lower. They breathe together, in the same space. It's a tentative kiss. Slow, gentle. She moves her fingers to rest on his chest. It's been a long time since Caddie's been kissed. The sport of making herself shiny before going out to trigger a random seduction—she's never had the knack. She's forgotten the joy of it. The sweet, tentative soft-against-soft, the smoky, molten taste of a stranger. She's breathing heavier. She doesn't want it to end, yet she ends it.

'It's late.' She looks up at her window. 'I better go.'

He nods. 'Sure,' he says. 'OK. Good.'

'Good night.'

'OK, great. Thanks.' He frowns. 'No, not thanks. Thanks isn't exactly what I meant. But. OK, yes. Thanks.' He bites his bottom lip. 'Wow, I sound really.'

'Really what?'

'Really, I don't know. I can't English anymore, apparently.'

She feels warm towards him, the street, the world. She can feel dimples appearing in her cheeks. 'Thanks to you too, then.'

She heads under the house to lock up her bike, then up

the back stairs. Jamie waits on the footpath until he sees her light go out.

The question is motive. Why would the German-American Bund want Inga Karlson dead? And there's still the question of Rachel. Rachel becomes part of Caddie's imaginings. She lurks in the corner of Caddie's eye at the bookstore. In the city, every old woman catches her attention. What did Rachel look like when she was Caddie's age? What was her temperament? Her manner? Every day both of the imagined Rachels, young and old, change in personality and in appearance. Sometimes young Rachel is a petite thing with mousey hair and alert brown eyes. Sometimes she is taller, paler; arms like sun-bleached bones and eyes like water. She is chatty and composed and angry and ambitious.

Are they the same Rachel: the woman outside the gallery and the woman who sent the flowers? It's not an exotic name. Caddie tries to remember every detail about the woman she met, as if she's in front of a police sketch artist, but she'd be the worst witness ever. Height? Weight? No idea. She remembers the tone of her voice. She seemed the kind of person who writes her sevens with a stroke across the middle, but that's no use at all. Late sixties to mid-seventies. Her voice—there was a slight accent, if Caddie remembers correctly. If she imagines correctly, wishes correctly. Not enough to betray her as an American but what does that prove? An actor can sound native-born in a matter of hours. What could be achieved in decades if someone made a determined effort not to sound foreign? Rachel, somewhere in her twenties at the time of

Samuel Fischer's funeral: yes, it could have been her.

But this is all conjecture. What does Caddie know for sure? She knows that Samuel Fischer was a Nazi and that Rachel Lehrer had money. The flowers that Marty Fischer described were not cheap. This Rachel did not know the Fischer family well, even though Marty's mother knew her, or knew of her—no one reacts with such fury to a gift from a stranger. The young observant Marty had never heard of her before the day of the funeral. Nor was Rachel herself there sitting in a pew with her head draped in black lace; and this fact wasn't remarked upon.

But how could a woman from New York end up living in Brisbane? Important visitors here are so rare that those who've graced the town with their presence pass into legend: people still talk about General MacArthur; the young Queen in 1954; Vivien Leigh and Laurence Olivier being presented with a pineapple on arrival at Archerfield Airport in 1948. Except for Terese and Terese's brothers and her mother, Caddie can count the people she knows who've been overseas, much less come from there, on one hand.

It's useless. It seems to Caddie she is marking off a check-list like a birdwatcher: her call is like so, the colour of her beak is like so, this type of place is her natural habitat. This is the pattern on the underside of her wing, on the shell of her eggs, on the down of her breast. As if by all these things she can be identified. But people are not birds. They are not consistent from one day to the next or in the company of one person as opposed to another. They shape-shift, they justify, they wriggle, they turn and turn again. If Caddie has already met Rachel, their encounter ran for—what?—two minutes? Three? Not enough to tell her anything.

It could be a mere coincidence that both women, the giver of the flowers and the woman outside the art gallery, are named Rachel. Or maybe Marty was right: the New York Rachel was having an affair with Samuel and had nothing to do with his work. Or she was a girlhood friend of Marty's mother who betrayed her over—over anything. A stolen cake recipe. Or perhaps Marty's mother was one of those women quick to anger. Perhaps she simply hated lilies or chrysanthemums, or her husband was dead and Rachel Lehrer's was alive and the thought of that made her want to smash everything in sight. And that's if the whole thing wasn't invented by a traumatised boy with an imagination raised on *Detective Picture Stories*.

But. But what if Rachel had also read the manuscript, somehow? If she suspected that whoever killed Samuel Fischer would also come for her? That could explain why a young woman would leave the greatest metropolis on earth to move to the other side of the world—she was on the run.

And Jamie. What is she supposed to think about him? As much as she wants to find Rachel, she also wants to be somewhere alone with Jamie, on an island or in a forest with no books, no problems to solve. No Rachel, no Samuel, no Inga. Caddie feels a pulse inside her when she thinks of him but she knows what she'd say if this was happening to someone else: it's their common purpose that's giving an illusion of closeness.

*

Monday morning, he calls her at the shop. She's with a customer. By lunchtime, her imagination is away. She thinks of his skin against hers, of her backed against a wall with her arms around his neck, of him holding her, suspended with her feet off the floor. The prickles on his cheek, how far they extend down his throat and whether he has hair on his chest or a line descending on his stomach. The shock on his face when she kissed him, his bumbling for words. Just thinking of it, she can't keep her mind on her work. She imagines sitting astride him, the look on his face. Making him gasp.

When she answers the phone in the mid-afternoon, she's miles away.

'Caddie? It's Jamie.'

It's her turn to be surprised. 'Hi. I just. Wasn't.' She looks towards the bookshop—there are no customers and Christine isn't hovering. Caddie doesn't know if that's a good thing or not. 'Hello.'

'Hello to you too.'

There's a pause, but not for long. 'So. I found some books we had in storage, about fascism in the 1930s. And I also spoke with a friend of a friend who put me in touch with someone with a special interest in FDR. The US, in the late thirties. Politics. All that.'

The pro-Nazi German-American Bund, Jamie tells her, wanted America to stay out of the coming world war. 'They were big in the isolationist movement. It was pretty obvious a war was coming. They knew Roosevelt would want to join in.' He told her about the Bund's clandestine relationship with the America First Committee, a pressure group formed in 1940 to ensure America stayed out of the war in Europe, that had 800,000 members at its peak.

'The Bund was massive. Just a few weeks after the fire, they held a rally in Madison Square Garden and almost twenty thousand people showed up. Roosevelt was a Bolshevik and a Jewish puppet, that kind of rubbish. They even had their own stormtroopers. And all kinds of plots—blowing up military installations, stealing weapons and explosives, the whole bit.'

'Impressive. You've been busy.'

'Aah, yep. I could not get to sleep for some reason. I went in to the office at six a.m.'

'Too much coffee?'

'No. No, no. Could not stop thinking. Anyway. You. Thinking about you.'

'Me?'

'Yes. And if I think about you now, and if I try to talk about this over the phone it'll take me hours to regain the ability to speak in full sentences and I'm pretty sure full sentences will come in handy some time today so back to the point of my call. Short answer: taking out one warehouse and two civilians was definitely something the Bund could manage.'

'But why? Why kill Inga, and destroy the book?'

'She was famously pro-Europe and anti-fascist. Maybe *The Days, the Minutes* had something in it that would influence people to support a more interventionist policy? I don't know. But you haven't even begun to look properly. It might take some time, but you'll find a motive, I've got no doubt.'

She doesn't speak.

'Caddie? Are you there?'

'Me?'

'Of course you. This is all yours. You can have the letter from Marty Fischer. It'll be easier with a university behind you. You'll need to go over, meet with him, interview everyone who remembers Samuel. There'll be records. In the FBI files, maybe?'

'I can't do any of that. I'm not a researcher. I have a job.'

'Caddie.' His voice is deeper now. Serious. 'This is important. This is the most substantial lead on the Karlson murder I've seen in decades. Someone will hire you, or fund you, or give you a scholarship to do this. There's a thesis here, if you want an academic career. Or a book if you don't. This is the kind of idea that can change your life.'

'I need to think.'

'Sure,' he says, but his tone says, *What the hell is there to think about?* 'Listen, I have an auction tomorrow night and I lost some time on this Nazi business. I'll give you a call in a few days, OK?'

She agrees but after he hangs up, she rings Philip. She's not sure why. Because her head is swirling, because he's the only person she knows in a position of power at a university. She rings him even at the risk of making things worse. She pictures the phone on his desk, she pictures him reaching for it, holding it in his clever hand. She wonders if this is an elaborate excuse to hear his voice. Philip's voice, saying her name. She thinks: do I know myself so little? Is this entire course of action me betraying myself? She has no idea what she'll say when he answers.

The phone in his office rings out. She exhales. That was close. She relaxes, and in that instant the call is transferred to the departmental switchboard. A woman answers—*English Department, University of Queensland*—and here again is her chance. *Sorry, wrong number.* That's all she has to say.

Instead, she tells the operator she's looking for Philip. There's a delay while the woman looks up some kind of sheet.

'He's on leave,' the operator tells her. 'Family emergency. Mr Binks is covering his classes. Are you a student, love? Do you want me to put you through?'

Caddie feels sick to her stomach. Really? she thinks. Philip? Dropping everything for someone else?

'How terrible. I'm an old friend of the family. I hope it's not his mother, in Geneva. She's all alone over there. He's the youngest son.'

'Don't know who it is,' the woman says, 'but it's overseas all right, so it must of been important. Not Geneva, I don't think, so his mum's in the clear. I believe one of the girls said he's in New York. I can take a message?'

'No. No message.'

A sudden trip to New York—what are the odds? She hangs up without saying goodbye.

16

New York City, 1938

By the end of the week her shifts are shorter and the Irish girls are, if not exactly speaking to her, at least nodding in her direction. Tommy, one of the busboys, has been fresh but he's sixteen, three years younger than Rachel: it's a calculated feint in front of witnesses designed more to further his reputation than to reel her in. She's not fazed. When she and her father were in public together, even when her mother was there, Walter's head would swivel like a barn owl's. Tommy doesn't know her experience on that particular battleground. On his best day, he couldn't trouble the likes of her.

On Friday afternoon in this late September, the restaurant has a holiday air. The afternoon carries, if not exactly warmth, then at least a memory of it. The days of bare arms and cotton dresses and ice cream in the park are over now, and the city is bracing itself for months of cold. Mrs O'Loughlin is in the kitchen umpiring a dispute between two of the cooks. The waitresses and hostesses and busboys fall into line with one sharp stare but it's the cooks who defeat Mrs O'Loughlin. They fight over spatulas that look indistinguishable to every-one else and point out sugar grains in each other's butter cream frosting. *You'll have no complaints from me when it's all automatic*, Mrs O'Loughlin says to the waitresses, crack-ing her knuckles like a sailor. *I've seen that pancake machine on Broadway. Mark my words, the days are numbered for those blessed cooks and that's a fact.*

At around two, there's a lull in the crowd. The door opens and Rachel can't tear her gaze from—what?—a door? There's something eerie about it, how she can't look away, how she knows who'll be on the other side of the glass and chrome before she ought to.

It's the blonde girl with the plait and the same man's coat. Her steps are light: an interloper, a predator. She again glances around as she enters, as though someone might throw her out.

One look and Rachel realises how often she's thought of her since Monday. Walking to work through the brightening streets, she saw a man in a fitted jacket made from a similar material to the girl's coat; not wearing it as well, Rachel thought. Last night, Carol asked Rachel to plait her hair on the side because she'd seen it that way on a subway poster. Every woman who ordered a hot chocolate, every man who bought bon bons. Rachel's been half-expecting her to walk through the door all week.

The hostess smiles, no recognition, and gestures to the coat rack near the door. The girl shakes her head and pulls the coat tighter around, tying it with a long strap that's grubby from trailing on the ground. The hostess sits her in Maureen's section.

Rachel forces her legs to move. She brings an extra napkin for a trio of women celebrating a birthday, ferries clean cutlery to a lady who's dropped hers on the floor, but all the while she watches. The girl orders her hot chocolate and Rachel watches her drink it, then stand. Pick up the check. Walk toward the cashier then detour via the candy counter.

By this time Mrs O'Loughlin is back from the kitchen and standing next to the hostess, nodding at customers as they pass. Only Rachel can tell where her attention is focused by the direction her right foot is pointing.

The girl picks up a jar of jam and inspects it—for what, Rachel couldn't guess. Puts it down.

Mrs O'Loughlin nods at Tommy and another busboy called Kurt. They deposit their trays under the refill station and, as if by coincidence, meander over and stand on either side of the door.

Rachel turns on her heel, order book and pen in hand, and walks toward the candy counter. They are close to the same height, she and the girl, and a similar build. As she passes her, Rachel shifts her shoulder and jolts the girl, hard. There seems little flesh on her; Rachel feels the taut skin near her collarbone even through her sleeve. Rachel's order book flutters to the floor.

'I beg your pardon, miss,' says Rachel. She waits for just a heartbeat; she tries to stare into the girl's eyes. Close up, the girl's skin is dewy. Her eyelids flicker as though she's waking up. Rachel drops to her knees to collect the order book.

The girl drops to her knees also, and reaches for the book. 'They're onto you,' whispers Rachel, soft and close.

She stands, slips the book in the pocket of her apron, thanks the girl for her trouble and apologises again. She heads behind the soda fountain and makes herself look busy, straightening the line of syrups and wiping under their sticky nozzles. Her pulse is thumping but there is no reaction, none at all, from the girl. Her face remains clear and bright.

Perhaps she's deaf, Rachel thinks. Perhaps she's simple and shouldn't be let out without her attendant.

The girl is untroubled. She continues on her inspection. Picks up a box, examines it, puts it back.

The next one, she drops in her pocket.

Rachel feels it like a blow to the chest. What can she do? The door is too far away, on the other side of a sea of people and guarded by Tommy and Kurt besides. She'd have to manhandle the girl in front of everyone to force her to put the box back on the shelf. The jig would be up. Rachel looks at Mrs O'Loughlin: she saw it this time all right, there's no mistaking that set to her shark face. Mrs O'Loughlin nods at the boys and follows the girl to the cashier. She stands behind as she pays the bill. Rachel wrings her apron as if it's wet and comes closer so she can hear. The girl collects her change.

'You'll be coming out the back while one of the boys fetches a policeman,' says Mrs O'Loughlin, leaning in. 'And the less fuss you cause us the better it'll be.'

The girl blinks her big eyes at her. She doesn't move.

'This silent business won't change where you're headed,' Mrs O'Loughlin says. 'I'll have the boys carry you, just see if I won't. There is no excuse for thievery. Every box in this shop is under my eye and the good lord knows I will do my duty.'

Rachel feels as if she's leaning over a canyon, suspended in air.

The girl opens her mouth. 'I do beg your pardon. Madam?' Her accent is European, her voice is low and guttural.

'A foreigner,' says Bridget, in her brogue. She and Maureen are standing behind Rachel, eyes agog. 'I shoulda known.'

'Don't you madam me and all,' says Mrs O'Loughlin. 'There's a cell waiting for the likes of you.'

'Forgive my English,' the girl says. 'But to what do you refer?'

'I refer to the box in your pocket, you sneaky little thief.'

The girl frowns and pats one pocket. It's empty, but it's the wrong one. Mrs O'Loughlin rolls her eyes. The girl pats the other pocket. There's something there, it's obvious. She extracts a tin of chocolate-covered cherries tied with a velvet bow.

'Abraca-blessed-dabra.' Mrs O'Loughlin runs her tongue around the front of her teeth.

The girl looks as if she could cry. 'Excuse me, please.'

'You can keep your please, where you're going.'

Rachel takes a step closer, then another. She would give everything she has to stop time, make everyone pause so she could take the box from the girl's hand and replace it on the counter.

'My mind,' the girl says, and her voice softens now to become crystal-thin and lace-edged. 'It wanders. I cannot keep it fixed to its work. I can only offer a thousand apologies.'

'Out the back now, I said, toot sweet,' says Mrs O'Loughlin.

'Perhaps I pay? And a tip for your trouble?'

From the same pocket, the girl extracts a fat wad of notes wrapped with a rubber band. She peels off two—no, three, notes. Rachel doesn't know how much one of those boxes costs because she's never bought one but she knows a Hershey's is a nickel. The box of cherries might be thirty-five cents, maybe even forty.

Mrs O'Loughlin stares at the notes.

'It is all the fuss,' the girl continues. 'Since the book. My head, it is full of stories. I apologise again.'

'Book?' says Mrs O'Loughlin. 'Don't play games with me.'

'Holy father,' says Bridget, from behind Rachel. 'Sure and I know who that is. That's whatshername, isn't it?'

'That's her all right,' says Maureen. 'I read that book from the library. It's got her picture right on the back. I shoulda seen it before now. She'd be almost thirty, would she? She'd pass for a teen.'

'That book made me cry like a babe,' Bridget says. 'Thought my eyes would fall out when Cadence finds the note.'

The restaurant falls dead quiet. 'It's Inga Karlson,' says Rachel, at the precise moment the girl says to Mrs O'Loughlin, 'My name is Inga Karlson.'

'You never are,' Mrs O'Loughlin says.

The girl smiles. 'I always am.'

For a few seconds, there is a frozen tableau of staff and customers, all of whom seem to have heard at least the last part. A woman at a nearby table begins to clap and the applause spreads in a wave, with occasional whispers of clarification, from table to table. One group of three women—post-matinee tea and rock cakes—stand. Before long, half the restaurant is standing and clapping, their sweets and salads forgotten.

Inga turns around to face them and Rachel sees that her skin is no longer ivory—her pale throat is rose now, and her cheeks are tinted cherry.

'You are too kind,' she says to the room, and she gives a small, stiff bow. 'I will never forget.' And to Mrs O'Loughlin, 'Again, I can only apologise for my oversight. But I think now I have interrupted. Excuse me, what were you saying?'

'I was saying,' Mrs O'Loughlin says, 'what a pleasure it is to serve you, Miss Karlson.'

17

Brisbane, Queensland, 1986

It's two days later, and Caddie's dining table is covered in magazines and glossy brochures and paper stock in various dusky pinks. There are squares of lace in ivory, pearl, bone, frost. Cubes of fruitcake in foil wrappers and fraying strips of satin in salmon, shell, coral, fuchsia. Caddie is sitting at the table next to Terese, writing in a notebook. Pretty is lying on the couch, watching TV with the sound low. Terese's mum, Olympia, is visiting. She's sitting at the table with her left leg, the one with the aching veins, resting on a chair. Caddie can feel a heat rash prickling behind her knees.

'I think this one.' Terese picks up one of the lace squares. 'It's not too floral. More geometric. Less chance of clashing with the actual flowers. If you think it'll go with the bridesmaids' pink?'

'Which is the bridesmaids' pink again? This bubblegum one?' Caddie says, reaching for a strip of slippery satin.

'Shit no,' Terese says. 'What is wrong with you? I'm not

standing at the altar with an entourage of Barbies. Besides, it'll be the same pink on the cummerbunds and that'd look sickly on Pretty.'

'All these pinks look sickly to me,' Caddie says.

'Good thing it's not your wedding then, isn't it?' says Terese.

'I had a soft spot for the mauve,' Olympia says. She winks at Caddie. 'It'd match my hair.'

'Let me make one thing clear, Mum, we're not revisiting the mauve,' Terese says.

'She's winding you up, babe,' calls Pretty from the couch.

'A white suit for you, I think, Ionnis. You'd look just like Johnny Young.'

'Kill me now,' he says.

In August, when the westerlies come through Brisbane, everyone curses the gappy timber and deep shade but now it's blessedly dark inside the house, and cool. Relatively. These old houses have verandahs and eaves and low doorways. The sensible spot to sit would be underneath the house among the grove of stumps, but in Brisbane that's reserved for cars and washing machines and the beer fridge. Still, the gloom upstairs has a solemn air. If it was his house, Pretty often says, he'd put in a skylight.

'Do you know how long it took to choose the pink? Back me up here.' Terese waves the swatches in the air.

'The pink is great, babe,' Pretty says. 'Whichever pink you want.'

'Do you want me to play the piano, Terese?' Olympia says. 'Anything you like. Doesn't have to be Streisand.'

Pretty drops his head back and stares at the ceiling. 'Olympia. Please.'

'I fail to see why you should pay some, whatisit, string quartet. Save it. Put it towards your deposit.'

My little caboose, Olympia would call Terese when they were children, because Terese's two older brothers were in high school by the time she was born. Olympia was older than the other mothers at school, and more glamorous. Caddie remembers waiting at the top of the car park for Olympia to pick them up after school. Terese's shirt untucked, shoes around her neck, laces tied together. Caddie's own hair in blonde pigtails, grazes on her knees from playing elastics, both of them carrying their cardboard ports and Olympia, stepping from her car and shocking the other mothers into silence with her blue eyeshadow and mini-dresses and platform heels and the long strands of beads that Caddie coveted above anything else. On afternoons when her father was in work, she'd stay at Terese's. Her house was chaos and noise; at the home Caddie shared with her father, everything was deliberate and calm. Two boys and the fug of their rooms, the vibration of their every word and every footstep and Olympia in constant motion, rushing out to singing classes and Irish dancing—her own, not the children's—shoving bowls of spaghetti at her and Terese to eat on the couch, or dragging furniture around so they could hang a sheet on a broom handle to make a stage curtain.

'You're the mother of the bride, that's a big enough job,' Terese says. 'Besides, you'll be looking after the flower girls.'

'Girls?' says Pretty. 'Plural?'

'We need three. Elena, Thea and Yolanda. Can't manage with less than three, because of the size of the train.' Then, to Olympia: 'Did you order the flower girls' dresses, at least?'

'Of course. I went with one size bigger than what you wrote down.'

'Mum, no,' says Terese. 'I took the girls for their fitting. The size was perfect.'

'And what if they grow in the meantime? If a dress is too big you can pin it, big deal. If it's too small, big problem. Hope for the best and prepare for the worst.'

'That does sound logical, Terese,' says Caddie.

'Thank you, Cadence,' says Olympia. 'You are a sensible girl.'

'All right, fine. Good idea, Mum. Now, the bridesmaids' dresses.' Terese picks up one of the wedding magazines and flicks pages. 'Come on, bridesmaid. Give me a hand.'

Caddie grabs a magazine and also starts flicking.

'You still working at the bookshop, Cadence?' Olympia says.

Terese looks to the ceiling. 'We've all told her, over and over. There's a big wide world out there, Cads.'

'I like it.' She loves the routines of bookselling: restoring order to the chaos of the shelves, delivering the perfect title into someone's hands. The delight of the new releases, the warm memories of the classics, the abstract beauty of the jackets.

'If I was your age again, what I'd get up to. Adventure. More mischief, definitely. That's what I regret. And men. More men.'

'Mum. Gross.'

'You should be going to nightclubs, Cadence. Images, is that the one? I've seen the ad on the telly.'

Caddie reaches for another magazine and fans the pages. There are no dresses in this one, she thinks idly. Then she sees that it's not a bridal magazine at all. *Professional Photography Magazine*, it says. February 1986.

'Should this be here?'

'That's me,' Pretty says, from the couch. 'Classy photos, that's what I want. The photos actually matter. They're what we'll be showing our kids, and everyone else. I'm not having just anyone. God, remember Sonja and Steven's?'

Hard to forget. Every time the photographer knelt down to take a shot of the happy couple at the altar he revealed his plumber's crack to the congregation.

'What about the video?' says Olympia. 'I could probably give a hand there. I do have performing experience, if you remember.'

Once, when they were twelve, Olympia told everyone she was starring in a television commercial and invited the neighbours over to watch it during the second half of *Number 96*. She served toothpicks threated with cubes of cheddar, salami and pickled onions the colour of traffic lights. Asti Spumante in champagne saucers with hollow stems. The whole street, fifteen people or more, sat huddled around the set in Terese's lounge room. At last the ad appeared and there was Olympia: a dancing tube of toothpaste recognisable only by her gorgeous legs, her body a gleaming white tube capped with a jaunty lid.

Terese spent the whole evening outside in her treehouse.

'Yes, the video. A video is a must. Which Mum will not be helping with.'

Caddie flips the magazine's pages, past advertisements for Canons and Nikons and Hasselblads, past articles on lighting and chemicals and endorsements of reflectors. Then she sees the yellow eye.

On the far left-hand column of the page: a narrow advertisement for the Brisbane Camera Club. All residents welcome, it says, to socialise with other photographers, develop their skills and engage in friendly competition. The logo of the club is a representation of a yellow shutter inside a circle.

Caddie blinks. She feels a taut strumming inside. She's seen that logo before. It was on the shirt of the chatty photographer who stood next to her in the queue at the Karlson exhibition.

18

New York City, 1938

Schrafft's has had famous customers before. Many of them are immortalised on the long back wall of signed photos. Mayor La Guardia has lunched here, and Ethel Merman, more than once. Frances Alda. Sheila Barrett. New York is a town powered by fame: most of the shop girls and waitresses and cigarette girls and busboys and delivery boys have travelled to this heaving city to become the person they know they can be. The thin skin between the life you have and the life you desire—this is a good part of New York's charm. Yet Schrafft's has never seen a customer like Inga.

For a good twenty minutes she goes from table to table shaking hands, thanking people. She is self-deprecating, blushing. Two of the women have *All Has an End* in their bags, if you can believe it, and she signs them with kindness and wit. She pays for sundaes for the children, she buys boxes of chocolate-coated cherries for the staff, all twenty-two of them, even the cooks, and apologises to all of them for the trouble she has caused. They gush at her. They loved her book, they adored it, they all tell her. All except Rachel, who seems to have lost the power of speech around this woman. Mrs O'Loughlin has Tommy fetch the photographer who works from the store around the corner and he captures Inga surrounded by the staff. A wonderful addition to their photo wall. Then everyone lines up and Inga moves along like royalty, shaking hands, and Inga is warm and shakes hands with everyone the same, with no special recognition toward anyone.

When Inga smiles at Bridget and Maureen exactly the same as she smiles at Rachel, she could cry.

After everything's been settled, after Inga's offered to pay for the cherries, again, and Mrs O'Loughlin has again waved it away, a strange expression comes over Inga's face. She pales. She stretches out a hand to settle herself against a table, making the glassware wobble. Everyone startles.

'I beg your pardon,' Inga says. 'I feel. Forgive me. My old trouble, it is returning. It has nothing to do with your food, I assure you. Even if I were to collapse upon your doorstep, no one would think that, I am sure.'

Mrs O'Loughlin's eyes bulge. Does Inga need a glass of water? A place to lie down? Should they call her a taxi?

'A taxi, yes,' Inga says. 'But I fear I may faint. Could someone possibly accompany me? Perhaps that girl there? If she is not too busy?'

Inga raises her quivering arm, open-palmed, and gestures toward Rachel.

*

It's almost four o'clock. They're outside now, and there's a powdery quality to the city air. Rachel's grabbed her coat and bag. Inga's leaning against her as they start up Fifth Avenue and Rachel can feel the weight of her and her fine bones and she smells cut grass and laundry soap. Her solid farm-girl feet next to Inga's dainty, bowed heels. What will she do if Inga collapses? Does she have the strength to carry her? Mrs O'Loughlin wanted to send Tommy out to hail a taxi but Inga dissuaded her. A stroll for a block or two, through Union Square, perhaps even Madison Square; that would revive her. She's been spending too much time indoors. She's been not eating right—leading inevitably to her lapse in concentration just now, with the cherries. With someone beside her she won't fear being overcome. There are not words enough to thank Mrs O'Loughlin for her kindness.

About a block up Fifth Avenue, Inga straightens and stands on her own without Rachel's help. Rachel's arms are empty now and she's conscious of them, of the sudden lack of Inga's body that's kept her from floating up to the clouds. Inga charges ahead and swings a sharp left along West Fourteenth. They're not heading for Union Square, then.

'Are you feeling better, Miss Karlson?' Rachel says.

'Miles.' She's walking better too. Faster.

'Would you rather I left you here?'

Inga slows and smiles at Rachel. 'Silly,' she says. Her eyes could melt snow.

As far as Rachel can see, a swaying field of bobbing hats. They pass men in fedoras and a few women in felt berets and turbans, all in sharp suits of grey and brown. Cars, gleaming. Trucks and buses.

Inga stops dead in the middle of the sidewalk. Rachel almost collides with her.

'Where shall we go?'

Where? Does she mean which doctor? Which hospital?

'Honestly, you should be under glass. No, I'm not ready for a quack just yet. The zoo? There's a tiglon or maybe a liger or something. Half of one thing, half of the other, poor pet. Or the Museum of Modern Art? We could catch something at the Roxy or, I don't know, have you been to Argosy? We could browse the maps. Or shopping. I could take you shopping for a hat.'

'Miss Karlson. If you've recovered, I should go back I think. I'm on till six.'

'That is a terrible idea,' says Inga, with finality.

It dawns: Rachel is being given an afternoon, as if she is a queen with no commitments. There is much at risk if she is discovered but Inga Karlson won't betray her, she's sure of that. No one will know.

'The park,' Rachel says, without hesitation. 'I want to see what grows when no one is looking.'

As it turns out, a great many things grow in Central Park when no one is looking. The cab drops them at East 61st and the park's still green this warmish fall. It's eerie—against the charging skyline of the towers, dozens of trees lie wrecked and broken, downed in last week's storm. Other visitors are few but there are men with axes clearing paths, others barrowing away the smaller limbs. Rachel and Inga meander around the choppy lake and cross the Gapstow Bridge and squirrels peer at them, evaluating their snack-source potential.

'You could have gone anywhere you liked,' Inga says.

'I have,' Rachel says.

Her skin is itchy and there's a restless current in her limbs at the prospect of being out of doors. At the idea of Inga, barely a foot away. Everywhere is mud but she spies something in the distance and darts off the path, skipping over puddles, and kneels beside an elm, its heavy trunk snapped clean through. She parts the loose dirt with her hands to release a thin root.

'See? This purplish burr, with the flat leaves, like elephant ears? It's burdock.' Then, to Inga's blank expression: 'Surely you know what burdock is?'

'If I ever did, I've worked very hard to forget it.'

'It's good.' Rachel unfolds her handkerchief flat and wraps the root before thinking better of it—Inga is looking at her as if she's the tiglon in the zoo. Perhaps she's being greedy. 'Do you have a handkerchief?' she says to Inga. 'We can split them. There's enough for two.'

'I'm full up to here with burdock, as it happens. Couldn't manage another bite.'

A little further along, in a shady part that seems miles away from the the honking traffic, Rachel finds plantains and sheep's sorrel and purslane. She's tender with them. She gentles them into her palm, brushes them clean. These low ground-dwellers have survived the wind, the blustering rain. She wraps them in her handkerchief with the burdock and charges on, Inga behind her. A blackberry bush clinging to its trellis, the fruit spoiled and mushy on the ground. Black cherries also, smashed and leaking blood-juice, savaged by birds, on the path.

'Such a waste,' Rachel says, and raises her head to find Inga frowning at her.

'I would have bought you a hat, if you'd asked,' Inga says.

'I have a hat.'

'Most girls I know would have spent a happy afternoon just staring in the windows at Bergdorf's. What do you propose to do with this strange collection?'

'Why, eat them, of course.'

'You can buy food.'

'But if you don't have to. If you can manage enough to eat and you can sleep out of the rain, then you don't have to put up with anything.'

Inga tilts her head. 'Has there been much you've had to put up with?'

At once it strikes Rachel that a being as sublime as Inga Karlson should not be standing in the mud watching her forage in a deserted park. Porcelain skin and astral hair; it's like forcing a ballerina to stand in the laundry and work the mangle. The wrongheadedness of it a sudden ball in her throat. Rachel looks down at her shoes. 'Some. Not so much as other girls, I'm sure. A girl can put up with so much. So much is fine. But not one bit more.'

'Is that so?' Inga says.

'You have to be strong about it, like swallowing cod liver oil on a spoon,' Rachel says. 'Hold your nose, get it down. No sense doing one thing and wishing for another.'

'No sense at all,' Inga says.

'Besides. Look at them. No one plants them, no one waters them. They just grow and grow. They're miracles.'

The day is cooling. They wander back to 59th Street, along muddy paths, crunching small twigs against rocks.

'I'll deliver you back,' Inga says.

At the taxi, Inga opens the door for Rachel and tucks the edge of her skirt so it's not trapped by the door. The taxi driver rolls his eyes at the state of their shoes.

Back downtown, taxi paid. It's close to seven and the sun is setting. They stand there on the sidewalk. Rachel's bag is heavy with weeds, sweetly wrapped.

'Thank you, Miss Karlson,' Rachel says. She clasps her bag to her chest but she doesn't move her feet. She feels a cobweb of tension holding her to Inga and she—she who turned her back on her family in a swoop, she who never checks the mail holding her breath, never scrawls the briefest note to her mother and toys with mailing it—cannot force herself away.

Inga blinks, hands on her hips. 'Now listen here. Have you not read my book?'

'Of course I have,' Rachel says. 'Everyone has.'

'Yet you were the only one who didn't tell me so, back there at the restaurant. Even that tartar of yours praised it to the skies, though that might well mean she'd never heard of it before today.'

'It's a private thing, a book,' Rachel says. 'It's hard to…It made me happy. Sad happy.'

187

Inga will ask now about the thing she said. *They're onto you*, whispered while kneeling at Inga's side. An act of disloyalty toward her employer. She'll ask, any moment, Rachel thinks.

But Inga doesn't ask. She says, 'I know what you mean.' She starts walking away, then turns back to Rachel.

'No, I don't believe we're finished yet, Rachel. Come on then. Do keep up.'

Inga turns left again under the El, casting a ladder of long shadows on the road. Sparks fly as a train passes overhead. They're heading further downtown.

One thing Rachel's realised in the time she's been here: this is not one city but dozens, and each could be in a different country. The only things in common are the garbage and the rats. She's never been this way before. They pass a building on the corner: leather coats, suede windbreakers, the sign says. *Complete Line of Riding Apparel.* Another few blocks, and things are becoming grimmer. Boys in caps, loitering on steps, staring at them. A black man, sweeping. Two nuns, fearsome in their flowing black habits and black veils and white coifs.

They pass the courthouse and Inga veers around the women's prison and they are clipping along when, with no warning, she swerves into a narrow alley obscured by carts and broken crates and a chair missing its seat. Rachel trots behind her. They pass a stack of cardboard that might be a night-time shelter, a huge steel dumpster with *Bureau of Sanitation* on the side and a cluster of orange cats of various sizes that stare at their ankles like watchmen. Rachel thinks she sees a rat move fast behind some round trash cans at the blind end but the cats are unmoved. It all smells like sour piss and rotting fruit and foreign sausage.

Halfway down the alley, Inga stops in front of a khaki metal door. There's a button in the right-hand jamb that Rachel wouldn't have noticed if Inga hadn't pushed it. She stands there, grinning, with her hands in her pockets.

'What now, Miss Karlson?'

'My name is Inga. Now we wait.'

They don't wait long. A panel slides open and dark eyes appear, then the panel closes again. There's a delay—Inga scrapes the sole of her shoe against a ledge—and the door opens. There's no evidence of any person inside but there is a narrow, shadowy staircase heading down. A wind rushes up toward them; it smells like a greasy sea.

Inga starts down. When Rachel is barely inside, the door smacks shut.

She stands at the top. The stairs are steep. The walls are uneven and flinty; they might have been dug with picks and shovels by the Dutch when this city was New Amsterdam. She needs to walk back to Schrafft's, she thinks, before this goes any further.

Inga is a dozen steps down when she turns back. 'We don't have all night.'

Rachel opens her coat and pulls at her apron, touches the netted cap. Her ugly flat shoes, for the long days on her feet. 'I really should go.'

Inga rolls her eyes, comes back up the stairs and stands close to Rachel, in this small space at the top of the stairs, and she slips her hands inside Rachel's coat, around her waist.

Rachel's breath catches. Her arms float away from her sides, trembling. Inga is undoing the bow of her apron at the back. Rachel feels it tighten as Inga unpicks the knot, then the constriction at her waist disappears and it's lifted over her head. Inga rolls the apron tight and stuffs it in one of the voluminous coat pockets. Then, with her face a breath from Rachel's, she reaches up and pulls one pin from Rachel's hair, then another, and there is nothing Rachel can do to suck air into her lungs. She couldn't feel the pins before but now she shuts her eyes and she feels every sharp grip drawn away. The cap is removed and her skull feels lighter, as if the top of her head might lift off and float to the sky. Her curls drop against the skin of her face. She opens her eyes to the sight of Inga leaning in closer still and sifting Rachel's curls between her fingers, loosening them. The gentle tugs as her hair snags in the V of Inga's fingers. Now Inga undoes Rachel's top button with warm hands, then another button, and opens her collar wider. She folds up Rachel's coat sleeves past the pale flesh of her inner arm to above the crook of her elbow, and she rubs her thumbs over Rachel's cheekbones and pinches the skin. She stands half a pace back.

'There,' says Inga. 'That's better.'

19

Brisbane, Queensland, 1986

It only took two phone calls to track down the mysterious photographer. When the secretary of the club phoned Caddie back, he knew straight away the man she was chasing.

'Rodney,' he said. 'Rodney Free? The shots, from the gallery? He told us all about it? The hoops he had to jump through? Showed a lack of respect for photography as an art, he said.' He would ring Rodney and give him her number. 'You got a job for him?'

'Kind of. I'm interested in some photos he's taken.'

''Cause Rodney's usually chasing a job.'

Rodney called back ten minutes later. He would meet her for coffee, no problem.

So on Saturday Caddie runs for the bus home when the bookstore closes at noon. She's arranged to meet Jamie first, outside Spagalini's.

Caddie walks up her street to Milton Road. It's a nice

suburb, Auchenflower. Happy families live in these houses; she suspects theirs is the only rundown rental. In the backyards, kids are running through sprinklers in their togs, laughing, while their mums watch from kitchen windows. Crisp blue sky, flat as a plate, and still air the temperature of skin. Cicadas in shrubs, humming, and the tops of trees peeking over iron roofs.

She turns the corner towards the Night Owl. She crosses Milton Road and she can see him as she approaches: Jamie, standing on the footpath, looking the other way. It's as if he senses she's there. He turns around towards her.

'Hey.' He looks at her, then at the footpath, then at her again. 'The game's afoot.'

'Follow your spirit, indeed.' She kisses him on the cheek, smiling.

He grins like she's given him a present. 'Most people think that was Conan Doyle.'

'I'm not most people,' she says. 'I know my *Henry V.*'

She centres herself, focuses. Jamie opens the door for her. Inside there's a pizza oven behind the counter and a few tables out front covered with red-and-white checked cloth. Rodney Free is sitting in the corner. His hair is shorter and shinier. His camera lies unpacked, ready to fire next to his cappuccino—to establish his bona fides, perhaps—and his black bag has a seat of its own. They order coffees at the counter on the way to the table. Rodney looks up as they approach but shows no sign of recognition. She introduces Jamie, who shakes Rodney's hand, then herself. She reminds him about the fragments, the exhibition. The more Caddie speaks, the blanker he looks.

'Peppermint?' He holds a crumpled paper bag open for them. It's half-filled with smooth white balls.

She shakes her head, as does Jamie. Rodney sniffs and helps himself to two, then rolls the bag closed and returns it to his pocket.

'We stood next to each other in a queue? If you say so.'

She reminds him of his fondness for air conditioning, books and paintings. It was only a month ago.

'I must of made quite an impression,' Rodney says as a peppermint draft wafts towards her.

Her coffee comes with a high frothy head that reminds her of a poorly drawn pot. Rodney cheeks his peppermints and takes a sip of his cappuccino. The chocolate moustache that remains makes him look like a large Don Ameche.

'No drama. Not good with faces.' The peppermints are two strange growths in his cheek pouches. He waves his palm in the air as if erasing an invisible blackboard. 'All a big blur. I meet that many people.'

She smiles at him. He's right, it doesn't matter. She just wants to look at his photos from the exhibition.

'They're right here.' He unzips the side pocket of the bag and inside there's a black portfolio with his name across the front. It looks expensive. Rodney strokes it as though it's a small dog. 'Strange request, this. What's it all about?'

'I'm trying to find a woman.' As soon as Caddie says it, she knows it doesn't sound right.

'Not like that,' Jamie says. 'Caddie met someone.'

That sounds even worse. Caddie and Jamie look at each other.

'The woman. I think she knows something.' She tries again. 'We had a fascinating conversation, one I haven't stopped thinking about.'

The front door opens: three teenage boys, here to pick up takeaway pizza. *Which one is the Auchenflower special?* one of the boys says. This isn't the way Caddie imagined this conversation progressing. She wants to say, *I have no idea why I'm doing this.* She looks at Jamie.

'Meeting someone you really click with, it doesn't happen every day,' Jamie says. He blinks. 'Caddie would like something to remember her by.'

That's it exactly. The single conversation under a baking sky when a stranger saw you for who you are. A small miracle that could vanish if she doesn't capture it, regardless of whatever the woman may or may not know about Inga Karlson or her work. Perhaps these tiny arcs of recognition have sparked around her before and she hasn't noticed. She tries to face Rodney but can't stop looking at Jamie.

'Lucky I'm a professional. You know, fashion. Runways and location, for magazines. Or I nearly am. Right now, I do a lot of groceries.'

'Groceries?'

'Catalogues. Vitamin bottles, that's my specialty. They're a lot harder than they look, vitamin bottles. They've got to look serious, like proper medicine, but not too serious, because they're not poisons? The bottles are made from plastic but you've got to make them look like glass. And I do a lot of graduations. And funerals.'

'People hire a photographer for their funeral?' Jamie says.

'Not for *their* funeral. They're dead, mate.' He pops another peppermint. 'Freelancing's not what it used to be. Cameras are cheap now, see? Every man and his dog thinks he's Lord Snowdon.'

'That must be hard,' she says.

Rodney Free sighs. 'Film, petrol, new lenses. Mum's physio. It adds up.'

Jamie takes his wallet from the back pocket of his trousers and extracts a ten. 'You must let us give you a little something.'

'That's very kind, very kind,' Rodney says, and his hand snakes out to grab the note. 'Nice to meet people who understand fair recompense vis-a-vis a man's stock and trade.'

Jamie drops another ten on the table.

Rodney nods as if performing an act of benevolence and slides the photos out of his portfolio and across the table.

'Tell you what,' he says. 'Help yourself.'

There are almost fifty. Some of them are of the fragments and other Inga artefacts, but the reflection off the glass obscures almost everything. Most of the others are blurry. One is Rodney's shoe, a tan and shiny lace-up. Caddie hopes Rodney has a second job.

And then she sees her. Rachel.

'These.'

In a few minutes, the exchange is over. Rodney Free folds the notes and slips them in the top pocket of his shirt, next to his pens and a tiny Spirax notebook.

'A pleasure doing business with you,' he says to Jamie, as he packs up his camera, his portfolio and his black bag. Then he's out the door without paying for his coffee.

195

Jamie leans towards her and edges the photos around so they can both see them. She can scarcely believe it. In one, everything is blurred. The cases holding the fragments, the jostling crowd. There's a sense of bustling energy. It's not the same atmosphere as Caddie recalls: the feeling in the room was something like a crowded memorial, while Rodney Free's photos make it look like a disco. Even the display cases seem to be spinning.

Rachel is there all right. She's at the left of the shot but Rodney's exposed it over and over and she's shattered into a dozen ghosts of herself. She is holding a multitude of arms aloft. She's noticed Rodney and she's waving her hand, her many hands, in the general direction of the camera in an attempt to block the picture. This, Caddie realises, is the second photo, chronologically.

The other photo must have been taken first. It also features a blurred figure in the foreground—it's Caddie herself. She sees the way her hair falls around her face, her rapt expression. Is this really how she looks?

Rachel, dead centre and sharp. She hasn't seen Rodney's camera yet. She looks exactly as Caddie remembers, but her expression is different. She's staring up and to the side, towards the heavens. She has a look of—the word that comes into Caddie's mind is adoration. As though she's in the presence of the most wondrous thing that could possibly exist.

'She's old,' Jamie says.

Caddie is also surprised. It's the research they've been doing, imagining young Rachel in the 1930s. Here are her thin arms, her white hair. In the first photo, she's completely unguarded and in the second, frantically defensive. So vulnerable, so exposed. Caddie wishes now she'd paid more attention to Rodney's camera on the day and stood between them as a shield; though of course then she wouldn't have the photos. Still. That delicate old face. So utterly guileless. Despite the way she spoke, it's clear now she is as devoted to Inga as everyone else. Caddie herself was there for ages, probably with the same expression on her face. Imagine someone looking at you like that, thinks Caddie. You'd feel it from wherever you were in the world.

There's an uneasy spot, too, in Caddie's thoughts. It hovers just out of reach. Something to do with tracking down candid photos of unsuspecting elderly women and keeping them like trophies.

Jamie taps his finger on the photo. She's seen his hand before, of course. She even held it the other night when they kissed, but now she notices how large it is—but narrower, more defined than she'd expected, and bony, with tendons like ridges. His wrists, too, are broader and firmer.

'Love,' he says.

Caddie keeps her gaze on the photographs. 'Is it that easy to spot?'

'Sometimes. In this case. What's she looking at?'

'A photo of Inga, but I'm not sure which one. The big one, in the centre? I can't tell from this angle where she's standing. Do you remember what was there, in her line of sight?'

'I haven't been to see the fragments,' Jamie says.

Somehow, it's never come up.

'What do you mean, you haven't seen them? You've spent

years studying her, and you haven't been?'

'Is it stuffy in here?' Jamie says. 'I need some air.'

As they leave Spagalini's the heat hits her like a wall. By the time they turn the corner back into Caddie's street the trees seem to have drooped and the grass on the footpath has thinned and yellowed. The background hum of cicadas is so pervasive she wonders if they're real or if the sound is inside her head. They walk along the footpath past a poinsettia hanging over a rusted chain-mesh fence and the sight of it throbs behind her temples.

'I owe you twenty bucks, plus two coffees,' she says.

He raises an eyebrow. 'Don't leave town.'

Her damp shirt clings to her back. 'So tell me.'

He holds up a hand to shield his eyes. 'Nothing to tell. I fell out of love with Inga, that's all.'

'Right. Because that's easy to do.'

They keep walking, stepping around a small boy coming up the hill on a tricycle, his mother close behind, pushing a stroller.

'I had a falling-out with Philip, OK?'

She grabs his arm and pulls him to a stop. 'When? What happened?'

'He was my supervisor. In the early days of my thesis I was trying to find a new way to interpret *All Has an End*. A major revision of the symbolism, the way she inverts all the Nazi images that we're used to seeing.' He looks to the heavens. 'It seems such a minor thing now. It's hard to even remember being that kind of person. When a single paper was life and death to me.'

Philip's big success, the article that made his name.

'I gave him the paper for one final check. He'd send it off, he said. I thought the referees were taking ages because the journal hadn't been in touch with me. The work wasn't up to scratch, that's what I thought.' He laughs and bites his thumbnail. 'Philip told me not to worry, he said these things take time. It wasn't until it appeared in print that I saw he was named as the lead author.'

'And your name didn't appear at all?'

'It appeared all right. In the acknowledgments. He thanked me for my invaluable support.'

A house a few doors from the corner has a stand of pawpaws in the backyard near the side fence. Two are ripe and yellow and one overripe, soft and blackly swollen.

'Did you say something?'

'Loudly, and with some colourful adjectives. That was not to my credit. I was a young idiot. It was called paying the rent, he told me. Everyone did it and I was immature to be upset. I had no idea how the world worked.'

Caddie turns and starts walking again. The exact same words. She had also been *immature to be upset*, she also had *no idea how the world worked*, according to Philip. She had believed him, but now she sees that these things were not peculiar to her. They were things he said to Jamie, perhaps to others as well.

'Just accept it and the rest of my PhD would be easy, that's what he said. And to his credit, it was.'

And just like that, Caddie feels the weight of the past slip from her shoulders. These words of Philip's she's been carrying around—they don't have anything to do with her. She can put them down now, wherever she likes.

'That doesn't explain your leaving. You'd already paid the price.'

'It seems crazy, doesn't it? I did my post-doc but…I never felt the same about academia after that. I bummed around overseas for a while. And then my parents died. And I came home.'

Giving up. Turning your back on everything you'd dreamed of.

They're in front of her house. She makes no attempt to go inside. They lean against the back of Terese's Escort, parked in the driveway. Jamie's taller than her so he slides his feet out to sink down to her level. They chat about nothing.

'I shouldn't have said anything,' he says. 'About Philip.' Along the side fence there's a long stem of grass topped with a seed head. He breaks it off and twirls it between his fingers.

'It's OK. I understand.'

'No. It wasn't professional. I'm sure he's very different in his personal life. A great guy, I'll bet.'

This is her cue to say something. Not such a great guy, actually.

'You were obviously close,' Jamie says. He takes a step towards her, rests his elbow on the roof of the car near her shoulder. They are almost touching. She can smell the warmth of him, the scent of Fabulon released by the sun.

This is the danger. Two people with the same wound, a triangle with both of them defined by their feelings towards Philip. Two little sparrows huddling from a wedgetail. Or worse: a kind of revenge. She wishes they had nothing in common now, nothing at all. That he was a butcher, an engineer, someone in sales who'd never heard of Inga Karlson. There's something important hovering out of reach and there's nothing she can do to bring it closer. Philip is a chasm between them, not a bridge. She has no idea how to cross to the other side.

'I need to think,' she says. 'About my future. What to do about Rachel and Inga and Fischer and all of that.'

'Right,' he says. He swallows and looks at the ground then straightens and buries his hands in his pockets. 'Of course.'

'There's a lot going on right now.'

'There is. A lot going on.' He walks down the drive towards the footpath. 'I'll give you a call. Or you could call me. When you've thought.'

'I will,' she says.

Jamie's car is parked back at the restaurant. She waits by the side of the road until he reaches the corner, then heads inside. She closes the door; she headbutts it once, twice. *You, Caddie Walker, are an idiot*, she thinks. Now that he's gone, she misses him. They could be having sex right now—she's imagined it for the last few nights. The whole morning is almost gone, and what has she achieved? And she needs to go back to the exhibition, to see what Rachel was looking at so intently.

Jamie will be back at his place in half an hour—she could call him. Say she's sorry, ask if she could come over. Despite Terese's car in the drive, there's no one else home. Caddie's clothes are sticking to her skin again so she strips off in the hall for a quick shower.

The doorbell rings just as she's stepped under. Her heart beats faster. She has a chance to fix this, right now. She turns the water off and wraps her hair in one towel and her body in another.

'Did you forget something?' she says, as she opens the door.

She hears a low whistle. 'Not a chance.'

It's Philip.

20

New York City, 1938

Before they reach the bottom of the stairs the walls grow damp and patches of green lichen appear. Rachel can hear music rising around them and at first it seems a riot of instruments fighting in a sack with wails and blurts and trills, but as she listens she finds she can pick out an underlying spine of melody that each separate sound pulls and pushes against. It's lazy yet somehow tense, like a lion resting after a meal, flicking its tail. The air around Rachel vibrates from the blares of the horn; she can feel it in the cavity of her chest. The blood in her ears seems to leap. And then they reach another heavy door and it swings open in a roar of sound and heat and it's hard for her to believe that this many people are drinking and dancing and yelling in so little space, and so early in the evening.

The ceiling is high: she didn't expect that either. The walls are solid like a cave and hung with mirrors and strange art. There are tuxedos and furs and jewels and feathers, there are men resembling boxers and plumbers and others who might be hospital patients or bums. The crowd swells like the sea, moving as one in a wave with the music. At street level, people walk and shop and drive their cars in the fading daylight without any idea that this seething, laughing mass exists. She can see women wearing next to nothing, smoking, arm in arm with men with no jackets and filthy shirts and others in tails. The musicians on stage are Negroes. A cigarette girl walks past her; she is naked from the waist up.

Inga weaves through the crowd. Rachel is a tender in her wake.

They squeeze along the bar, beside two men speaking a foreign language. Inga orders two champagne ciders and they carry them to a small booth on the far side, away from the stage. It's hot but not stuffy. Inga swills her drink; Rachel sips hers. It's sweet but still burns its way down her throat and the aftertaste is the way rubbing alcohol smells. If this really is champagne, Rachel thinks, she doesn't see what the fuss is about.

'All these people must have come straight from work,' Rachel says, over the noise.

'"Work." Yes, they've all come straight from schools and hospitals and offices, where they work.'

'Really?'

Inga laughs, sharp, like a bark. 'No, not really. It's like this down here from the middle afternoon until well after you've served breakfast to the working stiffs. Mostly ne'er-do-wells, with the odd whore, gangster, artist and subversive. Dope peddlers. Anyone who wants a party, almost any time.'

'I didn't imagine that people like you—' Rachel begins.

'You didn't imagine that people *like* me?' Inga's eyes widen and she folds her hands over her heart, an approximation of being pierced with an arrow. 'I'm highly likeable, or so I'm told. There are fan clubs. Letters from small children. They pray for me, so they say. Sitting at my lonesome desk, toiling every day for the greater good.'

'No, no. I didn't. I'm sure that people *like* you. I mean people who *are* like you. Authors, I mean. I didn't imagine you in a place like this.'

'But this is the best place to be,' Inga says. 'At home there's just you and your thoughts. Your bright, white, unsullied pages. Out on the street, there's always the danger that someone will see you. Sometimes that's fine, sometimes I'm in the mood for that. But usually I just want to be by myself. Listen.'

Rachel tries, but she can't make out any sounds apart from the noise of the continual party. She can't hear a thing, she says.

'Exactly,' Inga says.

'Excuse me, beautiful ladies.'

Rachel looks up to see a man with a painted necktie, shiny black hair and a lush moustache. He smiles with the tips of his teeth touching. He raises his eyebrows like he's trying to stretch them to the ceiling.

'Fuck off,' Inga says, without looking at him. 'What was I saying?'

Rachel swallows. The man has obediently fucked off, fading into the dancers on the floor, seemingly none the worse for meeting Inga. 'You just want to be by yourself.'

'Exactly.' She calls to the bar for more drinks, waving a note. 'But when even myself is too much to bear, I come here.'

The drinks arrive and, as the waiter leaves, another man comes to stand beside their table.

'Are you deaf or stupid? I just told you,' says Inga. This time her eyes are on her drink.

Rachel could have told her that it isn't the same man as before. He has no moustache, for a start. His hair is dark grey and wavy with lighter grey patches above the temples. His nose is bulbous and his lips are fuller. He's older, wearing round wire glasses that sit low on his nose. His eyes are bloodshot and he is wearing what appears to be a short silk bathrobe over tweed trousers with a white scarf almost to his knees. He looks to Rachel like a man who's just woken up and staggered downstairs to find a couple of hundred strangers dancing and drinking in his living room.

'What did you tell me?' the man says. 'I know what. Nothing, that's what.'

'Darling Charles,' Inga says. 'How funny to see you here. What a treat.'

'A treat?' He holds a squat glass of amber liquid and, as he speaks, it sloshes onto the floor. 'I've been calling you for three days. I've sent a messenger around, and I've sent Marion even though I can't spare her, and the phone rings and rings. I've even had someone deliver a side of salmon from Nova Scotia because I don't know anyone who won't open the door to Canadian salmon. Except for you, apparently. I was just about to scout the streets with a bloodhound trained on the scent of your indifference.'

'Yes, yes, mea culpa.'

'I've been here every evening for two weeks. She'll show her face down here at some stage, I'm thinking. My poor hardworking liver's taking a bullet for you.'

'Don't go on, honestly. Sit down, have another drink. This is Rachel.'

Rachel the waitress, she thinks, Rachel from Allentown, Pennsylvania who is as much at home here as she would be in an airship floating over the city. She shuffles around the booth to make space for him. The man, Charles, sits as if his knees give way and shakes her hand.

'Rachel is my Galahad, Charles. I met her just this afternoon when she risked all to save me from a dragon.'

'I think that was Gawain but in any case, the pleasure is mine,' Charles says. 'Please tell me she hasn't been out making mischief. Just this afternoon, did Inga say? I can tell from your fresh complexion that it's a recent acquaintanceship. Me, I looked like Tyrone Power when I first met Inga. That was several hundred years ago, shortly after the siege of Yorktown.'

'Don't you listen to him, Rachel. He would have died of boredom years ago without me. I'm like a tonic for him,' says Inga. 'Now, what shall we talk about? Mrs Roosevelt's charming friend? Gloria Vanderbilt's grippe?'

Charles removes his glasses and polishes them with his jacket. The light is soft where they're sitting but Rachel can still see the red flush on his cheeks and angry vessels around the side of his nose. The band launches into 'Caravan': Rachel has heard of Duke Ellington, though she's never heard jazz played live before.

'What about your next draft,' Charles says, louder, over the music. 'Let's talk about that.'

'You're not very nice,' says Inga. 'No wonder people avoid you.'

'That's unkind and untrue. You think I'm nice, don't you, Rachel?' he says.

She looks from one to the other. 'I'm not sure,' she says. 'I've only just met you.'

'Good lord, I've found an honest New Yorker,' says Inga. 'Hold the presses.'

'Speaking of presses,' says Charles. He jerks his shoulder to the far side of the room.

Rachel can't identify what or who he's pointing out, among the sea of people. Inga, though: she can see. She takes another long sip.

'Charles,' she says, calmer now, cooler. 'If he comes over we're leaving.'

'He's been helping me track you down. Doing the rounds of the bars, in case you popped up somewhere else. Not because it's his job—it isn't. Because nothing's too much trouble. He's been a trooper.'

'Did you say trooper? Or traitor?'

'You can't always have your own way,' Charles says.

'Whose name is on the cover? Whose sweat and blood is on the inside? I'd rather set fire to every copy than have that man come anywhere near it.' She squeezes her glass like she's about to snap the stem. 'Americans. You are all children, playing at things. You joke, you take nothing seriously. This is serious, Charles.'

It's a different Inga now, Rachel thinks. No longer flippant, no longer the lost little girl at the restaurant. How many Ingas are there?

'He's on board. We pay him a little extra, he keeps all the trouble away. And he's good at his job.'

'A protection racket,' says Inga. 'Him and his thugs.'

'A smart business alliance,' says Charles.

'Rachel,' Inga says, leaning toward her. 'Do you see that man over there? The one in the white shirt with the suspenders, leering at the woman in the unfortunate blouse? He's one of your very own American Nazis. Homegrown.'

'Inga,' Charles says.

'That's why America is a beacon for immigrants. All these Jewish quota people coming from Germany by the boatload, even humble me crossing the oceans for Lady Liberty. Because America can beat the rest of the world at anything. Even fascism.'

'She's overreacting,' Charles says to Rachel. 'They're patriots, that's all, Americans proud of their German heritage. They're worried about the commies, just like we are.'

'That's what they do out at Yaphank, I'm sure. They sit around like proud Americans and worry about the commies.'

Charles rubs his face like he's drying it with a towel. 'Inga. It's a free country.' His voice is louder than it needs to be. 'They own their own property, which is what we do here in America, and besides, it's a picnic ground. Children sing around the fire, probably. They eat bratwurst and sauerkraut and sing, I don't know, the Horst Wessel Song.'

Inga drains her glass. 'He's a pill. You don't know what they're like.'

'I know I bend over backwards to keep you happy. You're like the neurotic younger sister I never had. But I'm not going to fire a good worker with a family just when people are getting back on their feet. It's not two years ago we had soup kitchens on every other block in this city. Have you forgotten what it's like to be broke? Besides, he's ambitious. Hardworking. Wants to make something of himself. More people should have half his drive.'

While they're talking, Rachel can see the man with the suspenders winding his way across the crowded dance floor toward them. He's smiling, and every now and then he waves in an awkward attempt to catch their eye. He's knock-kneed, she sees, as he darts to avoid a reckless dip. And then he's in front of them, a smallish, soft-haired man with a sheepish smile and a long, thin face. His fair hair is parted dead in the middle of a low hairline. He wears round, fine glasses. His small eyes sparkle.

'Well, good evening to you,' he says. 'Mr Cleborn. Miss Karlson.'

'Samuel,' Charles says.

'I'm very glad you're found, Miss Karlson.'

Inga says nothing.

'This is Miss…' says Charles.

Lehrer, Rachel tells him.

Inga laughs. 'Lehrer? Truly? Are you Jewish?'

'Maybe my father's grandfather, I think? A long time back. We're Presbyterian.'

'Still, how wonderful. Isn't that wonderful? Don't you think it's wonderful, Fischer?' says Inga.

He smiles, showing all his teeth. 'I wouldn't know, Miss Karlson. A pleasure to make your acquaintance, ma'am,' Samuel Fischer says to Rachel.

Samuel Fischer blinks a lot, and every so often he uses his forehead and the muscles of his cheeks to make a stronger, firmer blink, as though he's straining to prevent a sneeze. Sometimes he bites his bottom lip, and looks frightened. His busy face makes Rachel think of warm milk in an anodised cup and liverwurst on white with the crusts cut off.

'I wouldn't have imagined you here, Fischer,' Inga says. 'The band. Look up there. As black as…well, a *Schutzstaffel* uniform, every last one of them.'

Fischer bows his head and smiles. 'Germans and Americans, they're not so different, Miss Karlson. American values are world values these days. The Reich doesn't aim to fight with anyone except the reds, just like us. It's true that they think people are best if they keep to their own kind. Much like our own Southern states.'

'Yet here you are,' Inga says. 'Mixing with people who aren't your kind.'

'Inga,' Charles says. 'Sam's only here as a favour to me, remember? Because of your vanishing act? Let's all take the night off.'

'It's no trouble, Mr Cleborn,' Samuel says. 'It's good to clear this up. I'm a loyal American, Miss Karlson, first, second and third.'

'And what are your thoughts about what's happening in

Europe? You're an isolationist, I'd make a bet.'

'I think a man ought to look after himself and his family, and I think that's a good rule for our country too. Yes, ma'am. I think we oughta stay out of it.'

'Do you think Italy will stay out of it? If Franco takes Spain, will—'

'Inga,' Charles interrupts. 'He's not running for Congress.'

Fischer bows his head. 'If I am lucky enough to typeset your book, I'd consider it an honour and a privilege to play my small part in what I am sure will be another triumph, Miss Karlson.'

'Holy hell,' says Inga.

'Now can we put this behind us?' Charles says, loud. 'Another round? I'm buying.'

None of them wants to go home, so there is another round, and then another. The music plays on. Trumpets and trombones, sound so rich you could lean on it. The four of them, alive, together, down in that cavern, and Rachel the waitress among them. She doesn't know much, but she is watching.

21

Brisbane, Queensland, 1986

Caddie clutches her towel, excuses herself and disappears into her bedroom to dress. Philip's grinning at the sight of her. He strolls up the hall with his hands behind his back like he's in a museum. She sees him as she crosses the hall back to the bathroom to dry her hair. He's in chinos and a blue cotton knit. Boat shoes, and sunglasses perched on his head like an American movie star on holidays. He's fine and neat and bony.

'I didn't expect you'd be home. I thought you worked in a bookstore. Retail hours. Nine to five,' he calls out.

'It's Saturday,' she calls back from the bathroom. 'Midday closing?'

He laughs. 'Silly me. You forget that kind of thing when you've been overseas.'

When she returns to the lounge she's reminded of when she was eight and had her tonsils removed and spent days home from school alone. Motes of dust rise in the air. There's a brown-speckled mango in a timber bowl on the kitchen bench and cereal bowls filled with milky water and the odd floating soggy flake of sugary grain in the sink. On the window ledge, a cortege of three dead flies. The dining table is covered in Pretty and Terese's embarrassing wedding paraphernalia. She puts the kettle on.

'Not yours, I hope?' Philip says, nodding at the table.

She flips two cups draining on the sink and drops teabags in them. 'You'll be the first to know.'

They take their tea and go out to the back garden and she wipes down the rusty iron furniture that Pretty found in a skip. It's unkempt out here. Ferns and a wild bougainvillea and what was once a row of red hibiscus all throw shoots towards the sky. The table is rickety, not to be trusted, so they rest their cups on the cracked cement.

'Your hair's longer now, isn't it?' he says. 'It suits you.'

Did Philip have opinions about her hair when they were together? In all those burning months, she can't remember one comment about it. Or about her face, or her eyes, or her skin or her clothes. She looks down at her hands, neat and unremarkable, folded in her lap, to reassure herself that she is visible, that she does exist in his company.

'You didn't come over here to discuss my hair.'

'Straight to the point. Classic Caddie. I need you to tell me what you know. About the woman.'

She remembers sitting in his office like a postulant, babbling foolishly. Confident that he was a tamed part of her past. She won't make that mistake again. Now she smiles, thinly, to bite down what she feels, which is close to rage. She thinks it might be at herself.

'What woman?'

'You want to keep it for yourself. I can understand. But think about the level of interest. The worldwide tour of the fragments, all those people, all the publicity. Now is the time.' He pauses. 'I've just come back from New York, where I found something very interesting.'

It takes an act of will to stop her knee from bouncing. 'Oh yes?' she says. 'What did you find out in New York?'

He smiles, sheepish, and runs his hand through his hair. That familiar gesture, it jolts her. He's warm and solid and he's Philip. Hours of her life when she should have been learning spent gormlessly in lecture halls, leaning on one elbow, watching him run his hand through his hair.

'After our conversation I couldn't stop thinking about the possibility of someone else having read *The Days, the Minutes*. Someone who could remember it. My thought was this: all that Karlson publicity must be translating to serious sales for *All Has an End*. Serious royalties. "Follow the money", that's what I thought. *All Has an End* is still in copyright. The royalties must go somewhere. Right?'

It's not something she has thought about, but yes.

'Right. So I fly all the way over there. The trouble, the *expense*, I can't tell you. But I go to the publishing house that holds the copyright—Greenbridge Press, it's called. I still have a few contacts over there, you know, from my post-doc. Anyway. I make the acquaintance of someone in the accounts department who has this information.'

'Let me guess—this someone in the accounts department. A woman?'

'Caddie.' He smiles. 'That little green-eyed monster. Yes, it was a woman, but believe me it was a sacrifice for the sake of higher knowledge. You've got nothing to worry about there. Let's just say a woman who works at the house that publishes Karlson felt well disposed towards me. She gave me the details of the person who gets the cheques. Decades now. We're talking a fortune.'

'She just handed this information over?'

'It wasn't exactly a secret. Other people have asked the question over the years, of course, but it was never a big deal: a distant cousin or something. Only living relative, never even met Inga. That's what it says in the file, from way back when.'

'But that's not what you think.'

'I think—and you, also, you think—that quite possibly there's more to the story. And here's the kicker. You'll never guess where this person lives.'

'This person, the Karlson heir?'

'Yes,' says Philip.

'She lives here in Brisbane.'

It's only a hunch, but it would account for Philip's naked enthusiasm.

He slaps his knee and jumps to his feet. 'There we go. You've got a lead, haven't you? That thing about female typesetters—this mystery woman was Karlson's typesetter, wasn't she? Or someone else, maybe someone in Charles Cleborn's firm. You think she's actually read *The Days, the Minutes*. Don't you, Caddie? Could you absorb the actual text by typesetting it?—you asked me that. That's what you think, isn't it? Otherwise why would you have come to see me?'

'Maybe I just wanted to,' she says. 'Maybe I thought enough time had gone by.'

'Sweetie.' He smiles like she's a child.

A waft of eucalyptus from somewhere. A top note of something else; maybe a small dead creature. She shouldn't have gone to see him.

'So I asked myself: what could possibly have tempted you back to my office, the scene of such fun times in the past, unless it was something worth putting aside your feelings for?' He holds up his hand. 'I know how you feel, darling. I could tell how difficult it was for you to be in the same room with me.'

He plucks a leaf from one of the hibiscus and shreds it to ribbons, then looks around the garden as if appealing to an audience. 'Look, there's not much time. This woman's old. She could drop dead any minute. Life can be cruel like that. So here it is: the name of the woman who's been getting the cheques from the Karlson estate for the best part of fifty years is Rachel Lehrer.'

Caddie's heart thuds. 'Rachel Lehrer. Is that so?'

'I'm going to find her, Caddie.'

'You don't even know what she looks like,' Caddie says.

He narrows his eyes. 'What does that mean? That you do? Do you know what she looks like, Caddie?'

She thinks of the real-life woman. The photos of her, inside Caddie's bag on its hook near the door. By her feet, her cup of tea is cold, or as cold as room temperature gets here, and there are drowned fruit flies floating in it. She should throw out that sad mango inside before the house is full of them.

Philip is hers now. All she needs to do is stretch out her hand and take him. It was inevitable, him being here in her house, close enough to touch. Her life has been in limbo, as if she has spent seven years in a hurricane's calm, dead eye. What happened last year? The year before? How did she spend her last birthday, for instance, and every hour when she wasn't at work? She's been waiting for him to come to her, all this time.

She nods. 'Yes. I've met Rachel Lehrer. I've spoken with her.'

'You gorgeous girl,' he says. 'You star. You little beauty. Do you understand what this means? The implications? What if she remembers parts of it? It may even be possible to reconstruct some of the fragments.'

'It's a long shot. It's almost fifty years.'

'Yes, but think what would happen to the researcher who breaks this story—like the Hitler diaries, but real. You know how much that guy got? Over three million dollars, Caddie. Three. Million.' He leans towards her. 'This could be the discovery of the decade.'

'The odds of this woman that no one's heard of having read the manuscript, and remembering it for fifty years, is about three million to one.'

'Caddie. I've told you everything I know. Now you need to tell me. What makes you think she's read *The Days, the Minutes*?'

'I can't be sure.'

'I'm not asking you to be sure. What's your theory?'

She thinks of Jamie, on the phone. *This is the kind of idea that can change your life*, is what he said. Philip has already begun work. If she wants to stay involved, there's only one way.

'If I tell you what I know about Rachel Lehrer, what's in it for me?' she says.

He's not expecting this, she can tell from his face. 'What do you want?'

'I can help you find her, but I have something else in mind. Another project, one that I want to work on. I want a job as a research assistant, and I want to publish from it, and I want to write it up for my thesis.'

He laughs and leans his chair back on two legs. '*Two* projects? Caddie, darling. I'm not a magician. I can't just click my fingers and produce funding from thin air. Something like that would need the approval of the head.'

'That's a shame,' she says. 'Because I'm pretty sure I know who killed Inga Karlson. And I think there's a way to prove it.'

She wishes she had a camera trained on Philip's face. What are the five stages of grief? Denial (*You can't possibly, that's ridiculous*), anger (*There are people who'd give their right arm for this, me included*), bargaining (*Why don't you just let me to do both projects? Look for Rachel and investigate this arson theory?*). Depression and acceptance should come next, but Philip just gets more and more excited. Grinning, pacing, punching the air.

'You help me look into the arson,' she says, 'and I'll help you find Rachel Lehrer. I know what she looks like. I'm the only one who does.'

'Your project, this arson project,' he says. 'It's better odds than finding Rachel. Like you said: the chances of an old lady, even if she's read the book, remembering anything? Three million to one. On the other hand, your theory. Every few years, a new Karlson murder book pops up. Even if it comes to nothing, your career will be on track.'

'So?'

'So, you take over finding Rachel,' he says. 'I'll do the research on the arson.'

'No deal. Finding Rachel is your project. I'm doing the arson.'

A wave passes over his face, and for a moment he seems a different man. 'You broke my heart.'

Her breath catches. 'You broke your own heart.'

He stretches his neck from side to side, then from back to front. He grips his chair from the back and adjusts it two inches one way, then the other.

'All right,' he says. 'I'll go to the head now. I'll go to the dean, if I have to. I'll call my agent about a book deal. You'll have everything you need. If your theory about who killed Inga pays off—well. You'll be on your way.'

He offers her his hand. She shakes it.

'Well?' he says.

So she tells him about meeting Rachel outside the gallery, the extra words. She tells him about Charles Cleborn and the typesetting, the newspaper clipping of Samuel Fischer's death, the letter from Marty and their conversation, the Bund. She tells him everything. Almost everything. The photos in her bag, taken without Rachel's knowledge, she keeps to herself.

The flowers too. She remembers Marty Fischer, on the phone. *Private business should stay private.* Until she knows more, the personal life of Marty's parents is none of Philip's business.

Jamie Ganivet, also, she keeps to herself.

'This idea of yours might just be something,' Philip says. He holds up three fingers and mouths the words *three million bucks.* 'Look, this is why we need to work together. You can start work on the arson research. I know where they send the cheques—it's a PO box in Woolloongabba. You can identify her. Together, we can catch her. If she remembers any part of that book, if she even knew Karlson in any capacity at all, we'll be famous. She's a rat in a trap.'

'She's an old woman. What if she does remember but won't co-operate?'

'Then she'll regret it. There's a story to sell, with or without her input. The woman who remembers parts of *The Days, the Minutes* and refuses to share them? Karlson fans from everywhere will hunt her down. Photographers will lie in wait. She'll never have another day's peace as long as she lives.'

'You'd do that?'

'It's not my first option, obviously. I like old people, in general. But she needs to see that we mean business. If she tells us everything she knows, we can protect her. Worse comes to worst, I'll sleep out the front of the post office and wait for her to collect her mail.'

'What happens now?'

'Now? Now you quit your job and start working for me. Immediately, if not sooner.'

'I'll have to give notice.'

'Will you? It's only retail. OK, fine, just make it short. Bagging the old girl will be the first step. We've got to see if there's anything in it. After that, there's a stack of work to be done. More background, and a proper book proposal. Some chapters written—you can do that, you know my voice. And your project, the arson project. Of course.'

'And if everything works out? If Rachel knew Inga, and remembers some of the book?'

'Then we'll need publicity. We better get a pro. Expensive, but an investment. A press conference, maybe, for when we unveil her. Or an exclusive. *Sixty Minutes*. "Aussie researchers' world scoop".'

'I thought you were all about serious research?'

'I am, Cads, I am. But that populist nonsense, it's part of the game these days, the university eats it up. And my responsibility as an academic is to bring my work to the widest possible audience. Taxpayers are the bosses, they pay our wages. And I can just see it. Can't you? Jana, in front of that ticking clock; that gorgeous little frown she gets when she's concentrating.'

She can see it. 'I'll tell Christine tomorrow,' she says.

'Good.' He jumps up again. 'And give notice here as well.'

'Pardon?'

'No sense paying rent when you'll be spending all your time at my place anyway.'

'Why would I be spending all my time at your place?'

'I'm not running this out of the office, no way. We'll get you a desk but we're not keeping anything important there.'

He drops his voice to a coarse whisper. 'Academics sniff around, you wouldn't believe it. Is your name on the lease? They'll find someone else, no problem. It's a good house, this.' He leans one hand against the doorjamb, as if to reassure it that Caddie's imminent departure is nothing personal. 'For a share house, I mean. It doesn't have that usual share-house smell.'

'This is a job offer, Philip. That's all.'

'Of course, love.' He blinks. 'But whenever you're ready, you know where I am.'

She spent months dreaming of this moment, awake and asleep. She's spent years, when other girls her age were thinking of travel or career or research or makeup or clothes. And it's here. The photographs of Rachel are in her bag, over her shoulder. She still doesn't mention them. You can never go back, she thinks.

He walks to the sliding door and opens it as if he lives here. 'I'm going to find this Rachel. And you're going to have a proper career. Win–win.'

She watches him go, and it's as if the very air parts around him. His energy, his intensity. The irresistible pull of his wake.

22

New York City, 1938

This isn't the night they kiss. That comes later. But after that night in the club, the thought of Inga fizzes inside Rachel like the bubbles in her champagne cider.

She staggers home at almost two after the finest night of her life. She's been drinking and dancing and laughing with Inga, and Charles and yes, even the strange little man Fischer with the *aw shucks Miss Karlson* manner. The night progresses, and Fischer is the picked-upon younger brother, the butt of every joke. He doesn't seem to mind. He tags along behind them. He reminds Rachel of a boy from infant school back in Pennsylvania, Ethan Fairweather, who had a harelip and would take all kinds of abuse just to be included. Samuel Fischer fetches the cigarettes and the drinks and clears them space on the dance floor when Inga insists on teaching Rachel how to do the Big Apple. *The ladies need room*, he tells the sodden, leaning shufflers. *Miss Karlson needs some room*. He's the one who holds the table while they're dancing and finds their shoes at the end of the night, though no one can find Charles's keys or his scarf. Charles'll have to wake his wife to get inside, he tells them—an inglorious end to a glorious evening.

Sam offers to walk Rachel home but Inga dismisses him and takes her home to Hell's Kitchen herself. There's a full moon. On the front steps of the tenement, Inga holds Rachel's hand in both of hers and turns it over, front and back, as though she's trying to memorise every square inch of skin. Rachel can't find words and for a while neither can Inga.

'I'm glad I know where you live,' Inga says, finally. 'Who knows how many dragons are out there?'

The next day should be an exercise in exhaustion but Rachel is alert at the restaurant, moving faster than she can recall. *Who put coffee in your coffee?* Mrs O'Loughlin says. Then comes Sunday, and perhaps if Rachel was another kind of girl she'd start worrying now about when she might see Inga again. But Rachel is not that kind of girl: she does not expect to see Inga again. It would be like a lottery winner expecting straight away to see their numbers come up again. A night like that is something Rachel is certain she will not experience twice.

On Sunday morning, as she is hanging out her washing on the fire escape, she looks down to the street and—who is that, leaning against the steps out the front of the building? Even from this angle—the top of an ice-blonde head—there's no mistake. Rachel leans over the cold iron railing and calls down.

Inga steps back further onto the street so she can tilt her head back and for a moment Rachel is sure she'll be hit by a passing car.

'I knew you had to come out eventually,' Inga yells up to her. 'I need you to take me to the park. I'm completely out of burdock.'

Rachel scatters the last of the washing and dashes back through the window to grab her coat.

In the following week they see a movie, they go to a cocktail bar after work. Inga asks questions about the farm, the mill, her parents. Rachel tells her so much and no more.

'Come over on Sunday morning,' Inga says. 'We'll decide what to do when you get there.'

So here she is now, standing outside Inga's apartment, a newish brick building in Yorkville near the Carl Schurz Park. She stands out there until the doorman peers through the glass at her. There's something under her skin, she can feel it. She's still unused to premeditated action. Would she have gone upstairs if the woman waiting for her was someone other than Inga? It's moot. Inga is one of a kind: a planet, not a person. In the end, Rachel succumbs to the gravitational pull.

She knocks on the door. No answer. Does she have the time wrong, or the day? She almost leaves but for the thought of Inga waiting for her. She knocks again.

'What now?' Inga calls from inside.

'It's me. Rachel.'

'Oh. What the hell is the time?' The door swings open and Inga is there in a man's dressing-gown with caramel silk pyjamas peeking out. She holds the door for Rachel to come inside.

Inga's apartment is so unlike Rachel's it seems absurd to

use the same word. A cream and blue Chinese rug covers much of the parquetry, and the chairs—some green velvet with tortured arms and legs, others with tapestry seats and armrests and backs like soldiers—are standing stiff against the cream-papered walls. Heavy oil portraits of angry or dead-eyed women glare across the room. The far windows, framed with chintzy scalloped curtains, are sealed tight but the view she glimpses would be glorious across the East River to Roosevelt Island and maybe as far as Astoria; trees turning red and amber and gold. Rachel's shoes click on the floor; Inga is barefoot, each nail a tiny silver shell.

'It's lovely,' she says.

'What? Oh, the apartment. Is it?' Inga says. 'Charles organised it. Some friend of his, in Europe, I think. Italy? The paintings are ghoulish, don't you think? I might put them in a cupboard.' And then, 'Look, I know I said we'd go out but I've just had a thought I need to jot down. Could you wait a bit?'

Rachel sits on one of the green chairs, bag on her lap, while Inga sprawls on the floor, leaning back on a matching love seat. Around her are half-a-dozen coffee cups filled to different levels with inky liquid. There's also paper in messy stacks: typescript covered with handwriting. Inga has a pencil in her hand and another threaded in her hair. She shuffles through the papers, attacking each one so furiously the lead makes tiny holes.

Five minutes go by. Ten. Rachel tilts her head to read a sheet of paper that's slid across the floor close to where she's sitting. Inga notices.

'No you don't!' She snatches the paper up and places it

on top of the messy pile. 'No one reads until it's finished. Do you want coffee? Make yourself coffee.' Inga waves to a door behind her, not raising her eyes.

Rachel picks her way around a gleaming kitchen that might be part of a spaceship. She returns to the living room and sits back down on the green chair, sipping her coffee.

Another ten minutes. Twenty.

Then Inga throws the pencil toward the window and it bounces off the glass with an unsatisfying tink. She stands. She kicks the pile of paper at her feet and marches over to stand before her, hands on hips, and Rachel thinks she's in trouble.

Instead Inga bends at the waist, tilts Rachel's face up by the chin and kisses her, open-mouthed and soft.

There's no time even for the shock of it. Later, yes. But for now Rachel is pure reaction: the inside of her throat melts. She softens and renders and becomes a liquid thing. That there is someone in the world who wants to touch her like that, to taste her. That there is a way, a possible way, to exist in this life, and that the person who shows her this is Inga Karlson, her Inga Karlson.

'I can't get a thing done with you around,' says Inga, against her open mouth. 'There's nothing for it.'

Inga kneels in front of her and kisses the line of Rachel's jaw, the length of her throat. She slips off her own coat and Rachel's blouse. This is not how Rachel imagined it, if she imagined it at all. There were boys at school when they lived on the farm. Billy Amberson, who stuck out his freckled leg to trip her whenever she walked past his desk. Bradley Ellis, who never made it beyond the first reader and tried to lift her skirt once as they walked home. She remembers his hand, fat and clammy. The boys and men at the mill, cologne and pomade not quite covering their sweat-smell and dangerous edges, mostly steered clear of her. More than once she wondered at the difference between her and other girls, who were chased with such grim determination.

Inga is gentle. Soft and exquisite and relentless, an ecstasy that's almost more than Rachel can stand. More than once as her hands twist and clutch at the lush oriental pile, Rachel thinks it'll be the death of her.

Just like liquid the afternoon trickles away and Inga's mouth and tongue and fingers bring her this way and that. That afternoon, Inga gets no more work done and Rachel does not go home.

23

The next morning Caddie wakes at five with her legs twitching under the sheet and her mind darting like a mouse in a cage. She needs the open air, the dawn light, blood pumping in her veins. She dresses for work and heads east on Milton Road. The city in the distance is lit gold from behind; a corona, a halo, a blessing. It's forty-five minutes away if she heads straight past the brewery at the top of the rise. She's in no hurry. She turns right towards the river.

From the hill above Coro Drive the river is a murky brown and the other side is flat except for Torbreck in the distance. There are so many things to balance. She wonders what life must be like for Philip: to care for no one but yourself, to allow everyone around you to be broken in your service. If that's what it means to be successful.

She makes it through the work day, somehow. Every time the front door opens, her heart leaps. For no good reason except it might be Jamie. It's never Jamie.

As she and Christine are closing the shop, Caddie looks through the big front windows onto Adelaide Street. It's like a wildebeest migration: schoolboys with shirts untucked, backs bowed by their ports, jostling on the steps of a bus; trainee beauticians in smocks, with scrubbed faces, half-jogging across the road to the square; uniformed usherettes from the Regent with green eyeshadow and lips like candy teetering on their heels.

No one lives here, no one socialises here. She'll miss it, she realises. Being in the centre, being surrounded by books. She'll miss Christine. And yet Caddie stands in the small back room, and she quits her job.

Christine runs her hands through her hair before thrusting them deep in her pockets. Nods. 'If you're expecting me to talk you out of it, you can think again.'

'I'm not expecting anything.'

'Unless it's about money. Is it about money? We could talk about it, if it is.'

'It's not about money.'

'Good. I don't have any more money. Is it about bookselling? Because it's a good job, with a future. Solid, stable work.'

'I still love bookselling. It's not that.'

'Fine, go. I mean it. You've been here long enough. It's a job, not a life sentence.'

'God, Christine. Don't get all mushy on me.'

'Off travelling, I expect? You'll never know where in the world you belong unless you see more than one place.'

Caddie feels like laughing. 'I'm not going anywhere. But I

do have a project. An exciting new project. A once-in-a-life-time opportunity.'

'Something to do with the bloke that phoned? I can always tell.'

'Who? Oh. No, not him,' Caddie tells her. 'It's nothing to do with Jamie.'

'A different bloke, is it? Because changing direction for a bloke, regardless of what kind of bloke…' Christine scratches her scalp with her nails. 'Look. It's not really my job to tell you this kind of thing. But in lieu of. You know. Your dad. You've got to set your own sails. Following a man, it's not very smart.'

'I know what I'm doing,' Caddie says. She's already feeling not very smart.

When Caddie gets home from work, she sees a note that Terese has left near the phone in the hall: *JAMIE called! Call him back. (And tell me everything!)*

She'd like to call him back. She's itching to; she picks up the phone twice and holds it to her ear until the dial tone gives up and becomes one long beep.

She'll finish up on Thursday. There'll be a cake on her last day. Something nice, from Shingle Inn. All her favourite customers will say heartfelt things about books she's recommended that they've loved or their children have loved. About the trouble she always went to. About how her smile cheered them up on days when they needed it. Everyone will sign a giant card. Christine will choose a special book for her and wrap it in cellophane; hardback poetry, perhaps. Last year's A. D. Hope, or a Les Murray collection. In a week or two, no one will miss her at all.

On the Monday of her last week, she stays late to go through the invoices and ring customers with special orders, but she's also making her plan. When she gets home it's after nine. Pretty and Terese are out but there's a parcel wrapped in brown paper and string on the kitchen bench. It's addressed to her. She opens it: an old hardback edition of *A Room with a View*, published by Knopf in 1923. It's lovely. There's a note inside: *I'm off to Melbourne this arvo for a week or so, for meetings and some estate auctions. (Planned for ages but slipped my mind. Clearly something is affecting my concentration.) I'll be home next Friday. Perhaps a strategy coffee/dinner? Qan Heng's? Or JoJo's? Jamie.*

This is good, she thinks. Really. She has enough on her mind and doesn't need to think about coffee with Jamie, or dinner or anything else. The last thing she needs is for her mind to wander to lazy Sundays in the beer garden at the R.E. or weekends away at Broadbeach and swimming in the surf, the pull of the swell, the lift and tug of it.

None of this is helpful.

She needs time to plan, to prepare. This is good, she thinks, Jamie being away. Keep saying it, Caddie.

On her first day at her new job, Philip is overjoyed to see her and he hugs her instead of his usual double-cheek kiss.

'First, we write to Rachel. University letterhead, the good one. *Opportunity to contribute to international scholarship. Long-awaited recognition for your unique place in history.* Charm offensive,' he says.

'And if she doesn't respond?'

'Unlikely. But she has to collect her mail some time, so.' His eyes light up and he seems almost boyish. 'Stakeout!'

She feels a strange calm. 'What about that other Karlson expert. You mentioned her once,' she says. 'You weren't tempted to get her involved?'

'It's a he, so you can sheathe the claws. And no: non-starter. We were close at one point but he just didn't have the *cojones* for research.'

Why's that, she asks.

He rolls his eyes. 'What you have there is a textbook case of overprivilege. Someone who doesn't appreciate opportunities. I called in favours to get him a post-doc, a really great post-doc actually, because he was one of us, and then he just threw it all in. Went off to bum around Europe. Now he's running the family business. Disappointed everyone. Not hungry enough, that was the trouble.'

She feels a creeping on her skin. 'You mean, not capable of hunting down a little old lady.'

He leans across the desk, chin resting on his knitted fingers. 'Caddie. There is no higher calling than knowledge. It's what humanity *is*. We owe it to the future to uncover the truth and we shouldn't be letting self-indulgent sentimentality stand in our way. Besides, I went out on a limb for that man. I even tried to talk him into coming jogging with me, because he frankly could've done with the exercise.' Philip puffs out his cheeks then releases the air in a whoosh. 'Like talking to a doughnut.'

'And he runs the family business?' she says.

'I don't know, his parents got sick or something. Some

kind of cancer? Both of them, which was unlucky. Book nerd. You know the type.'

'I do,' Caddie says.

'A bit of a dork. He's uncool, frankly.'

Uncool.

Oh. This is who she's siding with. This is the alliance she's chosen. A deal with the devil, to deliver Rachel into Philip's hands. She thinks back to that vulnerable old woman in the photographs. It's her fault that Rachel is in Philip's cross-hairs.

'If I hadn't come to see you,' she says, 'would you have found me?'

His strong, clean profile. Poetry in skin and bone.

'Sure, of course. Eventually.' He itches one side of his nose. 'A little shove from a lovely girl, that's what we all need. And you waited for me, I appreciate that. We make a good team, Caddie. And look, if you're genuinely concerned about the old woman, better to be inside the tent.'

'I feel responsible,' she says. She wishes she could warn Rachel somehow. Stand beside her and take her by the elbow and say *Someone's onto you.*

'Exactly. You can soften the blow. Look after her interests.' Philip looks at his watch. 'Shit, is that the time? I've got Chaucer at ten and I can't miss another one.'

Those corded wrists. There's no fat on him anywhere, not an inch. It's the kind of thin that comes from unwavering discipline and exercise. Part of her understands that these are admirable qualities.

24

New York City, 1938

When Rachel first moved to the city, she was too dazed and hungry to feel its troubled beat. The aftershocks of the Great War, the seismic tremors of financial collapse; the whole arrhythmic mess juddering against the distant rumbles of European calamity. Now she can feel the nervous energy in the streets, though; the bubbling and jumping at shadows. The Munich agreement at the end of September brings a city-wide exhalation, it seems. To everyone except Inga. She obsesses over the state of the world, reads as many newspapers as she can. Rants, periodically, about what she sees there.

'They think they can sell the Czechs down the river and that'll be the end of it,' she says. 'No one who's ever dealt with a bully would believe that.'

The *War of the Worlds* broadcast at the end of October has the city again in a panic. It feels the same as Inga's edginess, Rachel thinks. It feels paranoid. She'd never say, but she thinks Inga is jumping at shadows.

But the weeks pass into winter and there are dinners and holding hands in the dark at Loew's on 175th and there are shows: *My Man Godfrey* and *Show Boat*. They walk in Central Park often, despite the cold, and Inga picks up every white stone she can find and constructs miniature pyramids beneath the trees. It's about time, she says, that man-made structures are dwarfed by nature. Sometimes it's as if Rachel is a tourist and Inga the native, like when Inga takes her hand and points out the way the Standard Oil Building curves with the street. The pride she takes in the marble lobby of the Singer Building—as though she built it herself, each engraved needle, every thread and bobbin.

They browse in Sumner Healey's antique shop on Third Avenue, clowning among the statues of dogs and Indians, and Inga buys her a gold and green Ransbottom planter for one of the aspidistras in her growing collection. One evening they go to dinner at Villa Vallée and Rachel does not recognise herself in a sky blue satin gown of Inga's that falls in soft folds from her hips to graze the floor. Inga is in white that night: resplendent, commanding. Rudy himself kisses their hands and brings them champagne and flirts with Inga and asks her about the new book, which is only months away. Claudette Colbert can*not* be cast as Cadence in the film of *All Has an End*, he says: too old, surely! He asks with more than a casual interest who will play Jurgen.

Inga does not introduce Rachel to him. To anybody. Whenever they go out, since that first night when Rachel met Charles and Fischer, Inga has neglected to introduce her or, if pressed, gives her a random name with an airy wave. When they're alone, Inga calls her Punjab: the magical protector of Little Orphan Annie in the comic strip.

Mostly they stay in. Rachel makes eggs and bacon and rubs Inga's shoulders while she finishes redrafting. From the windows they can see fluffy clouds and their shadows through skyscraper alleys in the day and, at night, a checkerboard of lights and flooding beams. They listen to *Amos 'n' Andy* or play chess in the flickering dark. They read: Inga adores *The Unvanquished* and *Murphy*, and Rachel *Rebecca* and *The Sword in the Stone*. What Rachel wants most to read, of course, is *The Days, the Minutes*, but she hasn't asked. That first afternoon when Inga pulled the page away from her—it's vivid in her mind.

A few months. Not much, over the span of a life. Time enough to make a world.

Charles drops around sometimes for a drink and he's happy, so happy. No one else has read the new book yet, not one page, but the anticipation is already wild. He shows Inga the copy for some ads he plans to run. He doesn't talk about the typesetter again but he sends Inga a basket of South Carolina peaches with a note that says *Thank you*, and they eat them together, she and Rachel, naked in Inga's big white bath. They light candles that seem like tiny yellow spirits dancing while peach juice runs down their sticky chins into the perfumed water. Rachel feels like a yellow chick, warm and fed inside a porcelain shell. She cannot believe that such days exist.

Then Rachel's roommate Carol decides to move out from the tenement on Ninth Street. Carol is a door-to-door saleswoman of brushes and brooms—or used to be, until she discovered chain letters, but the craze is not what it was. The arrival of the mail makes Carol feel lonely now, when only months ago hundreds of letters would arrive every week from people around the country sending pennies and luck. Besides, Rachel has new friends these days, Carol sniffs, though she hasn't had the pleasure of making their acquaintance. Sometimes Carol goes a week without seeing Rachel and then, when she does come home, she's only there to water the blessed plants. Carol's had enough. She's going back to Kansas but will arrange for the post office to forward her mail so she won't miss out when the pennies start rolling in again.

'I'll need another roommate,' Rachel says to Inga, 'or else move into a boarding house.'

They're eating at Jack Dempsey's. She likes it here: the big glass windows out onto Broadway; the feeling of being an observer.

'A roommate? Don't.' Inga picks at her fillet of sole as though this is casual conversation.

Rachel's *now*—this glorious, unheralded present—should be enough. But Inga says *Don't*, and maybe Rachel has been waiting for something to happen. Maybe what she has been waiting for is this one word. *Don't*.

Could it be that Rachel sees herself differently? For the first time she wishes Aunt Vera would pass her in the street. She even wishes her mother could see her, upright and handsome, wearing Inga's clothes, at Inga's table, eating alligator pear and Long Island scallops. The very word *Don't* is making her greedy.

'I have to live somewhere.'

'Lord, you're funny. I'm not proposing, dear thing. Keep your place,' Inga says. 'Just don't get another roommate.'

Inga's apartment is modest, all things considered, but by choice. Rachel's apartment has unidentified smells and crawling insects and thin walls. But Inga likes it when Carol is away at her sister's out in Queens and they can stay there. It's like a holiday, camping in that tiny horrid room, snuggling on the single bed away from Inga's books, from her typewriter, from Charles and the rest of the world. No one knows she's there. She sneaks in so Rachel's neighbours don't see her, as if they would care. Between one apartment and the other, Inga barely takes her out at all anymore. It's too much bother, Inga says. Rachel hasn't seen anyone other than Inga and her workmates in weeks. She tries not to think about any of this.

'I can't afford it,' she says.

'So quit that stupid job and come work for me,' Inga says. 'Don't make that face. It's only a few months until the new book is out and then, oh I can't bear the thought of it. The paperwork, the mail, the filing. Contracts. Letters from people who want autographs. You can be my secretary.'

'I can't.'

'What can't you? You can't file? It's just the alphabet. Write letters? You're smart, I can teach you. I have a system already, and you'll handle things as they come in. Twenty dollars a week should do it.'

It's almost double what Schrafft's pays her.

'No shifts, no carrying trays on straight arms,' Inga says. 'You can sit whenever you want. I might even ease up on the fingernail inspections. Just keep me organised, that's all I ask.'

Rachel thinks of her mother and how it would be for her after all these months with her father in that tiny house. Even a scrap of happiness, she knows, is a temporary thing.

'If I have to answer my own mail I'll jump from a window,' Inga says. 'And we could sleep at your place sometimes. Most times. If we went in separately, no one would even notice. From a distance you can hardly tell us apart.'

'I'll think about it,' Rachel says, but she already knows what her answer will be.

Inga can see her decision in her face. 'Good. Don't tell anyone. The last thing we need is visitors.'

It brings to Rachel's mind advice her father once gave her a thousand years ago, when he was of a mind to lecture her expansively on all the things she should and shouldn't do. Allentown sits on the banks of the Lehigh River and it's broad and well behaved when it goes through town. Just a little out of town, though, the Lehigh narrows and twists. It's faster. It makes white caps and hides rocks and broken trees that snag branches and the foetid bodies of animals that wander too close for a drink. Her father worked on a pile-driving gang on that river one summer before she was born, when the farm still belonged to his father. A man he knew went boating one warm night with a woman who was not his wife. They were both found some days later, bloated, washed up on the shore, eyeballs eaten by scavengers. Should you ever be in that position, her father told Rachel, swimming against the tide of it only wears you out. Give in to the force of the current, and float.

25

Brisbane, Queensland, 1986

There are no Lehrers in the Brisbane phone book. Philip rings the US Friendship Society with a story about tracking down a long-lost friend of his aunt's. They know of no one by that name.

Perhaps Rachel didn't emigrate from the US. Perhaps she was an Australian, in America for a short time. Yes, this makes more sense. A holiday, perhaps that was it.

At the post office, Caddie checks every phone book for all of Queensland and finds Brian and Joan Lehrer living on the Gold Coast. She rings: Brian's a retired postmaster and not due at bowls till two, he's happy to chat. His people are from Sydney, he tells her. Berlin originally, but no one talks about that now. He has some cousins down Wagga way but none of them are called Rachel. Rach, would they call her? he asks. Rachie? Or Shelly? *Sounds a bit Biblical for our lot, love. Me, I'm the product of a long line of heathens.*

She heads back to the library, to the card catalogue, in

case Rachel has become distinguished in a field. In any field. Nothing.

One of the bookstore's former casuals is now a cadet at the *Courier-Mail*, in the sports pages—she phones him, cajoles him into checking the internal library kept by Queensland News. Anyone who's anyone in Queensland is in those files; the *Courier-Mail* knows everything, though what it chooses to reveal is another matter. There is no record of Rachel.

One dark morning Caddie wakes to a storm already underway and goes to the Electoral Commission where she checks the rolls for each of the Brisbane districts while listening to rain drumming on the roof and gurgling down the drainpipe. She likes this kind of work. She would have made a good miner, she thinks, wielding a sharp pick to uncover things hidden in dark, moist rock. She can think better in enclosed spaces, too, between banks of bookshelves or filing cabinets, or the rows of names and addresses as she works her finger down the list of *L*s.

There is no Rachel Lehrer anywhere.

Her research on the Bund, though, is going well. She finds evidence of a plot to kill Jewish Americans in Los Angeles, and another to sabotage America's home defences. She writes to Marty Fischer, officially this time, and asks if she can meet with him, and she spends what seems like hours writing to Bund historians in the US and reading through textbooks and filling out forms for a research trip. She spends Friday driving between the university and Philip's home a few streets away, setting up her desk and dividing reference materials: general ones for the office that give nothing away; more specific files and journals at his home. Philip's mostly in meetings. He gives her the keys to his car, his house.

She lets herself in the front door, and straight away there are things she's forgotten, like the smell of the eucalypts from the garden. His office is downstairs, but she wanders. She can't help herself. The bedroom has new carpet, and dividing the dining room from the lounge is a fish tank a metre long. Neon tetras with red flashes in their tails and yellow angel fish and bright green underwater trees sway in the current generated by a heating motor disguised as an ironic castle. The fish are flying dashes of colour and they dance and somersault just for her. She imagines Philip measuring their food with a tiny spoon and taking the temperature of their water every day. In the kitchen, she swings open the cupboard doors. There's still only one frypan: Philip prefers to eat out. There's still no television. That'll be the day I give up on life, Philip used to say. He's bought a rug for the lounge-room floor, though, some kind of tribal pattern in ochres and browns. It's wool, and looks expensive.

She's glad to see the rug, and the fish. Philip didn't have them before so they're evidence that years really have passed. She's older now. She's wiser.

At four o'clock she's back at the uni office, setting up things on her desk. There's a knock on the door and she swings it open. Standing there in the hall—an old-fashioned corridor, wide, with a vinyl floor—is a man holding a brown paper parcel. Jamie.

Something rises up inside her. Was his face always that shape? His eyes, faintly almond? He's unshaven, untrimmed, taller than she remembered. He's in corduroy pants, for heaven's sake, and a pale blue shirt, untucked, sleeves rolled. Floppy fringe that makes her fingers itch. A dusting of acne scars across his lower cheeks. His collar fraying at the point. The rays of the sun prefer him to anything around him.

Oh God, she thinks. She's aware of the shape of his skull, the fan of small bones on the back of his square hand as he cradles the package. She can feel the blood in her own veins. She places her palm on her forehead: she's roasting. She sees his face change.

'Caddie.'

She can't reply. She's lost all confidence in her vocal cords.

'What are you doing here?' he says.

'I thought you were away. Melbourne.'

'I was. I'm back.'

A feeling sweeps over her, out of nowhere. The gap between the instant a glass of water slips from your fingers and seeing the shards across the kitchen floor.

'I'm working here now. For Philip.' Her voice is too much, her words are too fast. There's too much air in her lungs. Why didn't she think about this in advance? 'Philip is my boss. We're doing both projects. I'm working on the Bund. He wants to find Rachel.'

'Philip's helping you find Rachel? Philip Carmichael?'

'This was your idea. A research project, you said.'

He blinks. 'You don't need to explain to me.'

She opens her mouth to reply when Philip walks around the corner.

245

'You've met. Excellent,' he says. 'It's Caddie's first week as my new right-hand girl. Finally someone to whip me into shape, long overdue. Caddie, I supervised Jamie's PhD an age ago. I was telling you about him at your place that time, remember? My old friend, the antiquarian bookseller? Ooh, is that my Rilke? Lovely.'

She's never seen them stand together. Philip is lighter in all aspects. He's crisp, sharpened, polished. Jamie is bigger, taller, scruffy. Tousled. His eyes are hazel; did she notice earlier? Philip takes the parcel from Jamie's hands.

'New job,' Jamie says. 'That's exciting for you.'

His lips are thin—she knows they're not usually thin.

'Yes,' Caddie says. 'I guess.'

'You look exhausted, mate,' Philip says. 'More sleep, more exercise, that's what you need. And you didn't have to drop it in yourself. You could have mailed it.' He moves past them and takes a pair of scissors from his desk.

'I was over this side of town anyway,' says Jamie. 'I had an appointment tonight. I might go home instead, though. I'm absolutely buggered.'

'You want an assistant. Worth their weight in gold. Hey, Caddie?' Philip unwraps the brown paper and then opens the Rilke, carefully, testing the repaired spine. 'They've done a good job. This is a little treasure.'

The pulse bulges in her wrists; at the base of her throat. She brings her chest in and out so her breath will follow. She feels like she's dying. She wishes she had something to cover her shoulders, a cloak or a wrap.

'I'd better go if I'm going to beat the traffic.' Jamie's stare is steady and focused on the middle-distance. That fascinating chair leg.

'I'll walk you out,' Caddie says. 'I'm exhausted too. You don't mind, do you Philip?'

'Well, actually there's another load to take back to my place,' Philip says. 'Have you still got the key?'

Jamie steps back from the door and at last their gazes catch and hold. Then he looks away.

'Yes, what kind of impression would that make, leaving early in your new job?' Jamie says, to the floor. 'Congratulations again, Caddie. Philip.'

There's a buzzing in Caddie's ears. Tonight, she knows already, she'll walk to Toowong and walk home again under the streetlights of Milton Road past purposeful cars with somewhere to be. She could walk all the way to Montezuma's if she felt like it, for a chicken and cheese enchilada, and take the backstreets home, surprising possums on fences. Walking the length of Miskin Street to ease the pacing of her mind. The perfume of late star jasmine leading her home and the lost chance of something precious, something that cannot be replaced. She will cast her gaze to the sky and wonder if, to really know a place, you have to leave it.

In the years to come, even after everything she'll achieve and everything she'll attain, she'll remember tonight with a knot of anguish. Looking up and wondering if there is any sight so beautiful and brutal as the night sky of your hometown.

26

New York City, 1938

The week before Christmas, Inga is asleep on Rachel's single bed. The curtains are open and in the weak afternoon light the ice on the ledges across the street makes it seem like the world has been dusted with diamonds. Rachel is on the floor beside the bed, turning the last page of a set of printer's galleys. It's late. She's reading Inga's new book, *The Days, the Minutes*. It's about to be printed. It's only weeks away from appearing on shelves.

Since that first time when Inga snatched the page away, Rachel hasn't asked if she could read *The Days, the Minutes*. She didn't know how. Early this morning, Rachel woke to see Inga sitting up in bed, looking down on her.

'You can read it, if you like,' Inga said. 'If you want to. You don't have to.'

'I want to,' Rachel said. 'I'm dying to.'

In the final stages, as she wrote and rewrote, Inga worked for sometimes twenty hours straight with her shoulders hunched and her head jutting out from her neck in a way that didn't look human. She napped on the chaise longue fully clothed and kept the windows closed because the traffic noise irritated her; she drank black coffee and swallowed Benzedrine and picked at the sandwiches Rachel made, her pinpoint pupils sharp as a crow's beak. Sometimes she asked Rachel questions about how a natural-born American would say things. Rachel answered without thinking and afterwards felt pressed flat by the responsibility, the fear of having led Inga astray. Inga became thinner. Sometimes she cried at the fates of her characters even as she polished the words that doomed them, but she didn't stop. She couldn't stop.

That was weeks ago. Now Inga's paying the price for all that relentless energy because the closer the book comes to publication, the more exhausted she becomes, as if this new work continues to sap her even as it comes to life without her. The champagne cocktail months are over: Inga dozes and eats buttered toast and eggs and drinks milky tea with too much sugar.

Rachel's work, on the other hand, is energising her. Inga's filing system, it turns out, was a waist-high stack of coffee tins hidden in a cupboard, stuffed with sheets of paper folded tight and wedged together. Rachel finds quiet peace in extracting these and smoothing the creases, in making files and labelling them in block letters, in copying out Inga's standard replies to correspondence in her own hand and signing them because Inga never wants to be disturbed.

This worried Rachel at the beginning, but now she sees it as a necessary evil. Better this, she believes, than readers thinking that Inga is too stuck up to acknowledge them.

Only three other people have seen the manuscript—Inga herself, Charles and Samuel Fischer, when he was typesetting it.

Finally Rachel turns the last page on the floor beside her. When she began, she felt the weight of how she should react. Now that she's finished, the air has a different texture. Her heart feels different. She doesn't have to analyse her own response. She can't. She's in the thick of Inga's story, feeling the world she has made, and it is a fragile thing and everyone is connected and there is space in her heart for everyone, even people who do terrible things and must be opposed.

'Well?' says Inga, without opening her eyes. She is lying on her side, knees tucked up to her waist, her hands in a prayer pillow under her cheek.

'Did I wake you?' Rachel says.

'If you thought I could sleep while you read my book, you've hugely misjudged me.'

'I thought you didn't care what anyone thought of it.'

Inga flicks her eyes open. 'You're not anyone.'

And all Rachel can think is: *Isn't it strange?* This vast city with its skyscraper canyons is famous across the seas yet everything important in it can fit inside this one room. Her heart feels lanced by a needle.

Perhaps when all this is over she and Inga can take a holiday. A week in Charles's cabin near Woodstock. It has its own dock onto the Esopus Creek, he says, where the water is wide and still, and a canoe and a stone fireplace. There are egrets and cranes and swans. Maybe she can find a rod and show Inga how to catch a trout.

'I think it's the most sad and glorious thing I've ever read,' she says. 'I think it'll change everyone who reads it. I think it'll change the world.'

Inga laughs, low and tinkling. 'You darling child. You don't really think books have that kind of power?'

'Of course,' Rachel says. 'You're only doubting it because this is a book that's on the side of good. If someone were to write an evil book, you'd believe in the damage that could do. And this…it's better than *All Has an End*, if that's possible. It'll make the world a better place.'

Inga smiles and stretches on the bed like a cat. 'Not everyone will agree,' she says.

Rachel knows that's true. She hasn't seen them all because they've been sent to Charles, but lately Inga's received some disturbing letters. Not just the usual crazy stuff: serious threats designed to stop publication of the book. She's part of the worldwide Jewish conspiracy. She's a traitor to her own people and part of the government's plot to drag America into Europe's troubles. One letter, milder than some, was written in rust-coloured ink that uncannily blobbed and thickened. The books will never go on sale, another letter said.

Inga's worried, though she tries not to show it. Charles has had advice and will lock the plates away in his private warehouse with the books as soon as they're back from the printers. He's the only one with the key. The books and the plates will be safe there. Charles has given Inga his word. Rachel doesn't doubt him exactly, but suspects that he is moved by commercial nous more than realistic fear. The excitement about this new book is so great he fears a copy will be stolen before publication day and leaked to a disreputable paper, or even printed illegally and sold on the streets. All kinds of journalists and two-bit private detectives and assorted types have been nosing around. These pages, the galleys Rachel is reading, are the only ones outside of Charles's control. Inga told him they'd already burnt them: stuffed them in the wood stove on a particularly cold December night.

'This is the book you were born to write,' Rachel says.

'Let's see if it makes that revolting man Fischer see the error of his ways. I still can't believe I gave in to Charles and let him touch it. I feel sad for my poor words, to have had his eyeballs on them.'

Rachel shuffles across the floor to bring her face in line with Inga's.

'But you had to let him work on it, don't you see? That's exactly what your book is about. Oppose these people, yes, by all means. Do anything you can to stop them, and protect everyone else from them. But you can do all these things while pitying them at the same time. Kindness and opposition, they're not mutually exclusive. He has a family. They have to eat.'

'Your gorgeous heart. These Nazis—Fischer and his Bund boys. People seem to think it's all flag-waving and nicely pressed uniforms and a little playful thuggery. But these people really believe there are whole categories of humans who don't deserve to exist.' She shudders and forces a laugh. 'Now if *they* thought my book had world-changing power I would really be worried.' Inga kisses her, saucy and quick. 'You're a doll, you know that?'

Rachel knows all of Inga's kisses by now: the one that means *I care for you* and the one that means *Make love with me* and this one, which means *Let's talk about something else.*

'Maybe we should move some of the plants over to your place,' Rachel says.

'Not a chance. They'd never make it—it's a botanical graveyard over there. When are you going to tell me the secret of your green thumb?'

With what seems like no effort, Rachel's collection of plants has grown. Inga bought her some, along with a red enamelled watering can, and others she has plucked as cuttings from the park while still others were donated by Charles as hospital cases from his house. Somehow she understands which ones need more sunlight and which ones less, which like wet feet as opposed to draining on pebbles.

'I don't know,' Rachel says. 'The plants tell me what they want. That's all.'

Inga hugs a pillow to her chest. 'Spurned again. I'll have to keep hanging around until you spill. Tell you what, when all this fuss is over I'll buy you a farm, what do you say about that? And we'll live together like a couple of old maids and you can grow anything you like.'

'You, a farmer?'

'And why not? I grew up on a farm.'

'You love this city. You'd never leave it.'

'I do love it here. But I come from across the seas.' She shrugs. 'Everywhere is temporary—who knows where we'll end up?'

'I'd love to live in another country some day.'

'Would you? Where?'

'Anywhere.' Rachel laughs. 'No, not anywhere. Somewhere with no tall buildings. I like them, I do, but it's hard to relax in a city like this. If I had a place of my own, it'd be somewhere sleepy. Somewhere warm; no snow. I come from a long line of people who've never been outside of Pennsylvania. Well, that's not quite true. My mother came from here, originally. And my father once went to a funeral in West Virginia.'

'All right, forget the farm. How about I make you this promise: one day, I'll take you to another country. A faraway place, as far as you like. Whirl a globe and stab a pin and we'll go. How would you like that?'

Later that night, Rachel can't sleep. Inga lies beside her, breathing in and out through her soft mouth. Rachel gets up, gently. The galleys are on the coffee table where she left them last night. Tomorrow they'll go in the fire and she can't bear it, this beautiful thing of Inga's heart and mind turning to ash like yesterday's peelings. She wraps the pages in a scrap of oilskin, a piece of the flowery tablecloth that was in the apartment when she arrived, and then conceals the package inside the Ransbottom planter, curved around the outside of the coffee tin that holds the aspidistra.

The next day, alone at Inga's, Rachel is cleaning an ink stain from the bedside table when she spots yet another pile of papers poking out from underneath the bed. She's been trying to coax Inga out of her habit of folding papers into tiny accordions and squirrelling them away, but contracts and letters and files keep appearing in unlikely places. Inga also keeps money, substantial sums, in both their apartments, wedged between books and in washed-out vanishing-cream containers in the bathroom. Rachel doesn't consider this strange. It's sensible behaviour for anyone who lived through the hard times of the last ten years, particularly someone who's known the uncertainty of life as an immigrant. She herself hid Inga's manuscript yesterday, a small example among many of the ways that being with Inga has changed her. Dropping documents on the floor and, no doubt, kicking them under the bed was an improvement.

Rachel wipes her fingers on a cleaning rag then drops to her knees to pick the papers up. So she can file them.

She reads the first page, and the next, before she even registers what it says. *Last will and testament*, that's what it says. Before she can stop herself, she sees her name there. She sits back on her heels.

I give and bequeath to Rachel Hannah Lehrer.

I give and bequeath to Rachel Hannah Lehrer, it says, all of my copyright of my work and all of my personal property, same to be sold by my executor herein named. I give and bequeath to Rachel Hannah Lehrer. In witness thereof, I, the said Inga Eva Karlson, do herewith set my hand and seal this the ninth day of November, 1938.

Rachel turns each page and when she's read every one, drops the papers as if she's scorched. She has known Inga for less than four months. Should she say something to her? Perhaps she should. Inga never talks about relatives or friends back in Austria, or of the villagers who famously pooled everything they had to send her to school. She should ask Inga to reconsider. Or is that too rude and ungrateful? Would it ruin this delicate thing they have between them? She decides: she will speak to Inga. Yes, definitely. Tell her that this is a mistake.

But not this minute. Inga is exhausted, with the preparations for the release of the book still underway and the publicity yet to come. So Rachel puts the papers back where she found them in the same state of disarray, and says nothing about the will, or the copy of *The Days, the Minutes* she's hidden away.

And Christmas morning comes, and Inga gives her a necklace to match her own: Lalique glass, with yellow wasps. Rachel gives her a box of chocolate-coated cherries, which delights Inga, and a pair of kid gloves, cherry red. And New Year comes and goes, and they pass it in Inga's apartment sharing a bottle of champagne. Days pass, and the weeks pass, and the printing is finished, and Inga's new book, *The Days, the Minutes*, is safe in Charles's warehouse. Before Rachel knows, it's February.

February, 1939. And still Rachel says nothing about Inga's will.

Part 3

27

Brisbane, Queensland, 1986

Philip made a start when he was in America: the Benjamin R. Tucker papers, held by the New York Public Library, mention Karlson, and Philip went through every page; the Dos Passos collection has more, and for that he went all the way to the University of Virginia. She skim-reads dozens of books from academic libraries around the country, including biographies of every 1930s literary figure who might have run into Karlson. Or read her, or thought of her. You can't trust indexes, Philip says. Check them yourself. And she loves this sharp-eyed fossicking. She's been away from academia so long and now, with the work before her, she can't imagine why. She could have picked a topic any time and just begun. She never needed anyone's permission.

It's just after dawn. As her eyes open, she hauls a book from the pile on the unslept half of her bed and reads for an hour before she rises. She fills notepads with references and cross-references, and she finds plenty that's fascinating but nothing that's new. It's not surprising. Karlson's life has been picked over for decades. She finds no mention of a Rachel or anyone named Lehrer.

She doesn't give notice to Pretty and Terese about moving out, and Philip doesn't mention it again.

Philip leaves the arson project to Caddie while he focuses on the bigger picture of how to unveil Rachel, when they find her. How to maximise the media impact? The crowning glory, of course, will be whatever they can reconstitute of *The Days, the Minutes*: but what if Rachel Lehrer can remember nothing? Caddie pleads with him. Perhaps we shouldn't be organising things just yet. She's old, after all.

Philip sees her point. The woman's probably doddery. But a few sentences would be enough, particularly if they recast the story as his, Philip's, quest for truth: a literary detective story. Meta's big right now. It's the kind of audacious thinking most academics don't have the flair and confidence to pull off. No, they continue as planned. Philip finds a corkboard on wheels and sits in his office, playing with titles. *The Karlson Detective: The true story of the greatest literary mystery of all time* is his favourite, though he also has a soft spot for *Revealed: The Days and Minutes of Inga Karlson*.

She's thinking about these things—Philip, Rachel, her labyrinthine research—solely and precisely so she doesn't have to think about Jamie. It's been building for the past few weeks and, whenever she thinks about him she feels a wave of such intensity that she has to stop and close her eyes and fight to regain her focus. She can't think about Jamie now or she'll have no rational brain at all. She can't even say his name. Jamie. Jamie. Ten times, twenty times, Caddie has her hand on the phone. Twenty times, fifty times, she thinks of jumping on the bus straight to his shop. But what would she say? Her only hope is to bring everything to a conclusion. It's not just Rachel's future that's resting on her shoulders—it's her own.

'Lunch?' Philip says late one morning as she's filing.

At his place, they spread their research over the Herman Miller Eames table. Philip makes a salad. He eats a lot of salad. He owns taupe linen napkins. The table is covered by protective vinyl cut to size and it feels to Caddie like they're working on a shower curtain. Philip's art—big, textural splashes of colour on unframed canvases, vaguely Japanese— looks down at her. She's had so much on her mind she's forgotten to wonder what they're supposed to be. He pours her a glass of nice rosé.

'Just a drop,' she says. 'I want to keep my mind on what I'm doing.'

He twists the bottle as he finishes the pour. 'I'm not entirely oblivious to subtext. As much as I find it personally disappointing—it's for the best, I agree. I don't want anything to distract you.'

She keeps at what she's doing, doesn't even look up.

'Look, I've been thinking,' he says. 'The exhibition of the fragments closes in a couple of weeks. A small gathering to announce our discovery of Rachel and drop a few teasers about your project, on the fire—where better to hold it than at the exhibition itself?'

'But we haven't found her.'

Finding Rachel. The most important part of Philip's strategy was the first thing they talked about. How to approach Rachel, and when. How to get her to speak to them. From the day Caddie started working for Philip, they've been sending letters to Rachel's post-office box. Official-looking ones from the university, promising attention—all old people want attention, Philip said. And almost straight away a reply came addressed to Philip, with Rachel's PO box as a return address.

> Professor Carmichael,
> Kindly leave me alone.
> Regards
> Rachel Lehrer

So they began sending friendlier, more personal ones on feminine stationery, handwritten by Caddie. Eventually, another reply came.

> Ms Walker,
> Now is not the time.
> Regards
> Rachel Lehrer

Now Philip wants to escalate.

'Look, this wasn't an easy decision to make. What if other people get wind of her? I have rivals. The timing, on the other hand. It's too good an opportunity to pass up.'

'I'm worried it'll be anti-climactic. If she can't remember anything, or if we've got it wrong.'

'Unlikely. We already have enough to make it interesting: the heir to the Karlson estate, living right here in Brisbane. That angle alone, as a beginning. An announcement, made in front of the fragments themselves: it's a delectable entrée for the whole story.

Caddie begs him, she pleads against it. He won't listen. And that's not all. From now on, Philip will wait in front of the post office for Rachel, for however long it takes. It's time he took charge.

'I feel responsible,' says Caddie. 'She's an old woman. Why don't I go instead? I'm sure I'll have a better chance with her. You are…well. You're a bit intimidating, professor.'

'Tough,' he says. 'I'm annoyed now. Now I like the idea of surprising her as she collects her mail. In fact, you know what? We could film it. Me, microphone in hand. Get a cameraman. The whole bit.'

Caddie suggests, gently, that to surprise her like that, with lights and strangers, could damage their chances of getting what they want. Besides, she might not even collect her own mail. A friend, a neighbour might go instead.

'Let me go alone. If she's there, I'll talk her around. That's why you hired me, because I know what she looks like. She knows me.'

He sighs. It's disappointing. It offends his sense of the dramatic, and of himself at the centre of things, but he agrees it's better for their plan if Caddie is by herself when she makes contact.

'Send another letter as well,' Philip says. 'Tell her what you've discovered about the fire. About Marty Fischer. Tell her we're releasing it on the last day of the exhibition, at a function. We won't, of course. Of course not—we'll give away the barest hint just to get some buzz started. Tell her she's cordially invited but we're going ahead, with or without her. Let's see if that brings her in.'

Security, evidently, isn't nearly as important for Caddie's project as it is for Philip's.

'But don't ask her anything and don't tell her anything. If you find her. Don't talk to her about the book at all. Just bring her to me. I need to be there from the very beginning. I need to see her face when we ask her. My own impressions.'

'Got it.'

'I suppose we can always hire some old actress if it comes to that,' he says. 'Re-enact it.'

Caddie knocks over her rosé. A pink spill spreads across the table; Philip rights the glass and scrambles to pick up his notes and books.

'A tea towel, sweetie,' he says. 'Quick.'

'What did you say?' Caddie says.

'A. Tea. Towel. This is exactly why the table is covered in vinyl. Quick, or it'll be on the floor.'

She bolts to the kitchen and brings back the tea towel that was hanging on the oven door.

'Honestly, can you not see that this is Irish linen?' Philip says, as the spill creeps closer to the edge. 'There's nothing for it now.' He presses it down upon the puddle. The notes are saved, the table is saved, the floor is saved. The tea towel is ruined. The fish are horrified: they make round mouths against the glass.

Caddie apologises as he swabs, straightens, then folds the stained tea towel. 'No big deal. Just try to be a bit more careful.'

'What were you saying before?'

'Oh. I thought—a documentary would be great, wouldn't it? It would be better if we filmed it actually happening but I appreciate the difficulties. I could play myself.'

'That's a really great idea,' Caddie says.

Philip finishes his wine then takes both glasses into the kitchen, yet all at once she's thirsty. She'd really like another glass of that rosé full to the top, that she could cup with both her hands.

It's the end of May. The next morning she wakes early so she can be at Philip's by six and head out again, driving his car. Woolloongabba, where the post office is, is on the other side of town. It's awkward, and it's annoying, but she must have the car. How would it be if she found this old woman, won her over then made her hike up Stanley Street looking for a taxi rank? Philip must walk to uni. He stands on the doorstep and watches her go. He's lighthearted. *Have a good day at the office, darling*, he says as he waves.

At around six in the evening, she returns without Rachel. Without even a sighting of Rachel.

This is to be expected, Philip explains. Most people do not collect their mail every day. Who would write to old people? The gas bill. Postcards from distant relations rubbing their *Women's Weekly* Discovery Tour in their retired face. A mail-order catalogue for fleecy cardigans and porcelain figurines of cats playing with wool or wall plates of Princess Diana. That's about it. They can't expect immediate success. Constant vigilance is the price of victory.

On the second day she wakes even earlier and packs a curried egg sandwich so she can eat it right there, leaning against the side wall of the old dispensary building across the road, and not take her eyes off the post office. No reading, definitely; any distraction and she could miss Rachel altogether. Old people, Philip warns her, are small and inconsequential. Old women particularly. Their features, the way ageing loosens their skin from their bones, make it hard to distinguish one from another. Focus, that's what she needs. This time she stays until ten at night.

She vows that when all this is over, she'll sleep until noon.

Each day she comes home without a glimpse of Rachel. At night she sleeps with books about 1930s New York open on her chest. She dreams she is diving leagues below the icy sea without a tank, and when she sees a clam on the ocean floor she prises its shell open with her hunting knife and levers the flesh aside until she finds a pearl. Tropical fish the size of cars gawk at her. In other dreams she is small again, and her father borrows a tinny from a friend and they spend the early morning on Bulimba Creek where the mangroves smell good and putrid, pulling crab pots. This really happened, when she was eight. They found three big muddies with dark green-grey shells like armour plating and only one small jenny they threw back. Caddie half-thrilled, half-terrified, squealing, avoiding those claws with the power to crush a slow finger. In the dream, though, she and her father haul each line and the pots seem heavy and unbalanced as they heave them over the side but they are empty, every one. The bait is in place inside the metal cage: eyeless snapper heads with seagrass beards, creek-washed but untouched. There are no crabs inside at all.

Before she turns out the light, she takes the photos of Rachel from her bag where she keeps them. She looks into Rachel's eyes and wishes she could ask her what she knows— about Inga, the book, the fire. Everything.

A week goes by. Philip is growing restless. He wants to take a taxi out to the post office himself in the middle of the day to keep watch when Caddie goes to the toilet. She keeps her liquid intake minimal during the day, as instructed. There's a loo in a nearby pub. She's quick. She's gone for four minutes; five, tops. What are the odds that Rachel arrives in those four minutes? But she can't dissuade him.

'I've booked that little reception room off the side of the exhibition, for the afternoon of the last day, for our soirée. I've rung everyone who matters. We're almost out of time. I'm coming,' he says.

So from now on, he arrives every day around one to relieve her. The post office is on a corner and she has a good view in both directions. Philip stands out the front for four minutes and even that drives him crazy.

'You're too busy for this,' she tells him.

He agrees. It's ridiculous, an associate professor travelling by taxi to sit outside a post office so his research assistant can pee. Not to mention her time, when there are chapters of their book to draft, letters to write, grants to apply for, files to request. He'll speak to the postmistress. After all, we're researchers. A little co-operation from members of the general public, it isn't too much to ask. She'll have contact details for everyone with a post-office box, and then we can go straight to Rachel's house. Leave it to me, he says to Caddie. I have a way with people.

But Philip does not have a way with the postmistress. She looks at him over her glasses and tells him she will under no circumstances divulge either the street address of her customers or their phone number, nor will she even confirm or deny their very existence. And if he dares to accost people on her property or attempt to bribe a Commonwealth employee, she'll have no hesitation in calling the police.

No progress. The head of the English Department is coming to their reception on the last day of the exhibition, and Malcolm Kirby from the art gallery, and a few select scholars. No journalists, not yet. Philip wants rumours to begin to rustle but will wait until everything is packaged up before he gets the press bidding for the story. Informal, really. A handful of important people, a few nice drinks, some little things to eat. A chance for everyone to see Rachel Lehrer in the flesh. It's urgent now that they find her.

When Caddie drops the car off the next night, Philip lifts his head from his book. 'I'm calling in sick for the rest of the week and coming with you,' he says. 'I can hardly believe I'm saying this, but I'm going to loiter out the front of a suburban post office and wait for an old lady.'

'It won't make any difference if you're there or not if she doesn't come. It's a waste of your time.'

'But she will come, if I'm there,' says Philip. 'I feel it. A sense of destiny.'

'Please. Give me one more day.'

'One more day. The day after tomorrow,' Philip says, 'I'm coming with you.'

That night, she gets out of bed around two to open the door and sit on the front verandah in this verandah town. The night-time world is another place entirely. Bitumen gives up the heat of the day like spirits rising; yards are ruled by bolshie possums bigger than pregnant cats. The sky seems unnaturally bright. On the footpath under the streetlight, she can see two toads considering each other. Tomorrow morning is her point of no return.

But again, on the day of her final chance to bring Rachel in alone, there is no sign of her. At around 6 p.m. she pulls into the drive.

'No good?' Philip says, as she gets out of the car.

'I'm sorry,' Caddie says. 'I did everything I could.'

'Luckily I have better news.' Philip waves a letter at her. 'This is from Rachel Lehrer. She's coming to our little party.'

28

New York City, 1939

Thursday, 9 February 1939 dawns cold and cloudy. Rachel
sleeps late, which she does often despite the years of discipline
at home with her parents and later at the restaurant. Inga,
notwithstanding the general lethargy of her days, is up at first
light.

'It's not a reflection of my character, I assure you,' Inga tells
her. 'I'm the legacy of four generations of women who woke
at four a.m. to milk goats.'

This morning, Inga and Rachel are at Inga's place for
a change. They linger in their dressing-gowns over a slow
breakfast, reading the paper, which is a flurry of news that
Rachel knows she should care about but can't bring herself
to. France and Britain prepare to recognise the Franco regime
in Spain; a commerce commissioner she's never heard of is
warning that the United States is only five or ten years from
a fascist government. Inga reads every word of every article,
clicking her tongue. She holds the paper up, turns the pages

and folds them back. Rachel moves her chair closer so she can read the articles on the new back page.

'Look at those beauties,' says Rachel, as she smears butter across her toast as thick as she likes. 'If only newspapers were in colour.'

The table has been set by Rachel with Inga's mismatched silver butter dish, odd chipped plates, heavy knives with bone handles the colour of honey and fraying napkins that look like rags. There's a small lamp on the table with a red-fringed shade. It gives everything a wine tinge and intensifies the feeling that Rachel has, whenever she's here at Inga's, of being giddy and out of her own body. The drug of being close to Inga and, increasingly, even near her things.

'If only,' says Inga, from behind the paper.

'Cultivated for two thousand years, it says.'

'Hmm.'

'Does that mean they're older than roses, do you think?'

'I guess.' Inga braces the paper with one hand and extends the other to stir her tea. She taps the spoon on the side, *clink clink clink*. She doesn't take a sip. The paper doesn't even quiver. Rachel can't see her face.

'Hey, you,' Rachel says.

Nothing.

Rachel pulls down the paper to reveal Inga not reading, not even pretending. She blinks as though she's just waking. Rachel catches Inga's distorted reflection in the butter dish, her white chin long and pointed like a witch in a fairytale.

'What?' Inga says. A pulse at the base of her throat dances in and out.

'Carnations.' Rachel bends the paper so Inga can see a bouquet in a basket adorned with, for some reason, wooden clothespins. 'There's a convention at the Hotel Pennsylvania.'

'And that is relevant to me somehow?'

'Everything will be fine, dear,' Rachel says. 'The book will come out and everyone will love it and you won't have space on your mantel for the prizes.'

Inga's nostrils flare. She unfolds her legs and one knee strikes a table leg, making everything rattle. 'And you know that for certain, do you? All hail, Rachel, the psychic waitress, teller of fortunes, seer of mysteries. What do you know about it? Nothing, that's what. Honestly you speak such rubbish when you choose.'

The quiet that follows is a palpable thing. Oh, Rachel thinks, how much you must be hurting, my poor dear. And from that thought springs another: Rachel is her mother's daughter. She has a memory of her mother in a white cotton dress standing in front of a mirror and pressing on her livid, swollen eye, praying it went down before her father got home. Telling little Rachel to run to a neighbour for ice because she was worried for the pain it would cause him to look at what he'd done. Rachel looks down at the tablecloth. If that's Inga's best attempt at hurting her when she's tense, what a blessed life they'll lead.

Inga folds the paper and drops it on the table and reaches across for Rachel's hand. She unfurls Rachel's fingers and kisses the palm, then she rubs her thumb over the tender blue veins at her wrist. 'I'm not the best breakfast company, am I?' Inga says. 'Let's go out.'

They are lucky to find a matinee of *Gunga Din* at the Radio City Music Hall. It's just the thing—Cary Grant and Douglas Fairbanks Jr. fighting the Thuggee with no room at all for introspection.

After lunch they head to the end-of-winter sale at Russeks on Fifth Avenue and try on grey Persian lambs and black caraculs and a black silk velvet opera coat with an ermine collar. The changing-room curtains are red chiffon and the weight of the coats is comforting. Rachel stands in front of a floor-length mirror with her arms spread wide, warm inside another creature's skin.

She no longer wonders at the identity of this strange woman before her. She has grown accustomed to her new body now. The milk skin on the underside of her upper arm: she didn't have that before meeting Inga, surely. The muscles that enable her bent knuckles to make such tiny tremors of movement whenever she desires, the susceptible sinews behind her knees. Her feet are new in their entirety. To think how little she understood them before, believing them only good for walking and standing. How did she live so long in this body without her skin being awake, she wonders. Did her mother feel like this, in the presence of her father? Because that might go some way to explaining things. She can't believe it, though. She won't. Has anyone ever felt like this in the history of the world before?

'I could afford these, you know,' says Inga. She runs her fingers along an ermine collar as though it were still a living thing and she was giving it comfort. 'I could buy one for me and one for you, if you like.'

Rachel feels a chill despite the fur around her. 'Please don't,' she says. 'This is just for fun.'

Inga hardens her eyes. 'Is that what you think? That this is just for fun? We're just playing at dress-ups, like two children?'

Rachel cannot think what to say.

The saleswoman comes over, just in time to stretch out her arms and catch the fur that Inga might have dropped on the floor.

They don't speak all the way back to Inga's apartment. Perhaps, Rachel thinks, she should go to her own place tonight. A little space, that's what they need. Or is that a type of cowardice? She's read in magazines of couples who refuse to part angry, but the magazine meant a different kind of couple from them. Are they even a 'couple'? She wishes there was someone she could ask.

Before they've had time to take their coats off, the doorbell sounds. It's a boy in a pressed uniform with a telegram for Inga.

URGENT COME TO WAREHOUSE NOW STOP PROBLEM STOP
NEED YOUR IMMEDIATE ATTENTION AUTHORISE FIX STOP
CHARLES CLEBORN

The awkwardness of this strange day is at once forgotten. They tip the boy, grab coats and hats. As they're wrapping, Inga turns to Rachel.

'It's cold and I've been beastly today. If you wanted to stay home I wouldn't blame you.'

'Of course I'm coming,' Rachel says.

They're out the door and into a taxi before they even ask each other what could possibly have happened. Inga bites the inside of her cheek and wrings her cherry gloves. As they race through the grubby, frozen streets to Division Street, Rachel reaches for Inga's hand. Inga lets her take it.

'Faster, please,' Rachel says to the driver.

They look out their respective windows down Second Avenue, because there's nowhere else to look. Rachel has the sense of a kaleidoscope of images flashing past: the struts and gantries of the El; a woman with a red scarf pushing a buggy; a cafeteria with huge plate windows; a deli on a corner with boxes of lemons stacked outside; a bakery she's been to once where only a few months ago bread was sold by the slice. Down the sides of buildings: hanging lines of laundry, catching what little sun there is. The night is coming. Neon lights appear, blinking. Children are climbing stairs to go home for dinner and a bath. Storekeepers are pulling shutters down with hooked staffs.

Rachel holds Inga's hand tighter and thinks of everything that could have gone wrong with the books. A printing error? The text upside down or the pages inserted randomly? Surely that is not so terrible. Expensive to fix, but not calamitous. A lawsuit, some charlatan claiming that Inga has stolen his work? Or could someone have broken in, despite Charles's best intentions, and stolen copies, or vandalised them? Rachel pleads to a god she's long forgotten. Please let Inga be all right, whatever has happened.

The taxi lets them out in front of a tall reddish building

on the corner of a quiet street. The driver zooms away fast without offering Inga change. On the side of the building, Rachel can make out STABLE: large block letters in faded white paint. There are no other signs or markings that would give away what's inside.

Inga knocks on the door and waits. It opens: Charles, wrapped in a black trench and a thick grey scarf, looking weary.

'Come in, come in.' They scuttle inside. 'This way.'

He leads them through a glass-panelled antechamber, past a mess of an office and then along a narrow walkway between pallets of boxes, double-stacked. Rachel looks up: the building is at least two storeys high with no ceiling and there are panes of grimy glass set in the roof. High above their heads a network of beams heavy with dust; a few naked bulbs hanging down. The place is filthy. There's a smell too, as though the building was a garage or a mechanic's work-shop. In a few spots there are puddles. The gaps between the pallets show a few tall windows, each set with cobwebbed iron bars.

'What's that smell?' she says.

'It's a warehouse, Rachel,' Charles says. 'I don't get a maid in.'

He stops in front of a small clearing in the centre of a forest of pallets. There are a few boxes already open. A handful of copies of *The Days, the Minutes* scattered around. Inga picks one up and runs her hand over it. It's cloth-bound in rich red with Inga's name and the title in gold. The buckram is so fine that, in this light, it could pass for velvet.

'It's beautiful,' Rachel says. Simple, elegant, striking: exactly what Inga asked for.

'Yes, yes. So what? You gave me a heart attack. Seriously. I thought. I don't know what I thought. But look, Inga.' He rips opens another of the boxes on the top of a single pallet with strong hands and takes out a book. He flicks the pages. 'They're fine, see? I've checked half-a-dozen boxes and they're all here, thousands of them, and they're all fine. Pick a box, if you don't believe. A random one, any one you like. There's no cause to worry.'

'Me?' says Inga.

'And it's safe, this warehouse. I've gone to every precaution. I'm the only one with a key. All the windows are barred, all the doors are double-bolted. The plates are in the office. No one even knows they're here.'

'OK.'

'Not that I object to coming down here on a Thursday afternoon when I should be in the office with a million things to do. I don't mind at all. The most important thing is that you're comfortable.' He takes a large handkerchief from his pocket and wipes his nose. 'Sorry. Dust. Anyway. Don't do it again, that's all.'

'Do what?'

'Summon me. You are neither my wife nor my sergeant nor, for that matter, my mother and those are the only people allowed to push me around. OK, my accountant. My bar-tender, on rare occasions, but that's it.'

Rachel feels a pricking in her fingers.

'Are you drunk? I didn't summon you,' Inga says.

He reaches again into his pocket and pulls out what is clearly a telegram. 'Read it again. What is it, if not a summons? I mean it's OK, I'm joking, really. I'm half-joking. It's natural to have some nerves.'

The telegram in his hand reads:

ON MY WAY TO WAREHOUSE STOP MEET ME THERE NOW STOP
DONT BE LATE STOP INGA KARLSON

Inga reaches into the pocket of her coat and pulls out her own telegram. Charles reads it, frowning. He looks at a spot floating in space then he bolts back the way they came, along the canyons of pallets, back through the anteroom to the front door. They follow him. He goes to open it. He pushes on it with everything he has, then throws his shoulder against it for no good reason but still it doesn't move. There's something barricading it from the outside.

'Charles?' Inga says.

On this deserted corner of the city, in this packed warehouse that was once a stable. Standing there at the front door, none of them knows what to do.

29

Brisbane, Queensland, 1986

Caddie stays in the shower until the water runs cold. She rests both hands against the pink tiles, soaking her head, trying to wash away the image of Philip standing in his driveway waving Rachel's letter.

Rachel's changed her mind, Caddie thought at first. Rachel is happy: with their project, with Philip's intentions. Whatever Rachel knows about Inga Karlson, she is at last ready to stand in front of strangers and reveal it. Caddie felt the weight of responsibility lift.

Then she read the letter.

Professor Carmichael, Ms Walker,
I fail to see how any of this is your business. If you insist on this course of action, however, I will attend.

Regards
Rachel Lehrer

'It's not exactly a ringing endorsement, is it?' she said to Philip.

Philip—she could scarcely believe it—danced a gormless jig, then held the letter high and kissed it. 'Who cares? She'll be there, that's what matters. Hallelujah!' He folded the letter and sandwiched his palms around it in prayer—possibly also a first.

Now, in the shower, she sees the leaves of a palm sneaking over the sill of the casement, open to let the steam out. The narrow bathroom was renovated badly in the seventies and the ceiling and the walls are panelled in pale, knotty pine. When she turns her back to the shower rose and faces the length of it, she could be in a giant coffin.

Rachel Lehrer is the key to Caddie's new world. One old woman, close enough to a stranger. Philip won't stop: that's the simple truth. He has Rachel exactly where he wants her.

There's a thumping. She turns off the taps, dries herself and changes, wraps her hair in a towel and slides open the door.

'Mate,' says Pretty from the kitchen. 'You were a good twenty minutes.'

'Sorry,' Caddie says. 'I'm so sorry.'

'Whoa. Hey, no worries. I like cold showers. Good for the circulation. No, seriously Cads, it's not worth getting upset about.'

'I'm fine,' she says. 'Planning on throwing my career away but apart from that, absolutely fine.'

She skips dinner and instead sits cross-legged on the floor beside her bed, writing notes and drawing flowcharts then rolling the pages into balls and missing the bin. She writes down everything she knows about Philip; she tries to imagine any eventuality. She thinks on it from every angle but comes to the same conclusion: Rachel must be delivered from Philip's plans, that is not negotiable. She makes a phone call, she flicks through her wardrobe in search of something Philip would consider appropriate for their function tomorrow. When at last she sleeps, just after three, her legs cycle through the empty space in her bed and she dreams of someone holding her from behind. She'd give anything to call all this off but she knows full well that Philip will keep going until he builds his glittering future on the pile of Rachel Lehrer's bones.

Just a few hours from now, the Karlson exhibition will close in Brisbane. The fragments will be packed in their individual cases. They will be padded against shock, protected from light. Inga's letters will be lifted from their display by gloved hands, as will the press clippings and Inga Karlson's remaining belongings. All the objects will be sent to another city where they will be unpacked and displayed and Karlson fans young and old will queue to see them. Exhibitions like this belong to the world. They have no proper home at all.

In a private room off to the side of the exhibition, the staff have almost finished setting up for a small function. They are positioning a rostrum and a long table for drinks. Caterers have dropped off small food: tiny pancakes with smoked salmon and little meatballs with an apricot glaze. There's a table with champagne flutes and glasses for orange juice and water. Soon, twenty or so people will stand around chatting and sipping their drinks, and pounce on the snacks as they wait to discover from Philip why they've been invited.

Philip and Caddie arrive at the art gallery in a taxi a little before 1 p.m. He's in a sports coat and a new blue-checked shirt, though for some reason his collar and cuffs are both white. Caddie's in a brown suit she bought, for no good reason, at a sale last year at Shopping Town. She's carrying a briefcase that was actually her high-school port: battered tan leather with a pocket at the front and two buckled straps. Inside the port are two sets of overhead transparencies in manila folders: one set belongs to her, about the arson, with details of the mysterious but (as yet) unnamed typesetter who belonged to a paramilitary organisation; the other, Philip's, has Rachel's missing line and the revelation that she's Inga Karlson's heir. In the back seat of the taxi, while Philip rested with his eyes closed, Caddie picked at the skin around her thumbnail until it bled.

They're on their way up the brutal concrete gallery steps now, close to where Rachel sat when she was overcome by the heat that day. The river lurks at the bottom of the grassy slope and above them, the flat, pale sky looks like it's been coloured with crayon. It's as good a spot as any. Caddie stops, bends over with her hands wrapped around her waist. Philip was almost at the top, but he steps down again to stand beside her.

'It's only natural to be nervous,' Philip says. 'This is a big deal.'

Caddie straightens. 'I don't want to do this.'

She feels a dampness in the creases behind her knees and a wild compression in her chest. The sky above her, featureless in all directions. She's been brought up to be patriotic by instructions from everywhere. Even the television jingles command your allegiance: *You can count on a Queenslander. Love you, Brisbane. That's what I like about Queensland.* She's heard stories of pilots disoriented by cloud who can't tell which way is up; perhaps the result is the same.

'Just as well there's nothing much for you to do.' He straightens his collar and rolls his eyes. 'I'm giving the speech. Your details are up on the slide as the lead researcher for the arson project but all you have to do is stand beside me and say a few sentences. That's all.'

'No.' Caddie takes his arm. 'I mean: I don't want to do this. Whatever she knows or doesn't know, Rachel's right. It's none of our business.'

'Cold feet. It's not unheard of. In a few hours it'll all be over.'

'I'm calling it off.'

'Caddie, sweetie,' Philip says. He notices her face: the set of her jaw. Her hands are clenched, one thumb still wrapped in a tissue. 'You're serious.'

'Yes. I want to cancel the whole thing.'

'This is literally your job. The job you wanted. We've been working on this for weeks.'

'I've changed my mind.'

She can see him thinking. He lifts his sunglasses to the top of his head and scratches the side of his face, in front of his ear. 'No. I have a room full of people. I have to tell them something.'

'I can't do it, Philip.'

'It's not up to you anymore.'

She takes his arm. 'Philip, let's swap. You said yourself that the arson research is the better prospect. The one that'll definitely come off. A book at the very least, you said. The Rachel idea—three million to one. Remember? You take the arson. Samuel Fischer and the German-American Bund. Go in there and tell them you've solved the literary mystery of the century. I'll take Rachel; like you said, it's almost certainly a dead end. A little old lady no one knows, who probably doesn't remember what happened last week, much less fifty years ago.'

'A swap? You're giving me your project, just like that, just because you feel bad about some old dear?'

'Just like that.'

'Caddie. Angel.' He takes both her hands. 'This ridiculous empathy is the kind of thing that holds women back in their careers.'

'Do you want it or not?'

He bows. 'If that's what you want, I will oblige. But this is at your request. Don't forget that.'

'I'm not introducing Rachel,' she tells Philip. 'I'm putting her in a taxi and sending her home.'

'It's your project now,' Philip says as he turns back up the steps. 'Do what you want.'

There's less than an hour to go. They've commandeered one end of the information desk, and Caddie's borrowed stickytape and scissors. The transparencies for the Rachel presentation are in her port, tucked under the desk out of the way—she'll destroy these when she gets home. In front of her, spread out, are the transparencies Philip will need to present the arson investigation. They need to have her details removed. She lifts the scissors. There's time for Philip to back down, to take her side.

'Wait,' he says.

She looks up, swallows.

'Make sure you get rid of the footnote as well, the one with your contact info.'

So she does. She cuts her name out of the slides, out of the arson investigation, out of any credit for the work she started, and she writes Philip's details instead, then she patches the slides back together with tape.

Philip watches her. 'Very neat,' he says, examining them. 'Excellent craft skills.'

Then he heads outside to a quiet corner around the river side to practise his speech to the frangipani, and Caddie takes a minute in the ladies', pacing in front of the sink and holding a damp paper towel to the back of her neck. By the time she comes out, Philip is loitering in the foyer. It's a quarter to two. Caddie still needs to find Rachel when she arrives, and apologise, and send her home again.

'I'm going to wait for her here.'

'Look, I've got thirty people arriving and I'll need to manage it all by myself, thanks to you,' Philip says. 'Just give me a hand for a sec.'

So she follows him to the small function room, which is half-full: about two dozen men and three women are milling, sipping, chatting. Some of the men are in suits, so they're not academics. Media people, she thinks, but probably not journalists. She can see the head of the department and one of the classics professors against the far wall, laughing like schoolboys.

'Gentlemen,' Philip says, to the nearest cluster. He waltzes around the room, nodding here and shaking hands there, from group to group, calling everyone by name, welcoming everyone. Down the back, near the drinks table, she can see Malcolm Kirby, the director of exhibits, in deep conversation with a tall man whose back is to her.

She knows. Of course she knows but she hopes she's wrong, and then he turns to hand his empty glass to a passing waiter and—yes, it's Jamie.

Every part of her flushes, from her toes to her earlobes. She should have asked Philip for the guest list. Of course he'd be invited. Of course. There's no way Philip would pass up the opportunity to condescend to Jamie in this moment of triumph. She's more surprised that Jamie said yes. She would have guessed he'd be scathing: Philip and his ilk scoffing hors d'oeuvres and small-talking in the middle of the afternoon. He looks at ease, though.

Then he sees her, and he excuses himself from Malcolm Kirby mid-sentence and comes straight over. On his way across the room he keeps his gaze on her as he lifts another white wine from a waiter.

She smiles, rummaging for an inconsequential remark.

'Hear me out,' he says, straight away. 'Think about what you're doing.'

'I've thought,' she says.

'Please. Just give me one moment?'

She nods, and he shepherds her to the doorway. He raises one arm to the wall behind and leans down to her, and close. Her throat tingles.

'Caddie, please. You can tell me to mind my own business. But this won't end well for you and it won't end well for Rachel, if you find her. It will only end well for Philip.'

If she shuts her eyes they could be standing on the footpath out the front of her house with her bike between them and their fingers intertwined. Yet despite all the time she's spent thinking about him, now she wants nothing more than to punch him in the head.

'I know what I'm doing.'

She feels a hand on her shoulder and looks up: it's Philip. He has a hand on Jamie's shoulder also.

'Two of my favourite people.' Philip gives them both a little shake. 'James, so good of you to come. What's it going to take for you to put that shop on the market and come back to the hallowed halls, hey?'

'I'm looking forward to your presentation.' Jamie takes a gulp of his wine.

'Well, not long to wait now.' Philip checks his watch ostentatiously, then steps further through the doorway to the foyer. 'But if you'll excuse me? It's almost two and my guest of honour is due.'

The hum of the room and the chink of glassware; a waiter has knocked over some empty glasses that had congregated on a ledge near the lectern. Jamie is standing so close. All of it, a faint buzzing at the edge of Caddie's awareness. For a moment, she's not sure she's heard properly.

'My guest, you mean.'

Philip smiles at her, with his lips curled inward, and shakes his head. 'Caddie, Caddie.'

'We agreed. She belongs to me now.'

'Who?' says Jamie. 'Who belongs?'

Philip holds Caddie at arms-length and makes the kind of sad-face reserved for infants. 'Don't be naive. I'm the lead investigator for *both* projects. It's my name on the files and on the grants. It's my name on the door.'

'No. We had a deal.'

'And I'm very grateful for all the great, the really solid work you've done. And you've got a good job out of it, and you will be acknowledged on every paper.'

A waiter appears beside them with a tray of small burnt fish fingers sweating on lace doilies around a bowl of liquid grass. 'Blackened goujon with herb vinaigrette?'

'Not right now, mate,' Philip says. 'Look, Cads, you'll do well out of this. You'll finish your thesis. The references I'll write for you.' He kisses his fingers: a cartoon chef.

'But you said. You agreed it was a long shot. That she might not remember anything, even if we found her.'

'Yes, it's a long shot. A lottery ticket. But who knows?' He winks. 'My numbers might come up. The arson's the main game, of course it is, but I'm happy to have a couple of bob on old Rachel.'

'Rachel?' says Jamie, looking from Philip to her and back again. 'You found her? She's here?'

'How do you—? Never mind. Just stay out of the way,' Philip says.

'Have you spoken to her?' says Jamie. 'Has she agreed to all this?'

Philip ignores him. He cracks his neck side to side and runs his tongue around the front of his teeth. He could be preparing for a date. 'If you'll excuse me.'

They follow him out into the foyer. The ceiling is high and it's markedly brighter here. A large group of older women are chatting and laughing close to the entrance: a club perhaps, or a group of friends out for one last look at the exhibition or a late lunch at the cafe. Straight-backed in tailored trousers with cardigans or jackets. Silver hair and chunky bead necklaces; rich auburn bobs. One outlier has ink-black hair worn long and loose.

'Which one is she?' Philip's gaze flicks from side to side, evaluating the women, weighing them.

Jamie dashes ahead and stands between the women and Philip and Caddie, facing them, hands up.

'Stop. Just stop. Has she spoken with a lawyer? Someone to look after her interests, before you pair parade her in front of everyone?' Jamie says.

'Caddie,' says Philip, quietly. 'I'll ask every old woman here, just watch me. And you, James, are in the way.'

Jamie looks from Philip's face to hers. Caddie understands how he feels. He wants to give Rachel a warning. It's the way she's felt herself: this urge to protect. It's not only because Rachel is old and vulnerable. It's more than that. There's something shiny and rare about her that anyone can see. She wants to put her hand on Jamie's. It'll be all right: she projects this thought towards him.

And all at once, something shifts in Jamie's eyes. He holds her gaze for a beat. Steps to one side and waves his arm. 'I guess I can't stop you.'

'Caddie?' Philip says.

Caddie swallows and raises her arm. 'Her. That's Rachel Lehrer.'

She points to the other side of the foyer, and Philip spots the woman sitting alone on a concrete bench against the wall. She's wearing a pale floral short-sleeved Queensland dress. Cotton. No gloves.

Philip waves at her from across the room. He beams. The woman stands and waves back.

'Leave this to me,' Philip says.

30

New York City, 1939

It strikes Rachel now that the strong smell is gasoline.

'We need to get out of here,' she says.

'I think you're right.' Charles heads toward the back door and tries to slide it open. It isn't budging.

'I don't understand,' Rachel says. 'No one knew the books were here.'

And Inga says: 'Fischer.'

On this corner of the city, in this packed warehouse that was once a stable, Inga looks up. One of the high windows is open and they can see a face in shadow between the bars.

'Fischer?' calls Charles. 'Sam?'

The man in the window raises a box of matches. He takes one out and strikes it. In the sudden small flare his face is visible before he flicks the match inside the warehouse. It lands close to where they're standing.

Inga finds it and stamps it out, but now they are all

running between the pallets in the dark warehouse. Fischer and his typesetter fingers are fast. The lit matches make graceful crescents and lie on the floor twinkling, Rachel thinks, like the fireflies that she would watch dancing on the grass on summer nights when she was a child. Fischer is lighting them, one, two, three, and they have no hope of finding them all in time.

A match lands on a puddle near a pallet of books to the right. There is no big explosion, no boom. The puddle flares into flames, beautiful in the gloom. The flames move up along the edge of the pallet, crackling. On the other side of the room the same thing is happening. The flames are dancing now, and hissing. They move quickly. They are living things.

The world has become a forest of fire. Somewhere in the centre of the warehouse, something snaps and crashes. One of the beams, perhaps, or part of the ceiling. The noise is like nothing Rachel's heard. Her eyes sting. She coughs once, twice.

'Up there,' Inga says, pointing to the high window.

Fischer is gone. The bars are solid and the space between them is narrow, but the window itself remains open. It must be sixteen feet from the ground.

'You just might fit,' says Charles.

Inga takes Rachel's arm.

'Now.' Charles takes off his scarf and wraps it around his face so that only his eyes are visible. 'There's no time. We'll lift her up. Then, when she's up, she can pull you up. The two of you can go for help.'

Inga can't meet his eyes. She knows, and he knows, how long that will take.

He reaches for a box of books, and then another, and he stacks a pile of them. She scrambles to the top. She's still a good five feet below the bottom of the window frame.

'On my back, quick.'

'I can't,' she says. She looks from one face to the other. 'You should go first.'

Charles says, 'Now. We don't have time for debate.'

'Please, do as he says. You have to try. Please. Please try.'

'When I'm up there, I can lift you up.' She tries her best to smile. 'Don't go anywhere.'

They all nod. When she is up there, she will help him to lift her up.

Later, she will realise there was no need to rush. If they had thought slower, acted slower, there would have been plenty of time. There was time to kiss them both, to put her soul in order. What hadn't she said? A million things.

Eat your vegetables. Rug up when it's cold out. I should have buried you in kisses, carved your name into my skin with an ivory pin.

There's another crash and the lights go out but she can see by the glow of the flames. Charles climbs up, bows low and she scrambles upon his back like a child. His knees sway and then, with a great force of will, he stands up straight. Growls and huffs like a bear. She reaches higher, leverages herself until she has a knee on his shoulder. She stretches until she can grab the bottom of the iron bars. They're already warm. Charles, below her, yells like a woman in labour.

She feels Charles's strong shoulders beneath her feet and she pulls herself up until her face is level with the bars. She

293

slides one arm through, followed by her shoulder and head. She can see the skyline sparkling in the distance, the narrow, dirty street below. Those blessed cobblestones, that garbage, those discarded tin cans and newspapers. There's no sign of another human, not even Fischer. The air is cold, brittle. Underneath the window are a number of timber crates, unevenly stacked, a makeshift ladder that Fischer must have constructed to climb up and light the fire. With her arm through the bars, she can almost touch the top crate. She inches forward but when she reaches the width of her chest, she's stuck. The space between the bars is too narrow.

From below, four hands push at her feet and legs and buttocks and back, taking the weight from her arms. She expels the air from her lungs, she sucks in her stomach and manoeuvres her breasts and rotates her chin.

She cannot manage it. There is nothing she can do to force herself through.

31

Brisbane, Queensland, 1986

Shop-worn and bruised—that's how Caddie feels, standing beside Jamie and watching Philip charge across the foyer towards the waving woman in the floral dress. In ten years, in twenty, in two hundred years this merciless concrete bunker will look exactly the same as it does now, while Caddie is immeasurably older than she was an hour ago. She's not finished yet, though. She needs to be standing out the front at exactly 2 p.m.

And then she catches a movement near the entrance in the corner of her vision. Another woman has stepped from the glare of outside into the quiet foyer. This woman is older again, perhaps seventy. Pale pink knee-length dress, large red tote. White gloves, to match her white pumps.

Caddie's hand goes to her mouth. She can hear Jamie's sharp inhale. Philip pauses halfway across the room to register this new arrival.

She's been distracted by Jamie's presence; it's later than she thought. Jamie, Caddie thinks, in a rush of hope. She turns to face him and angles her head towards the entrance. 'Is that lady here for you?'

'Oh.' Jamie squeezes her hand. 'Yes, I think she is.' Then he waves and calls to the woman: 'Hello! I'm so glad you could make it.' He passes Philip on his way across the foyer. 'One of my best buyers,' Jamie says. 'Serious collector of 1930s first editions. Hope you don't mind my inviting her.'

'Be my guest, mate.' Philip flicks his hand as though Jamie is a fly. He continues across the room and Caddie should ignore him and his schemes, should tell him to fuck off and never see him again but she can't, not yet. She jogs a few paces to catch him, after a quick glance over her shoulder to make sure that Jamie is fine, murmuring to the woman in pink and steering her towards the ticket counter.

Philip reaches the woman in the floral dress first and thrusts his hand forward. 'Associate Professor Philip Carmichael,' he says. 'We're honoured you could come.'

'Miss Lehrer,' the woman says, shaking Philip's hand. 'Miss Rachel Lehrer.'

Caddie stands beside Philip while he talks to Rachel Lehrer. In the background she can hear his VIP guests chatting and clinking glasses in the reception room, the arch murmur of academic gossip. She thinks about how hard she has worked as she smiles at Rachel Lehrer, here in the foyer of the gallery, and hears her tell Philip she doesn't understand what all this fuss is about. She has never met Inga Karlson, she says; has never read any manuscript.

'University people, I thinks to myself when I kept getting all those letters. They must know something I don't. Couldn't for the life of me guess what.' Her accent is broad and rich, old-fashioned Queensland.

Philip shrugs, can barely stop himself from grinning. 'Never mind. It was a flight of fancy of Ms Walker here, who has a bit to learn about textual analysis. I did warn her it was very unlikely.'

'If you don't mind telling us,' Caddie says, 'what exactly is your connection with Inga Karlson?'

Connection? Her father was some kind of cousin from Austria, she says. She might be the only living Karlson relative. She's grateful for the money, don't get her wrong. It's been a blessing all these years. She owns a nice little house, goes on a cruise every year. Helped her niece and nephew through university. She sponsors two African children. She writes them letters. Their photos are on her fridge. The rest goes to the church. She came to the exhibition on the first day out of curiosity, that was all. That was when she met the young lady here. She's never been one for made-up stories.

'That book must be good? Because new books come out all the time, don't they?' the woman says. 'Modern ones, you know. Danielle Steele.'

'So, you haven't read the manuscript?' Caddie says.

'What manuscript is that, love?'

'A misunderstanding.' Philip pats the woman's hand. 'You quoted a line at Caddie, is that what happened?'

'It was a bit dull, wasn't it? The exhibition. I tried to memorise some of the burnt bits. Like a little game, so it

297

wasn't all a waste of time. Did I stuff them up? Sorry, love.'

Philip chuckles. 'Don't give it a moment's thought. No harm done.'

'Why didn't you just say this, in your reply?' Caddie says. 'Why didn't you write back and tell us? Or ring? Why didn't you ring? You were so brusque. You could have explained. I thought. I thought you were hiding something.'

'Truth is, I don't like talking about the money,' Rachel Lehrer says to Philip. 'There's a lot of con artists about. My pastor is very particular about that. I must say he wasn't happy about me coming here at all. There's pictures of naked people in here, are you aware of that?'

'Surely not,' Philip says, eyes wide.

The woman pats his arm. 'Mind you, the love of God can transcend even the godless to put power in the hands of those willing to do his good works. Inga Karlson was godless, I understand.'

On the other side of the foyer, in the doorway of the reception room, Malcolm Kirby appears. 'Philip,' he calls out. 'Tick tock, mate.'

Philip gives each white cuff a tug. 'I'm going to leave Ms Walker to see you out. I have a presentation to give. An exciting development in the Karlson arson case.'

'Suit yourself,' the woman says. 'Any chance of cab fare back home?'

'This way, Miss Lehrer,' Caddie says, as she leads her towards the door.

'Ta, love.'

298

The woman seems unsteady on her feet after all the excitement, so Caddie takes her arm. Philip is still on her mind. She knows him well, has known him well for years. She listened when Jamie told her of his experience, too. So why is she disappointed? Because she hoped, despite the evidence, that he was a better man. Because she wasted so much time adoring a person like that. Because she's sad for him: to have been blessed with such gifts and yet be so small.

When a taxi pulls up, Caddie gives the woman a twenty and opens the rear door for her.

'Slightly off script, Miss Lehrer,' Caddie says, 'but still your best performance since that tube of toothpaste.'

'I'd been sitting there for a while. I was beginning to think you wouldn't need me.'

'I *hoped* I wouldn't need you. Still. A wise woman once told me: hope for the best, prepare for the worst.'

'It was the most fun I've had in ages. And your professor! What a spunk.' The woman kisses Caddie on the cheek. 'See you soon, Cadence.'

Caddie waves as the taxi takes off, then she jogs back inside, buys a ticket and heads for the exhibition. This is the return visit she promised herself, when was it? Five months ago? Everything in her life has changed. It no longer seems important to linger through the relics again, to pore over every artefact, including the sad ones about the fire. Now, in the final hour, there is no one here except for her and—she sees them on the far side—Jamie and the woman in pink.

From where Caddie stands, they seem like old friends.

At ease, chatting, pointing occasionally to something in a display case. They could be a young man and his grandmother, out for the day—albeit a young man who knows his grandmother's face only from photographs purchased in an Auchenflower pizzeria.

Jamie and the woman hear Caddie approaching and they both turn. Caddie's every step brings her closer; everything echoes with the click of her heels. To reach them, she walks past Inga's childhood, the display about the fire. The newspaper headlines, the blackened timbers recovered from the scene; Inga's pendant, the melted glass one with the bee design that was found in the ashes of the warehouse and used to identify the body.

She walks around the fragments themselves until she reaches the two of them.

'Here she is now.' Jamie smiles at her. 'May I present Caddie Walker?'

'We've met,' Caddie says.

The woman nods at Caddie. 'How could I forget your fond thoughts of evangelist readers? Also, you've sent me about a hundred letters.'

She extends her hand to shake Caddie's but before they touch, she stops. She inches off her left glove; she does the same with the right and slips the gloves in the outside pocket of her tote. She pulls up her sleeves and holds out her hand again. Caddie and Jamie can see her right forearm now. The long fingers are elegant but from the tips up to the woman's elbow, the skin is stretched and shiny: puckered as if drizzled with pink icing.

'I barely notice it these days. I just don't like to be gawked at.' The woman splays her fingers and flutters them as if playing an invisible piano. 'Works perfectly fine, though.'

She takes Caddie's hand. Her grip is strong and cool and the ridges are a secret message, telescoping years down to seconds.

Caddie swallows. 'You're a long way from home.'

'Not at all,' the woman says. 'This has been home for many years. I love it here.'

Jamie clears his throat. 'You knew Inga Karlson,' he says. 'You read her work.'

'To have known Inga Karlson,' Caddie says, wondering how she can even speak the words, considering the tragedy and the decades that have passed. 'That must have been a tremendous privilege.'

This close, the woman's face is laced with fine wrinkles and the whites of her eyes have a yellowish tinge. Her breathing, too, is shallow and laboured. Something passes over her face that could be a smile.

'I've reached the conclusion over my long life,' she says, 'that it's a tremendous privilege to know anyone.'

This is what Caddie's been hoping for, for so long: talking to this woman, asking her questions. Although in this moment that one line—*the seconds spent on this earth and the number of them that truly mattered*—that one line is almost enough.

The woman turns to Caddie. 'Your young man's been telling me what a brilliant researcher you are.'

The corners of her mouth twitch up; Jamie's face breaks into a wild grin.

'My *young man* is slightly biased. Anyway, I'm pretty sure I'm currently unemployed.'

'Even better. That means you've lots of free time. I've something you might like to read.'

She reaches into her tote and pulls out a thick parcel wrapped in a floral oilskin. She weighs it in her hands before handing it to Caddie. 'It's strange to hand this over. No one's read this in a very long time.'

'Is that—' Jamie says.

'God,' says Caddie, as she takes it. 'God.' Her hands are shaking and Jamie touches her forearm to steady it.

Resting the parcel in the crook of one arm, Caddie peels back a corner of the heavy wrapping. Inside is a dense pile of printer's galleys, slightly yellowed with a few crumbling corners. She flicks the pages: they're covered in faded type with the occasional annotation in pen.

At first, neither of them can move, or speak, or breathe. Then they both begin to laugh in the way of people overcome.

'Is this?' Caddie says at last. 'It can't be.'

'Can it be?' says Jamie. 'How can it be possible?'

The woman ignores their laughing and gaping. Businesslike, she opens her bag again and produces a manila envelope which she places on top of the manuscript. 'And here are some documents you'll need, a contract—there are some places you'll need to sign. Assorted bits and pieces. Use my lawyers, they're very good.'

'I don't think,' Caddie stammers. 'I'm not sure I'm the right person.'

'I'm quite sure. Someone who is definitely the wrong

person—your professor, for instance—wouldn't question it. It seems to me you'll be the perfect person.'

Caddie hugs the parcel to her chest with one hand. Her other hand finds Jamie's.

They hear footsteps behind them. The security guard: there's a few minutes left before the exhibition leaves Brisbane for good.

'Would you like some privacy?' Jamie says.

The woman looks up at Inga, on the wall. 'Not necessary. I have no idea why I keep coming back. It's not like I'm ever going to forget what she looks like.'

Outside, shadows are growing long and the air is beginning to cool. The traffic, the fountain, the horn of a ferry. The woman leaves Caddie and Jamie, and she walks towards the smaller photo on the wall. Inga in a restaurant, flanked by uniformed staff. She stands close, tilts her head back.

'Isn't she beautiful?' the woman says. 'Isn't she the most beautiful thing you've ever seen?'

32

New York City, 1939

She won't fit, that's her conviction. The bars are tight and close and the metal is now growing hotter. She's jammed at the widest point of her chest. She changes her angle, hopes she can slide between the bars like a slippery fish. She knows they won't be able to support her for much longer. The bars are even hotter.

It reminds her of when she was a child and she watched a goat being born back in the village in Austria. She was in tears, pulling on her mother's arm but her mother only laughed and then—how amazed she was at the sudden rush of it. The inevitability of gravity, and the small complete beast standing up almost immediately, surer on his feet even as she watched.

Something gives. She falls the few feet to the top crate, using her arms to cushion her, and then overbalances and tumbles down Fischer's makeshift ladder. She lands on dirty snow and earth. She's winded but not hurt—or at least she can't feel any injuries. It's quiet out here, like another world.

The noise and panic inside the warehouse are years away. She is reborn. She rises, fills her lungs with air. To blink, for salty liquid to clear the smoke from her eyes. In an instant, she turns around to the window.

It is an instant, surely. It can't have been more.

She climbs the crates again, her fingertips tearing on the splintered timber, until she reaches the top and plunges her hand back through the bars. The air inside is hotter than before. Another memory comes unbidden—again when she was small, opening their old pot-bellied wood heater and putting her hand inside only to be pulled back by her father and yelled at until she sobbed. There is no one to pull her back now. She stretches further. An iron bar—steaming, livid—sears the skin between her shoulder joint and breast. She can feel her blouse melting into the skin and still she stretches.

Her fingers touch nothing.

She reaches further, presses harder. Waves her arm as high and as low as she can reach. From side to side. Spreads her fingers until she can feel the webbing close to splitting, fighting every instinct that tells her to whisk her arm away. The smoke is thicker than before. She sees nothing. She feels nothing solid. She screams now. She screams Rachel's name, she screams to God, she screams for Charles.

The skin on her hands, she can feel it pucker. She touches nothing but oven air. The feeling she is praying for, the touch of skin and bones, of a hand she knows so well—it isn't there. She stretches. She presses. She screams.

*

Very soon after that, she hears the sirens. She stays at the window until the fire engine comes, until the hoses unfurl, then she climbs down on her hands and knees. She crosses the road to a quiet, sodden alley and lays her arm in the grubby mud because the pain has built brick by brick to become a monstrous heavy thing. The sky is clear now. The smoke has blown somewhere else, yet there's no wind. She can't recall ever seeing so many stars.

For a while, she lies on her back on the pavement in that alley on the other side of the quiet street, looking at the dark blue sky that pulses with the throb of her arm. She hears three loud explosions, and she thinks of all her words, tens of thousands of them, freed from the pages and flying through the sky in wild arcs. Her heart beats of its own accord, her chest moves up and moves down. It seems to her that the thrum of the city is quiet for the first time since she moved here and she longs to rest on fresh earth that still remembers people and animals living and breathing atop it. She wants to feel damp soil close around her and press her nose against it like a dog.

She thinks of the time she and Rachel first met, the way Rachel crossed the room to give her a warning.

Later she finds a stinking blanket in that alley across the street and huddles beneath it in a doorway to watch because she cannot leave, not yet.

Things go wrong just after the second engine arrives. Part of the roof of the warehouse collapses. A tall brick wall falls with an almighty crash. There are injuries. Yelling, running. She watches, impassive, as though all this happened years ago.

An ambulance comes and leaves with two injured firemen. Another ambulance comes and does not leave. The driver and his colleague wait, squatting on the gutter, smoking and chatting with their greatcoats wrapped tight around them. There will be no siren tonight. They've been told already that there is no hurry.

The night passes. She stays. The pain in her arm and in her hands ebbs and flows. It keeps her awake and remembering.

She stays in that alley until early the next day when two bodies are brought out in long sacks, one fireman at each end, and loaded into the ambulance. She stays as they are driven away and although she wants to follow them, she knows this is ludicrous and she must let them go. They have each other, after all. She pulls the blanket tighter with her unfeeling hands and begins to walk. Her hands are bloody and her face is ash. Rachel's tenement is the closer, and as she staggers through the streets toward it she looks like a tramp, another victim of the last few years. She thinks of water: drinking rivers of it; the feel of her hair, floating like kelp.

A block from Rachel's, she hears the newsboy shouting to the world that the famous author Inga Karlson is dead. He is close to crying as he calls it out, and she watches for a good half-hour as people hand him a coin and take a paper and then sob on the shoulders of strangers. A woman drops the paper in the street and Inga kneels down to read it where it lies. She is dead and Charles is dead, she reads. It is here, printed in black ink. She sits in the gutter, stunned, while close by the newsboy continues to call.

Two bodies, the boy cries.

Two bodies. She is dead. Charles is dead. Dear Charles, kind and brave Charles. In the swirl in her head she thinks of the scars that will form on her hand and arm: that they will be a kind of armour. She is immortal now. There is nothing more to fear. She is dead. The worst has happened, yet here she is.

She is free now, from everything. The world opens up before her. She has cash, she has a lot of cash and a way to get more. She has nothing left to lose. She will change her name and she will change her face—with money and courage and a little ingenuity, anything is possible. And Fischer will pay, and soon. She will cushion his family as best she can, but he will not draw one more breath than she can help. She will look him in the eyes and the last thing he will hear in this life will be Rachel's name. Wherever I go, I will make sure that people hear the name *Rachel*.

Two bodies found, the newsboy cries.

Rachel likes small things, humble things. She has feeling for people, and a kindness. She has a way of finding joy and for a short time, she gave that joy to Inga but Inga's life is over now. And her heart is light, so light that she starts to laugh right there on her knees on the sidewalk, as people detour around her. She wants to grab them by the ankles and tell them that Rachel is alive and everything will be well. Two bodies, and she is dead and Charles is dead and that must mean that Rachel, her beautiful Rachel, is alive. Rachel is alive, and the thought fills her with such joy.

ACKNOWLEDGMENTS

In researching this book, many people were kind enough to share their memories of 1980s Brisbane. Thanks especially to Monika Sudull. Robert Stanley-Turner pedalled around South Brisbane at short notice, taking photos when my memory failed. Thank you also to the staff at the Queensland Art Gallery, especially Cathy Premble-Smith, for their invaluable help. Any errors, of course, remain my own.

Paddy O'Reilly and Merle Thornton were insightful and generous first readers—thank you Paddy and Merle. Jane Novak is not only a wonderful agent but one of the best people I know. Emma Schwarcz lent me her keen eye and at Text Publishing, Michael Heyward remains an inspiration. I'm very lucky to work with him. Most importantly of all, all my love and thanks thanks thanks to Mandy Brett, who makes everything possible and whose work on this novel was unparalleled. (And thanks to John, for lending me his Sunday-night chef.)

An early draft of this manuscript was awarded a Varuna Fellowship. I'm grateful for time spent in quiet contemplation in Eleanor's beautiful home, and for the many kindnesses and good advice of Gabrielle Carey, Linda Jaivin, Judith Rossell and Dave Allan-Petale.